CHOICES

a novel

J.A. Stone

To the best editor,
thanks brenahes!!

2016

DEDICATION

For my children.

ACKNOWLEDGEMENTS

Life Choices exists because of the hard work of many people. I want to thank Jennifer and Kim at Killion Group, Inc. for making my publishing experience so easy. I thank my writing group and early readers for their many suggestions for revisions to the manuscript. What would I do without Melissa Rollins and Mimi Shannon handling my marketing and graphic design? And finally, I owe a huge debt of gratitude to my editor, Jane Lightcap Brown, who knew exactly what I wanted to say, even when I didn't.

CHAPTER ONE

Each step that Jessie Graham took in her brand new Jimmy Choo heels was a minor miracle. The shoes weren't easy to walk in under the best of circumstances, and they certainly hadn't been designed for climbing a steep, gravel hill. On another night, Nick might have driven her to the top of the hill and deposited her by the steps leading up to Benton Hall, as other solicitous husbands were currently doing. But because she had insisted he come to this wedding, he was punishing her with the likely ruin of her new shoes, and the distinct possibility of a twisted ankle.

"It's your partner who is getting married, so you have to go." Jessie had argued earlier in the day when Nick started trying to back out.

"I'm on call tonight. Everyone will understand."

"But I'll hardly know anybody there."

"Give me a break, Jessie!" Nick had retorted furiously. "You don't even have to go to the ceremony. Just go to the reception, sign the damn book, congratulate the happy couple, and come home. Surely you can manage that."

"I'm not going by myself," she'd said firmly.

"Oh, hell," Nick had exclaimed. "Why did I have to marry a child instead of a woman?"

Now Jessie wished she had come alone. At least then she could have paused long enough at the bottom of the driveway to appreciate the lights hung beautifully in the trees lining the road. But without so much as a glance toward her, Nick had started striding up the hill, taking broad, determined steps that left Jessie scrambling to keep up with him.

When they finally reached the top, both breathing hard, they stood as silent as strangers in a line waiting to enter the front door. Jessie's silvery sheath dress, dangly diamond earrings, and almost waist length blonde hair shimmered in the window's reflection to the right of the door. Jessie examined her image critically. She had been satisfied at home in front of her bedroom mirror. She'd bought a seemingly perfect dress two weeks ago and spent almost two hours adding the finishing touches to her hair and makeup this afternoon. And her efforts would all have been worth it had there been any acknowledgement from her husband. However, when she'd walked into the den, his eyes had remained glued to the television as he'd muttered, "Damn the Dodgers! I should have known better than to bet on them." When he'd finally looked from the screen to her, his only comment had been, "I thought only the bride was supposed to wear white."

Jessie's confidence had plummeted. "It's not white. It's silver. But maybe I should change?"

"Like we have time for that now?' Nick rose from the sofa, looking perfectly handsome in his black tuxedo that complemented his dark good looks. "If I have to go to this wedding, I certainly don't want to be late. The sooner we get there, the sooner we can leave."

Standing in the receiving line, Jessie recognized Betty, the office manager of Nick's physician's group, and her husband, Ethan, ten people or so in front of them. To their left was a massive wedding cake topped with roses that looked more centerpiece than dessert and reminded Jessie of her own monstrosity of a wedding cake. She hoped the similarity in their cakes wasn't a bad omen for this new bride.

Finally it was their turn to greet the bride and groom. Nick heartily shook the hand of Jonathon, his newest partner, while offering jubilant well wishes to the glowing bride. No one observing Nick's enthusiasm would have guessed that he'd literally been forced to attend the event. But Jessie had long ago ceased to be amazed by how easily Nick could turn on and off the charm.

Pleasantries done, she and Nick flowed smoothly into the middle of the ballroom.

"You want something to drink?" Nick asked, scanning the ballroom with an experienced eye.

"Tonic and lime," Jessie replied and then watched Nick walk off. She looked around for any familiar faces. Seeing none, she moved from the middle of the room to one side where she wasn't so obviously standing alone and where she could watch Nick's slow progress in the bar line.

From across the dance floor, she noticed a woman in a tight, short, sapphire blue dress move determinedly toward the bar. She was the kind of woman who demanded attention. Even in the muted light, Jessie noticed how the woman's dress was a perfect contrast to her brilliantly red, short-cropped hair. Surprisingly, the woman didn't stop at the end of the bar line but walked directly to where Nick was standing. Jessie didn't know this woman, but she recognized the proprietary hand she placed on Nick's arm. They chatted for a few moments before Nick finally reached the front of the line. Then, after he handed the woman a glass of wine, she turned and was quickly swallowed up by a crowd of people.

Jessie watched Nick walk back to the center of the ballroom where she had been standing before. Clearly irritated, he looked from one side of the room to the other. Jessie walked out of the shadows to join him.

"Where were you hiding?" he asked.

"Who was that woman you were talking to?"

Nick seemed surprised at her question. "What woman? Do you mean Daisy? Our new office assistant?"

"The woman you handed the drink to."

"Yeah, yeah, that's Daisy," he said quickly.

"I don't know her," Jessie said in what she hoped was a neutral voice, taking a sip of her drink.

"She's only been working at the office for about six months."

Jessie took another sip and said nothing. Yet his words seemed to echo inside her head. Six months, six months, six months. Was it only a coincidence that Nick had been on call more than usual and working a lot of late hours for the past six months?

From then on, Jessie looked everywhere, trying to catch a glimpse of Daisy, hoping she'd be accompanied by an adoring husband or a long-time boyfriend. Perhaps then Jessie would realize that her suspicions were ridiculous. After all, the woman had only placed her hand on Nick's arm. Maybe Jessie was becoming as paranoid as Nick often accused her of being.

A few minutes later when Nick's pager went off, she felt relieved. This night, which she had planned with such great expectations, had turned into an unmitigated disaster. Now, mercifully, it could come to an end.

"I'm going to the bathroom before we leave," Nick said, "Why don't you go ahead and get your wrap?"

Jessie nodded in agreement. There was no line at the cloakroom, and getting her wrap took only a moment or two. Instead of waiting at the front door as she normally would have done, Jessie decided to circle back to where the bathrooms were located just outside the ballroom and wait for Nick there. As she rounded the corner, she saw Nick and Daisy talking in the hallway. Without stopping to think, Jessie walked up to them and placed her hand on Nick's arm in much the same manner as Daisy had earlier. Their conversation stopped. And was it only Jessie's imagination, or did the conversation of the people standing near them in the hall also stop?

"I don't believe we've met," Jessie said brightly. "I'm Nick's wife, Jessie, and you are the new office assistant, Daisy, right?"

The woman's large blue eyes grew wider. "Yes, I'm Daisy Mitchell."

"Are you new to Atlanta?" Jessie imagined she saw a certain wariness in Daisy's demeanor.

"Yes. I moved here from Charlotte almost a year ago."

Nick interjected, "If we don't leave now, Jessie, I won't be able to drop you off on my way to the hospital." Was Nick anxious to end this conversation?

"Good-bye, Ms. or is it Mrs. Mitchell?" Jessie asked in a determined tone.

"Ms."

"Well, I must get by the office soon so I can get to know you better."

"I'll look forward to it," Daisy replied with what Jessie thought might be just a hint of a threat in her voice.

Outside, rain was falling lightly, and they hadn't brought an umbrella. In uncomfortable silence, Jessie walked excruciatingly slowly down the hill, trying to keep from slipping. Gusts of wind blew the tree branches wildly so that the lights mounted there created a psychedelic show as they went. In frustration, Nick finally reached out and took her elbow in an agitated manner, trying to speed her along. They were both drenched by the time they reached the car.

"Hasn't this been a lovely night?" Nick asked as he threw the red Mercedes E350 sports car he loved so much into reverse. Jessie looked out of her car window, unable to see anything through the suddenly heavy rain. The lights of Benton Hall appeared as a blur at the top of the hill.

"Perhaps we ought to sit here for a minute until the rain lets up," she suggested.

"Perhaps if you hadn't taken an eternity to get down that damn hill, we might be able to do so. But I've got to get to the hospital as soon as I can. Did you forget that someone's life depends on it?"

Jessie had grown to hate his profession as a surgeon because Nick used it as a trump card to get his way in any situation. "Well," she said, "what about going down Roswell Road instead of Riverside Drive? A four lane would be better on a night like this."

"Damn it, Jessie. Let me drive!"

A lightning bolt, the signature of an Atlanta spring storm, struck amazingly close and illuminated Nick's profile. Jessie felt a sliver of relief when she saw how hard he was concentrating on the road. Nick was always at his best when there was a crisis underway. It had been a crisis of sorts, after all, that had brought them together. She put her head back against the leather headrest, closed her eyes, and remembered how much she had disliked Nick the first time she met him. Why hadn't she paid better attention to those first impressions?

He had been flirting with her sorority sister, Wendy, all night. Jessie had thought him too smooth, too perfect, and too old for a college band party. Over Jessie's strenuous objections, Wendy had drunk lots of red wine and danced for hours with this mysterious older man, leaving Jessie with nothing to do but watch protectively.

Jessie recalled how Nick had been twirling Wendy as REM's latest hit came to a close. Suddenly Wendy began spewing the remains of a burrito and a lot of red wine onto the dance floor. The people surrounding them had moved backwards en masse, with looks of disgust. To Nick's credit, he hadn't backed away from Wendy, but had reached out to hold her so that she didn't crumple over onto the nasty dance floor.

"Will you help me get Wendy to my car?" Jessie had asked Nick after making her way to where they were.

"Sure." He'd scooped Wendy up as though she were a bride that he was carrying across the threshold. "Which way?"

Jessie pointed to the right and started clearing a path toward that side of the room. When they'd finally reached her car, Nick had carefully placed Wendy in the backseat and then had taken off his t-shirt to gently wipe her face clean. His thoughtfulness had softened Jessie's feelings toward him.

"Why don't I go with you and help you get her settled?" he offered. "I'm Nick Graham, and I'm a doctor, or almost. Right now, I'm a surgical resident at the Medical College in Augusta."

Jessie had almost said no thanks and sent Mr. Nick Graham on his way. But the fact that he was a doctor had been comforting, and the logistics of getting Wendy out of the car and into her apartment, if Wendy were unable to walk seemed daunting. "That would be great," she'd finally said. Just four small words. Now Jessie couldn't help wondering, if she had instead said, "No, thanks," would she now be on this rain-slick road feeling afraid and miserably lonely?

Five minutes or so more, and the rain seemed much lighter. Jessie felt her fear lessening. She let out the breath she hadn't realized she was holding.

Nick must have felt the danger was over as well because he turned to look at her for the first time since they left the wedding, "So what the hell was that bit of drama all about?"

"What do you mean?" Jessie asked hesitantly.

"Don't act all innocent now. When have you ever wanted to come by the office and get to know the office staff?"

Jessie felt anger begin to simmer, "Maybe when an office assistant places her hand intimately on her boss's arm in the bar line?"

"So what is it now?" Nick began angrily. "Am I not even allowed to speak to other women at public events? To have them touch my arm?"

Doubt flickered in Jessie's mind. Had she imagined there was more to his exchange with Daisy than there had been? Surely even he would draw the line at having an affair with someone who worked in his office.

"I do have my reasons for being suspicious, you know," she offered.

"Damn it, Jessie. Aren't you ever going to forgive me for my past mistakes? Isn't that what our very expensive marital therapist told you to do? Forgive me?"

"Yes, but he also said we should continue our therapy."

"I know how that stuff works," Nick said scornfully. "He was just trying to keep the income rolling in, and he wasn't that good anyway."

Jessie's anger flared again. "How would you know? You only went along with it long enough to pacify me. You never really participated in the process."

Nick looked at her coldly. "The process? Princess, here's the only process we need to follow. You need to concentrate on learning how to take care of your husband, and the house, and getting pregnant. You do those things, and we'll be just fine."

"Well, guess what?" Jessie said, finally letting her anger explode white and hot. "I am pregnant, and we don't seem fine to me!"

Nick looked at her with surprise. For just a moment, they locked eyes—two defiant eyes staring into two shocked ones. Then the darkness surrounding them exploded with bright lights that came from around the two-lane road's sharp corner. Nick's attention went back to the road, and Jessie watched him jerk the steering wheel suddenly. Then time seemed to stop as the car began to slide crazily. There was a rough jolt. Jessie felt as if she were on a stomach-lurching carnival ride as bright lights flowed over her and around her, and then she felt an excruciating pain in her head, followed by a delicious nothingness.

CHAPTER 2

Rain was falling in sheets when David Miller pulled onto Interstate 285, the highway that was more like a racetrack around the perimeter of Atlanta. According to the weather radar, the storm system was moving rapidly to the east, and he was heading north, so he hadn't expected the rain to be coming down quite so hard. Oh, well, it would take more than a little bit of rain to make him miss his date with the tantalizing Tizzy.

By the time he reached the Riverside Drive exit, the rain had become just a drizzle. Still, the winding road and the large puddles of standing water were no picnic to navigate. All of the sudden, his brother-in-law's name lit up his cell phone. David's sister, Amelia, had been in bed for a couple of weeks, trying to hold off the birth of their twins for as long as possible. David knew when he saw Mike's name that the wait was probably over. Then the excitement in Mike's voice when he answered the phone provided verification.

"Hello, Uncle David," Mike said.

"Everything okay?"

"Yeah, they're both about five pounds, which made the doctor real happy."

"And Amelia?"

"She's great. And listen, we've decided to go all traditional and name the first one after me and the second one after you, so don't go doing anything crazy to make us regret that decision, okay?"

"Wow, I ...." It was at that point that David rounded a sharp curve and suddenly the almost complete darkness was broken by intensely bright lights. For just a second, it had seemed that he was destined for a head-on collision with an oncoming red sports car. At the last moment, the other car veered to the right, spinning in a complete circle before going off the side of the road as if in slow motion.

"Shit!" David dropped the phone as he pulled his car quickly to the side of the road and stopped. He sat for a moment, his heart beating a staccato rhythm in his chest. He heard his brother-in-law's voice ask, "What's going on?" But David didn't pause to answer him.

He opened the door and ran to where the car had disappeared. He saw the red sports car—a jumble of twisted metal—upside down and pressed into a massive oak tree. The sports car's lights provided an eerie pathway from where he stood to the wreckage down the hill. He took a couple of faltering steps before remembering that he needed to call 911. He reached into his pocket for his cell phone. *Hell, he'd dropped the cell phone in the car.* The few steps back to his car seemed to take forever, as did the conversation with the 911 operator.

"Do you know where you are on Riverside Drive?" she'd asked matter-of-factly. "Do you see any crossroads?"

"I'm somewhere between Interstate 285 and Johnson Ferry," he'd replied tersely as he'd made his way back to the road's edge and started the slippery descent toward the wreck.

"It would help if you could be more specific," she'd continued.

"Damn it. I don't know any more than I've told you. I'm going to help the people in the car. Just send an ambulance. Now!" And he'd hung up.

David grabbed onto scrub pines for balance as he went slipping and sliding down the hill to the upside-down sports car. The driver's side had taken the brunt of the impact and was pancaked against the tree. The dark head slumped over the deployed air bag was covered in blood. With no visible way to open the door, David reached through the broken window to search for the man's pulse. His neck was wet with gushing blood, and in the darkness, David couldn't tell where the blood was coming from or find a heartbeat.

A blonde woman, who was dangling in the air on the passenger's side, began to moan. David ran around to the other side of the car. He managed to get the passenger door open with surprisingly little trouble and, even more surprisingly, the car's interior lights came on. The deployed airbag and seatbelt held the unconscious woman hanging in place like a perverted puppet. He reached in to hold her with one arm while fumbling at her waist to press the seatbelt release button. Nothing happened except the blonde's eyes fluttered open briefly. Sapphire blue eyes impaled him as she whispered, "Help me."

"You're going to be fine," he reassured her as her eyes began to close again. Thank God he could hear sirens in the distance becoming louder. He tried pulling on her seatbelt while pushing the seatbelt release again, and with an unexpected whoosh, the woman fell heavily into his arms. He noticed that her blonde hair was darkening rapidly with blood. He carefully and gently angled her body this way and that to maneuver her out of the little car and had just accomplished his task when he heard the sirens stop at the top of the hill. Moments later, two EMTs were at his side.

"We'll take her," one of them barked.

"Check the driver first," David said as he continued to cradle the unconscious woman.

One of the EMTs grabbed his bag and crawled into the passenger seat while the other one ran around to the driver's side of the car. "Not looking too good in here," the guy called from inside of the car.

A cacophony of sounds—more sirens, more voices—surrounded David as he watched two men with a stretcher making their way down the hill. Meanwhile, he held on tightly to the limp blonde as the girl's chest rose and fell steadily—a good sign.

The men with the stretcher reached his side. "Let's get her strapped in," one of them said. David slowly released his burden onto the stretcher, and the EMTs strapped her down. Then, at a sign from one of the EMTs, David grabbed the side of the stretcher and then the guy on the other side motioned for him to start walking. Slowly they began the steep ascent to the road. Once at the top, the woman was whisked into the open door of a waiting ambulance. David's last glimpse before they shut the door was of an EMT setting up an IV.

A large policeman who looked as if he could have been an NFL linebacker walked up to him. "Are you the driver of that car?" He pointed to David's Toyota Camry.

"Yes."

"Are you okay? I need to ask you some questions."

"Yeah, I'm okay."

The policeman pointed a finger toward a police cruiser that still had its lights flashing. "Let's go over there."

Once inside the cruiser, David patiently answered the usual questions. Name, address, occupation. Upon learning that David was an army doctor, the policeman's attitude softened considerably. "So, Doc, what happened?"

"To tell you the truth, I don't know. There's a bad curve and no streetlights. I rounded the corner in darkness and then was practically blinded by the headlights on that car. I thought it was about to hit me, like head-on, but then it jerked quickly to the side, started turning in circles, and slid off the road."

"Was it speeding?"

"I don't know. I couldn't tell." David ran his fingers through his hair. "It happened so quickly, and I'd just answered my cell phone."

"You were talking on a cell phone on a road like this and in this rain?" The policeman's voice had taken on a hard edge.

David noticed that the rain was falling hard again. Guilt surfaced for the first time. "It wasn't raining when I answered the phone," he said defensively. Could he possibly have drifted over the centerline while talking on the phone? He had no memory of his driving right before the accident. Mentally, he'd been with his sister and her newborn twins. He continued, "My sister had just delivered twins, and my brother-in-law called to tell me I am an uncle."

The policeman looked at him disgustedly. "You would still have been an uncle if you had let the call roll through to voicemail and called them back later. I'm going to get out and look around a bit. The detail guys will be here soon, and they'll likely have some more questions for you. Do you mind sitting here for a while?"

"Of course not," David said. Once the policeman was out of the car, David closed his eyes and tried to remember every detail about the accident. Soon the detail guys arrived and started asking him more questions, but he couldn't remember anything else of importance. He had rounded the curve, there had been bright lights, and he'd seen the red car spinning around in circles before falling off the side of the road.

Finally the linebacker-sized policeman walked back to him. "Well, we're guessing

the Mercedes was speeding, and since
there's a good bit of standing water, it
probably hydroplaned," he said. "Since
there's no evidence that you did anything
wrong, and we've got all of your
information, you can go now."

David felt a frisson of relief. He had to
believe that he hadn't carelessly caused
this wreck and potentially a man's death.
Once back in his car, he called his brother-
in-law.

"I'm sorry," David said as soon as Mike
answered. "I just witnessed a horrific
accident. I think the driver is dead, and I
had to get an injured girl out of the car."

"Oh, man, we've been going crazy here. I
must have called your cell phone ten times,
and we were looking up the number for the
Atlanta police."

"Listen, I'm fine. Give my sister and my
two nephews a kiss for me. I'll drive up
tomorrow morning. What's the name of the
hospital again?"

David had meant to stop and buy a
newspaper on his way out of Atlanta, but
he was an hour and half into his trip before
he remembered. He'd cancelled his date
with Tizzy. Then he'd gone home and taken
a long hot shower, and fallen into an
exhausted and dreamless sleep. He'd risen
later the next morning than he'd planned

and hurriedly packed some clothes. Now, with nothing to do but think about the wreck the night before, he wished he'd remembered the paper so that he might find some answers to the questions swirling around in his head. The woman's wounds hadn't seemed life threatening. But he still would have liked to know for sure that she was all right. And what about the man? Had David's assumptions been right? Had the man died?

Mike, a large bear of a man, greeted David in the hospital lobby with a hard handshake and an uncharacteristic grin on his ruddy, round face. "Amelia can't wait to see you and show you the babies. Sorry about that accident last night. You okay?"

"Yeah, I'm okay," David said as they exited the elevator.

Mike stopped in front of a window and put his hand up against the glass as if he might somehow reach the tiny babies lined up inside.

"Which one is my namesake?" asked David.

Sheepishly, Mike admitted, "To tell you the truth, I'm not sure. I worry that we'll get them mixed up when we take them home."

David smiled at him. "I'll make a small wager right now that it won't be a problem for Amelia."

Mike grinned back. "I know. Come on, Amelia will kill me if I keep you from her any longer."

When David followed Mike through the doorway, his sister's face lit up. "David!"

David felt a lump in his throat at the sight of the dark head in a sea of white sheets and blankets. *How could tiny little Amelia be old enough to be a mother?* He walked toward the bed and kissed her forehead. "You did good work, sis. They look remarkable."

Amelia pouted slightly. "You've already seen them?"

"Just looked at them as we walked by. I didn't find out any of the really important things, like which one is my namesake."

Amelia smiled, appeased by his words. "If they are eating normally and maintaining their temperature, we may be able to take them home when I leave the hospital."

"Having a doctor at our house might help make our case," Mike added hopefully.

"Hey, guys," David said. "It's been a long time since I did a pediatrics rotation, so I'm not sure I'd be much help in an emergency. Call me when they reach those tumultuous teenage years, and I'll be happy to counsel you. But right now, let's don't rush things."

Later, when the babies were brought to Amelia, David got to see his namesake up close. Although he had studied anatomy and knew in theory exactly how everything worked, it wasn't until he was standing there touching a miniscule David's finger that he realized how truly miraculous a baby was. Miraculous, but so vulnerable. Someone had to supply a newborn baby's every need.

A memory of newborn Amelia screaming, red-faced in her bassinet came unbidden. He remembered their mother crying silently while looking into the bassinet instead of picking Amelia up and feeding her. At those times, the seven-year David would get a bottle of milk from the refrigerator, heat it in a pan of water as he'd seen his mother do, and place it in the desperate mouth of his baby sister, calming her. One night his dad had come home to discover him feeding the newborn while their mother slept. His dad had pulled his mother roughly out of the bedroom, calling her all sorts of angry words. David hadn't recognized their meanings at the time but had still been frightened by his father's intensity. David recalled how his always fragile mother had crumpled to the floor beside Amelia's bassinet and wept hysterically until his tight-faced father finally picked her up and carried her back to their bedroom, slamming the door firmly shut behind them.

"Wanna go get something to eat?" Mike asked, looking pointedly at Amelia lying with her eyes half closed.

David shook off his uncomfortable memories. Amelia would be a great mother. She'd lovingly cared for a menagerie of animals her entire life. No, Amelia hadn't inherited their mother's craziness. But sometimes he worried that he might have.

CHAPTER 3

Thirteen months later, David sat at the bar of O'Leary's Irish Pub in Augusta, Georgia, waiting for his friend Andy Norton to arrive. With equal interest, he watched both the Braves game on the muted television above the bar and the locals' interactions with each other. Everyone seemed to know everyone else, and the raucous laughter coming from several of the tables indicated that happy hour had started much earlier than five o'clock.

David was invisible to the patrons sitting in the bar, but not to the female bartender, who had been engaging in flirtatious banter with him between filling her orders. When she asked if there was anything more she could do for him, David knew she was offering more than a drink. With true regret, he spotted Andy at the door. "Maybe," he replied, for after all, she was a feisty, cute blonde. "For starters, how about two more beers?"

Andy saw him and made his way to the bar, stopping to speak briefly to several people. He reached for David's hand with a jovial, "Great to see you, buddy. Sorry I'm late. My last patient was a real challenge."

"No problem. I've had cold beer and the Braves to watch." David nodded toward the television. "Braves are even winning."

"When did you get into town?"

"About an hour ago," David replied.

"Have any trouble finding this place?"

"Not at all. Nice neighborhood bar."

Andy smiled, nodding positively. "I knew you would like it. This area is 'The Hill' section of Augusta, several blocks of mostly historic homes where a lot of native Augustans live. My office is just around the corner, about two blocks from here."

"How convenient," David said, noticing that the people Andy had spoken to were now staring at them. He was no longer invisible.

"It's a nice change from Atlanta where you never know anybody, don't you think?" asked Andy. Without waiting for a reply, he continued, "The quality of life here is off the charts. Hardly any traffic, but plenty of golf, of course. And with the Savannah River running through downtown and a lake only a short distance away, we have fishing, canoeing, or whatever other water activities you might want to do. There's hunting less than an hour away and a growing fine arts community. It's really a great place to live."

"Why are you giving me such a hard sell?" David asked curiously.

"I'm going to cut to the chase," Andy answered. "My practice is growing, and I've reached a point where I need to add a partner. I want it to be you. Imagine…you and me, working together again."

David was surprised. "I don't know what to say."

"Say you'll take a hard look at the town and my practice while you're here and give my offer some thought." Andy looked at his watch and took a long swig of his beer. "We better finish these up. Jan's expecting us home by 6:30. Sorry my running late ruined our happy hour."

"It didn't ruin mine," David said, holding up a napkin with a telephone number on it and a nod toward the bartender.

"Some things never change," Andy laughed.

David felt self-conscious getting into his bug-splattered, ten-year-old Toyota Camry alongside Andy's sparkling clean, brand new Volvo SUV. When they pulled up outside a two-story brownstone with an immaculately manicured lawn and an inviting porch that boasted a white porch swing and large pots of red geraniums, David felt the chasm widen between Andy and himself. Andy's house screamed permanence, which was not something David had ever had much of in his life.

"Nice place you've got here," David said as he got out of his car.

Andy smiled. "I'd never be able to afford something like this in Atlanta. See, affordable housing is another benefit of living in Augusta."

"David!" Andy's wife, Jan, came running through the front door, her brown hair pulled back into a pony tail that made her look as if she were about twelve. "I can't believe we've finally gotten you here! We've been in our new house for over a year, and you've been promising to come ever since we moved in."

"I know, I know." David shook his head. "I've no good excuse for not coming. Would have served me right if you'd stopped inviting me." He gave her his most engaging smile.

Jan stood on the tips of her toes and stretched all of her five feet three inches until she could put her arms around David's neck. She gave him a hard hug and then stepped back to look at him. "You are still just as good looking as ever."

"I'm right here," Andy reminded them as he put a proprietary arm around Jan.

"I don't understand why you haven't let some woman gobble you up," Jan said with mock seriousness. "Come on in and see what you've been missing by refusing to be domesticated."

Later, enjoying a second cup of coffee that provided the perfect ending to the incredible meal Jan had fixed, Andy again broached the topic of David moving to Augusta.

"My practice really is getting too large for one person to manage. And we haven't told anyone yet, but Jan is expecting, so I'm thinking she's going to start demanding a bit more of my time."

"You've got that right!" Jan said.

"Congratulations, you two." David smiled warmly at Jan. Turning back to Andy, he said, "You've got it all now—a successful practice, a beautiful house, and soon a family."

"This could be yours, too," Andy said. "You just need to settle in one place long enough to put down some roots."

"And dating one girl at a time might help," Jan added with a smile.

David thought for a moment about how unsettled he'd felt since leaving the military. He'd been discharged for only two weeks, and already his plan to spend some time doing nothing was losing its appeal.

"Just imagine," Andy said, "you and me doing what we do best and actually getting paid what we're worth." He paused for a moment and then added with a cheeky grin, "Well, maybe not what we're worth, but a hell of a lot more than what they pay you in the military!"

CHAPTER 4

The blue sofa in the den of Jessie's mother's house, where Jessie currently reclined, was the epicenter of her universe. Originally a physical necessity because she couldn't navigate the stairs with her broken leg and cracked ribs resulting from the car crash, the couch had become the only place where she felt truly comfortable. She liked looking up and seeing her father gazing protectively down at her from his portrait over the mantel, and she liked hearing Maggie, her mother's housekeeper, as she bustled around in the kitchen. Jessie closed her eyes, allowing the familiar sounds and smells from the kitchen to transport her to a time when her life had seemed secure and full of wonderful possibilities.

"You are just being lazy today." Maggie's voice reached Jessie from the den doorway, and she opened her eyes.

"I didn't sleep well last night," she offered in her defense.

"Sleeping on that sofa might have something to do with it," Maggie said with a huff. "Anyway, I need you to go to the Fresh Market for me. I need onions for the pot roast I'm making for dinner."

Jessie knew that Maggie engineered these little errands to make her get out of the house. She rose wearily. *Why was she always so tired?* "I don't know why you bother to cook big meals anyway," she said. "I would just as soon eat a bowl of Campbell's chicken noodle soup."

"Well," said Maggie, "I like to cook. And I get tired of heating up Campbell's chicken noodle soup. Now you go on and get me two or so medium-sized Vidalia onions."

Twenty minutes later, Jessie parked and looked around furtively at the other cars to see if she recognized any of them. Then she realized how silly she was being. How could she recognize a car when most of the time she didn't even recognize the people who drove the cars? Maybe she'd be lucky today and get out of the store without having to talk to anyone.

Even before her accident, she'd hated running into people she was supposed to know but didn't. Familiar faces with no memory attached to them. She had been gone from Augusta for so long...longer than she'd lived in the city. Now she found it hard to believe that she had been living in Augusta for over a year. But did her life in the rehabilitation center, and all of the therapy she'd had to do after leaving the center, really qualify as living?

She entered the Fresh Market, made a swift turn to the right for the produce section, and made a beeline for the onions. Then she stopped mid-stride because the well-dressed, well-coiffed, and expertly made-up woman standing in front of the onions was someone Jessie recognized as a person she should know. She turned to walk in the other direction just as the woman looked up and spotted her with an immediate look of recognition.

"Jessica, it is so good to see you out and about," the woman said pleasantly.

"Thank you, ma'm. It's good to be out." Jessie searched her brain frantically for some scrap of memory about the woman, but her brained failed her.

"Is your mother still in New York? I was at the Smithson party with her the night before she left."

"Yes, ma'm. I think she should be back by the tenth."

"Quite a long trip, all things considered...." The woman's words trailed off. With more determination, she continued. "I want you to know that my Sunday School class has been praying for you since the accident."

Jessie felt her face flush red. She had yet to learn how to respond to comments like these without embarrassment. On one hand, it was nice that people cared. But she wished people didn't feel that she needed praying for. "I appreciate it," she said, knowing that she should say something more. She looked down at the onions. "Mother's housekeeper is waiting for me to bring her onions for a pot roast she wants to get started cooking." She reached into the bin, scooping out a couple of onions. "Nice to see you."

"You too, dear," Jessie heard the woman reply as she walked briskly to the register.

When Jessie handed the onions to Maggie, she could feel the earliest twinges of a headache, a constant occurrence since the accident. The doctor had said not to worry, as headaches were normal after a severe concussion. She rubbed the front of her head. "I'm taking Advil and closing the drapes. Why don't you go home early? I need total quiet more than pot roast."

Maggie peered intently into her eyes. Seemingly satisfied that her pain was real, Maggie said, "You go on and lay down. I'll get the roast ready for tomorrow and then go home."

Jessie smiled weakly. "Thanks." She went into the den, closed the drapes, and lay down on the sofa. She pulled the soft cashmere blanket up to her chin, glanced up at her father's comforting face in the portrait, closed her eyes, and drifted into a deep sleep.

Jessie was walking down a dimly lit corridor. She reached a bright window that revealed rows and rows of tightly swaddled babies in blue and pink blankets with dozens of nurses ministering to one baby and then to another. Jessie tapped lightly on the window to catch the attention of one of the nurses. She wanted her baby brought to her. But none of the nurses looked up. Jessie tapped harder against the window. Still, no one looked at her. Jessie's tapping transitioned into pounding, and soon she was slamming both fists against the glass.

"Miss, you need to stop that." A security guard appeared at her side from out of nowhere.

"You don't understand," Jessie replied without looking at the man. "I need them to bring me my baby."

"You don't have a baby," the security guard answered sternly. "Your baby died in the accident."

"Yes, I do have a baby!" she shouted, hitting the glass even harder. She opened her mouth to scream for a nurse, but instead of a yell, only a slight moan came out as the security guard suddenly grabbed her arm and started pulling roughly on it.

"You need to wake up. You're having a bad dream," he said in a voice that was strangely reminiscent of her mother's.

Jessie opened her eyes. Her mother was leaning over her, one perfectly manicured, red-nailed hand gripping her arm. Her mother let go of the arm when she saw that Jessie's eyes were open. Jessie felt confused by the dream and the sudden and unexpected appearance of her mother. She sat up slowly. "What are you doing here?"

"It's my house." As always, Rita looked as though she'd just stepped out of a magazine ad for an older, but very attractive and obviously very wealthy woman. She was wearing crisp white linen pants and an apricot silk blouse. Gold bracelets rattled on her wrist as she pulled her arm back, and gold earrings glittered against her silver hair that was pulled into her signature elegantly messy bun.

Jessie tried again. "I mean, I didn't expect you back for another week."

"Phoebe called me yesterday and told me that all of Augusta is worried that my daughter is going crazy. You don't return phone calls, and you don't go anywhere. And when you do go out and meet someone, you cannot carry on a coherent conversation."

Rita moved to the cream-colored club chair across from the sofa and sat down. She leaned to a lamp at her side and turned it on. "It's so dark in here. And why are you still sleeping on the sofa? I thought I told you when I left that you were to move up to your bedroom."

"I sleep better here." Jessie was becoming more alert.

Rita raised one of her highly arched eyebrows. Over the years, Jessie had learned to read Rita's moods through her eyebrows, just as a weatherman used a barometer to predict the weather. One arched eyebrow warned Jessie to be careful.

"Perhaps all of Augusta is right," Rita continued. "I will not allow you to continue to vegetate on this sofa. You are either being melodramatic, or you really do have mental problems. Either way, things are going to change. I'm going to get you in to see a therapist as soon as possible so maybe we can get some answers. I should have done it right after the accident."

"Mother, I don't want to go to a therapist. I went to one once, and it accomplished nothing. Besides, I'm an adult, not a child, so you can't make me go."

"Perhaps I can't. But you are living in MY house and sleeping on MY sofa. If you prefer, you can go back to YOUR house in Atlanta and vegetate there. And, by the way, has it ever crossed your mind to wonder whether the mortgage on YOUR house has been paid? Whether the grass is a mile high? I doubt you've given it a thought. If you're an adult, stop acting like a child. I've not wanted to burden you with such mundane matters. But if you are well enough to make these kinds of decisions, go back to Atlanta. Start living your own life. Or you can stay here. But staying here means you will start going to therapy. It makes no difference to me which you choose."

Rita rose regally from her seat. "I'm going to bed now. You can give me your answer in the morning. And why don't you try out that new TempurPedic mattress in your room?"

"I'd rather sleep here. If you don't mind."

Rita paused at the door of the room and gave Jessie a final withering glance, "Perhaps you are crazy after all," she said. Then she disappeared from sight.

The mention of her old life was unsettling to Jessie. She tried hard to imagine her house in Atlanta—a red brick, traditional two-story in a well-groomed neighborhood of upwardly mobile professionals. She tried even harder to remember her life in that house as it had been with Nick before the accident. But that house and her old life seemed less real to her than the movies she now watched almost continuously while lying on this sofa. She knew she wasn't ready to go back to Atlanta. And she couldn't think of anywhere else she could go. *Okay, mother,* Jessie thought to herself. *As always, you win. For now.*

CHAPTER 5

David put the last book on the shelf and stood back to admire the three long rows of leather-bound tomes in varying shades of brown, black, and tan. He'd never had an office with enough shelves to hold all of his medical and reference books. Of course, he'd also never had an office with floor to ceiling windows on one side, either. Government-issue offices were typically eight-by-ten windowless boxes in blue, green, or beige. He'd always thought them more likely to cause depression than promote a cure. Still, he'd grown used to those offices over time, and now this plush carpeted room filled with so much light seemed too large and too bright for the intimacy required for therapy.

"Not bad." Andy walked abruptly through the open door, the ivory carpet swallowing the sound of his footsteps as he went. "Personally, I prefer pictures and mementoes, but there's a certain high-brow professionalism associated with endless rows of textbooks, I suppose."

David smiled. "Maybe when I have some pictures of a wife as lovely as Jan, I'll redecorate. I'm honored you've managed to squeeze a social visit into your busy office schedule."

Andy plopped down into the navy chair in front of David's desk. "I've no time for social visits. This is a business call."

David sat down behind his desk, leaned in toward Andy, and said very seriously, "You and Jan need some marital counseling about how to bring the sizzle back to your love life during pregnancy?"

"Our sizzle is just fine, thank you very much," Andy said. "No, I'm here as the managing partner of this group. Now that you've moved, and," he gave a wave of his hand to the room, "finished decorating, we need to get you some patients. Right now you are 'Overhead' in my accounting statements, and I'm ready for you to become an income stream."

"Would like nothing better."

"Good. I received a call this morning that should be right up your alley."

"A wounded warrior making the transition back to real life?"

Andy shook his head. "Remember, you're in the real world now. In the real world, we see mostly depressed socialites and soccer moms dealing with infidelity and midlife crises. It's a tough transition for hardened combat doctors like us, but you'll get used to it."

David smiled. Andy had served only the minimum time necessary in return for his medical schooling and then gotten the hell out of the military. He wasn't exactly a hardened combat soldier. "So which is this?"

"Depressed socialite. Not sure what she's dealing with but she's too young for a mid-life crisis. And she's just what you need. Very old Augusta. You get her back to functioning normally, and you won't be suffering for patients in the future."

"If she's old Augusta, why is she willing to accept an outsider instead of insisting on Augusta's native son?"

Andy grinned sardonically. "She hasn't yet, but she will. I'm planning the old bait and switch. I'll get them in the door with an initial consult, and then I'll tell them I don't have the time she needs, which is why I've added the esteemed Dr. Miller to my staff. Then it's up to you. Smile that ruggedly handsome smile, turn those big brown puppy dog eyes on them, and I'm sure you'll have them begging you to be her doctor before it's over."

David felt a twinge of annoyance. He was going to have to get used to having to attract patients by selling himself, instead of receiving a steady supply, another difference between his new situation and the army. Then Andy's words caught his attention. "*Them*? I thought you said it was a depressed socialite. Who's *them*?"

"Actually," Andy cocked his eye at David, "it's her mother who made the appointment and who's bringing her in. Evidently the daughter isn't interested in therapy. So, in addition to selling yourself, you need to sell therapy to the daughter."

"Ummmm, that doesn't sound quite so simple after all."

Andy rose from the chair and headed toward the door. "Oh, and by the way, the mother is one of the wealthiest people in Augusta. Her husband died and left her with an ownership interest in everything of importance in this town—from the bank to the newspaper. So, be nice."

"I'm always nice."

"Yeah. Right. Anyway, they'll be in at 2:00 p.m. and I'm sure that, compared to some of the situations you've been in, this one will be a piece of cake."

Andy's office was on the opposite corner of the building from David's office. The next morning, Andy's door was slightly ajar when David arrived. He stood outside, listening to the muted voices and trying to decide if he should walk in or knock when Andy opened the door wide.

"Come on in, Dr. Miller," he said.

David walked into an office that oozed warmth and coziness, from the polished and welcoming wooden desk to the cheerful water color painting in muted greens and blues that hung over the tan leather sofa where two women now sat. The older one, stylish in a sophisticated crème colored silk suit, looked directly into his eyes, daring him to look away. The younger one wore black pants and a crisp white top, and sat with her eyes downcast. Her hair was a blondish brownish color, pulled back with a clip into a severe, blunt ponytail.

David stopped beside the sofa as Andy made the introductions.

"Rita Forrester, Jessica Graham, allow me to introduce my new partner and very old friend, David Miller."

David first offered his hand to the mother, who took it somewhat reluctantly as if she found it distasteful to take a hand in welcome. When David turned to the daughter, she raised startlingly blue eyes to his, and he felt a nagging familiarity. She didn't smile as she took his extended hand in a brief exchange.

Andy was in full salesman mode. "David has had a long and distinguished career in the military. And since he's just starting his private practice, he will be able to devote extensive amounts of time to his new patients—time, which unfortunately, I don't currently have available."

David stood awkwardly by as Andy continued hawking him to these people as if he were a used car.

Finally, the mother rose regally from her seat. "I think we've heard enough," she said dismissively. "We'll give Dr. Miller a try." She turned to leave the room.

For some reason, the older woman's dismissive tone of voice toward both her daughter and him grated on David's nerves. Didn't her daughter have any choice in deciding whether to accept him as her doctor? "Not so fast, Mrs. Forrester," he said.

Rita Forrester stopped mid-stride and looked back at him questioningly.

"I need to know what my prospective patient thinks first." Andy looked at David in surprise, and the older woman's entire countenance tightened. David said nothing as he waited for the younger woman to look at him again.

When she did, those blue eyes again stirred a vague uneasiness within him. Her voice was soft but with a faint hint of determination. "Dr. Miller, I don't want to do therapy at all. But since my mother has made it clear to me that my choice isn't available to me, I suppose you will do as well as anyone else."

"Very good, then." Andy jumped in to smooth things over. "Now that we've gotten everything settled, Cindy, our receptionist, will set you up with an appointment and give you some paperwork to fill out, including a medical questionnaire. How soon would you like to get started?"

"I'd have her start this very moment, if it were up to me," the older woman said caustically. "She doesn't have anything else going on in her life to keep her occupied."

David glanced at the girl for a reaction to her mother's sarcasm, but her eyes were downcast again. "How about tomorrow morning?" he asked.

"That sounds good," Andy interjected. "Let's go see Cindy now, and she can schedule an appointment for tomorrow morning."

CHAPTER 6

The July heat hit Jessie hard after the chilly doctor's office. She felt slightly dizzy and stumbled, and the appointment card slipped from her hand and fell to the gutter.

"Losing your appointment card won't get you out of the appointment," Rita said unsympathetically.

Jessie didn't think her mother's comment worthy of a reply. She picked up the brown card, recalling how Dr. Miller's brown eyes had made her uncomfortable, staring piercingly into hers while asking for her opinion. Was it because Nick's eyes had also been brown? Still, she supposed it was nice that he had asked for her opinion instead of simply going along with whatever her mother wanted. However, he was new to Augusta. Things would change after he'd been here for a while and understood the power of her mother's money.

Rita put the car into reverse and waited for a car to go by. "I'm wondering if we shouldn't have interviewed some other doctors instead of taking Andy's word about this ex-military doctor," she said.

Again, Jessie didn't feel inclined to comment. After the silence continued for a few more blocks, Rita added, "I mean, Andy does have a financial interest in his partner being successful."

Now that her mother's support for Dr. Miller was wavering, Jessie suddenly decided she wanted no one else. "I thought he seemed nice."

"I thought he seemed rude," Rita retorted. "I'd have much preferred young Andy Norton."

Jessie could feel the beginnings of a throbbing tightness in her head. "Maybe young Andy will make an exception for you if you call and offer him double or triple his usual rates. Doesn't everyone have a price?"

Rita glared at Jessie with a hard look. "Do you still believe I bought Nick for you?"

Jessie felt the tightness spread from her head to her heart. "Oh, I don't think you bought him," she replied flippantly. "But you did make a good down payment."

Rita's voice was cold, "Life is difficult, and marriage isn't a fairy tale. You and

Nick could have had a good marriage, had *you* only tried harder."

Jessie's anger dissolved as quickly as it had come. Nothing was ever gained by arguing with her mother. She turned to look out the car window, feeling suddenly overwhelmed by the hopelessness of her situation.

At ten o'clock sharp the next day, the receptionist ushered Jessie into a different office than she had been in the day before. Dr. David Miller's office was modern, full of chrome and glass. She supposed it was because he was new, but there was no hint of a personality in the room.

Jessie put the completed medical history questionnaire on his desk and sat down in a blue leather chair that faced the desk. It had taken her the better part of an hour the night before to fill out the form, and even then, there were blanks she wasn't sure about. She supposed a near-death experience and three days in a medically-induced coma left a lot of gaps in one's memories.

The door opened, and the doctor walked in. Jessie noted abstractedly that Dr. Miller wore crisp khaki slacks and a blue starched shirt that was almost the color of the chair she was sitting in. She was glad he wasn't wearing a white lab coat. After all of the hospitals and rehabs she'd been in, she'd be happy if she never saw another white lab coat for the rest of her life.

He held out his hand as he had the day before. Jessie put her white, slender hand into his much larger brown one and felt the warmth of his hand seep into her palm uncomfortably.

"Why don't we sit over here?" he said, indicating the ivory-colored sofa on the other side of the room. "All I want us to do today is get to know each other."

"I put my medical records on your desk," Jessie said before she moved to the sofa.

Surprisingly, he sat down next to her, and Jessie's body tensed. He was a little too close for her preference.

His brown eyes looked directly into hers, making her even more uncomfortable. "I want you to know that this is a safe place, Jessica."

"Only my mother calls me Jessica. I'm Jessie, please."

He smiled pleasantly. "Okay, Jessie. I want you to understand that therapy begins with trust. Everything you say to me is strictly confidential, and nothing is off limits. Your mother, even if she is the one paying for these sessions, has no right to know what we talk about here. And I won't provide her with any information unless you want me to. If we are to make any progress, we must develop a relationship based on mutual trust. My only purpose here is to help you. Do you think you can trust me?"

Jessie didn't quite know how to respond to his earnest question but finally managed, "I think trust comes with time."

She watched the doctor smile approvingly, "Yes, it does. And in time, you will find that you can trust me. Do you want to be helped?"

Jessie nodded.

"Okay, then, I like to start off by telling my patients a little bit about me. It sort of helps break the ice. My father was in the military. I grew up a military brat. You name a Southern town with a naval base, and I've probably lived there. After vowing never to join the military, I ended up joining so I could go to medical school. And I ended up staying in the Army much longer than was required. I don't know what that says about me, but we aren't here to analyze me, right?" The doctor smiled at her engagingly.

Jessie managed a slight smile in return.

"I have one sister, Amelia, who is seven years younger than me," David continued. "She's an artist who lives in the North Georgia mountains with her husband and twin boys. It's just the two of us now that both of our parents are dead.

Jessie realized she should probably respond in some way. "I'm sorry about your parents. When did they die?"

"My mother died when I was young. My father died from cancer a few years ago."

"What kind of artist is your sister?"

"She paints. I think she describes her work as impressionistic. Her husband is also an artist of sorts—a craftsman, I guess you'd call him. He makes furniture."

"Must be nice for them to have so much in common," Jessie said hesitantly.

"Yes. But in some ways, it would be better if one of them had a more traditional job—a steady income, insurance benefits, that kind of thing. Now, what about you?"

Jessie hated talking about herself. Hers was such a sad, depressing story, so she would make it quick. "I was born in Augusta. My father died of a stroke when I was thirteen. I was sent to Virginia to boarding school for high school. I got an English degree from the University of Georgia. I met Nick, my husband, while I was there. My husband and I were in a car accident last April. He died, and I was injured badly. When I was able to leave the hospital, my mother brought me back to Augusta to recuperate. Evidently my body heals a lot faster than my mind because here I am with you."

She watched him make some notes. "Where was your accident?"

"Atlanta. I don't know if you're familiar with the city, but it was on Riverside Drive." Jessie thought Dr. Miller suddenly had a most curious expression on his face.

"When was this accident?" he asked.

"April, a little over a year ago."

"What happened?"

"It was raining, and the police say our car likely hydroplaned. I can't remember anything so I don't know. We hit a tree on my husband's side of the car. I was told he died instantly."

By the time she had finished her recital of facts, Jessie thought Dr. Miller was looking at her strangely. Then, even more strangely, he proceeded to spend the remainder of her session quizzing her about the extent of her injuries from the wreck and her treatment afterward. She wondered why a psychiatrist seemed to be so interested in her medical background.

CHAPTER 7

After Jessie left, David stared at the pine tree branches swaying outside the windows of his office. He felt unable to fully comprehend what had just occurred. What were the odds of the woman he had pulled from a wreck in Atlanta coming to him as a patient in Augusta? A billion to one. Probably greater. No wonder he had felt such a sense of familiarity with her the previous day. But where was the stunning blonde he remembered from the accident? And her unemotional recital of facts stood in sharp contrast to his vivid memories of that night. He could still recall the stickiness of her husband's blood and the woman's sudden weight dropping into his arms. He could recall the sounds of the sirens and the lights from that night as clearly as if they had occurred only yesterday. Perhaps she was lucky to have no real memories of the accident.

"Want to grab a quick bite of lunch and tell me about your first session?" Andy asked from the doorway. Then looking at David's pale face, he asked, "You okay?"

"I've had the damn craziest thing happen this morning."

Andy walked in, immediately at attention, and sat down. "With the Graham girl? David nodded. "What happened? Seriously, you don't want to get on the wrong side of her mother."

"She's the girl I pulled out of that car accident last year."

"What?" Andy's eyes widened. "How's that possible? You didn't recognize her yesterday."

"She looks different now. The night of the accident was dark. It was raining. Hell, I don't know. All I know is that when she started talking about her accident, I realized who she was, and I froze. What could I say? 'Oh yeah... I was there too.'"

"What *did* you say?"

"I didn't say anything about me being there. She's fragile and suspicious of therapy, and I had just finished my speech about how she can trust me." David ran his fingers restlessly through his hair. "I find this situation hard enough to believe myself, and I can remember everything about that night. She doesn't remember much, if anything, so how can she believe this is just a coincidence?"

"I need to take over her treatment, then."

"I don't know," David said slowly. "I feel this connection to her."

Andy rubbed his forehead anxiously, "You feel a connection to her because of the accident. You've seen her only three times in your life, and the first time she was unconscious, right? Besides, you know what old Dr. Beans in medical ethics class would say about something like this?"

David smiled weakly at Andy's attempt to inject some humor. "I think we both know the answer to that question. Look, she's definitely depressed. I just don't know how severely yet. Give me some time to get a handle on her situation, and then I'll tell her the truth."

Andy appeared to be pondering his words. "It is such an unusual coincidence. I suppose there's no reason why you can't wait a little while, and I'm talking a very little while, you understand? When's your next appointment?"

"Monday."

"Mmm, I don't know, David. I still think it would be best for you to go ahead and turn her over to me."

"And how are you going to give her the time she needs? Have you got three extra hours or more each week?"

Andy slowly shook his head. "Okay," he said bringing the discussion to a close, "I hope you know what you're doing. Rita Forrester is a force of nature in Augusta. As far as I know, she's never had any business training, but she oversees several successful businesses that employ large numbers of people around this area. She's also able to donate large amounts of money to charities or politicians as the spirit moves her." He paused. "Basically, when Rita Forrester speaks, people stop and listen. If you mess things up with her daughter, it could be the end of both of our practices here."

David returned to his office, sat down at his computer, and typed up his notes about the session with Jessie.

Female, 27, manifests signs of clinical depression. Feels uninterested in all basic human functions. Suffers from migraine headaches that are likely the result of a concussion she suffered in a car accident. Medications: Advil as needed.

Should he make a note of his involvement in her accident? Probably the less said about that, the better. Professionally, he knew it would be safer for him if he told her the truth immediately and turned her over to Andy for treatment. But his gut was telling him that he was the

one who could help this girl. And his gut
had hardly, if ever, led him the wrong way.

CHAPTER 8

Jessie walked out of Dr. Miller's office feeling that she hadn't accomplished very much. The bright, warm sunshine felt good after the chill of the doctor's office. A lot of people were out and about, walking and running. A car coming toward her on Central Avenue was playing Earth, Wind, and Fire's song *September* rather loudly, and for just a moment she saw the bobbing head of a middle-aged woman as she went by. Jessie envied the carefree smile on the woman's face.

A college-age boy with a battered backpack sat on the top of a bus stop bench, texting furiously on his cellphone. He had such an intense look on his face that Jessie wondered if he was having an argument with someone, maybe a girlfriend. All of these people were living, she thought. They were exercising, going to work, going to school, just as they should be doing on an ordinary Thursday.

She, on the other hand, had not a clue as to what she wanted to do, or should be doing, on this ordinary Thursday. And thinking of all of the other Thursdays, and Fridays, and other purposeless days that lay before her for the rest of her life, she felt a deep sense of emptiness. At that moment, she couldn't think of one thing that seemed appealing to do.

Perhaps she should go back into Dr. Miller's office and ask for an emergency afternoon session. At least then she wouldn't have to go home to her mother's house. Instead, feeling worse than she had when she left to go to her appointment, she got into her mother's "fun" car, a white Range Rover, and went back to her mother's house to spend another afternoon on the sofa watching Turner Classic Movies.

When Jessie drove up, Rita was leaving the exercise/pool house, a white cottage nestled beside an infinity pool and situated tastefully behind the larger white house. Wearing a fitted black exercise outfit, Rita looked surprisingly fresh, although Jessie knew her mother had been walking on the treadmill, watching television, and making phone calls since Jessie left for her therapy session. Rita motioned with her hand for Jessie to wait for her.

"So, how'd it go?" Rita asked.

"Okay, I guess. Just sort of an introductory session."

"When does Dr. Miller want to see you again?" One of Rita's perfect eyebrows went up slightly over an almond shaped eye, indicating dislike or distrust, or both.

"Monday. He scheduled me to come three times a week for the first few months— Mondays, Wednesdays, and Fridays."

Rita's eyebrow went back down. "Well, at least I like that he's taking an intensive approach to your therapy. Are you interested in going to the club for lunch? I'm meeting Phoebe and Bit."

"I'm not really hungry now. I'll just stay here and eat something later."

Jessie watched Rita's eyebrows indicate skepticism, but she said nothing more as she started walking toward the house.

Jessie followed Rita silently inside and went upstairs to the bedroom that was hers but that contained nothing of her in it. The room was too white and too perfect. A French provincial magazine layout brought to life, designed for looking at, not for living in. Jessie suddenly recalled running to her mother with dirty hands when she couldn't have been more than four or five years old and being scolded fiercely for dirtying

Rita's new dress. Like this room, Rita was only for looking at and never touching.

CHAPTER 9

That night David had a date with a nurse whom Andy and Jan had introduced to him. Lillie was cute. A bit too talkative for his tastes and much more interested in moving their relationship along than he was. After only two dates, she was already texting him with ideas for things he might want to do, with the implicit expectation that he would want to do those things with her.

"Oh God, it's hot!" Lillie exclaimed when she opened the door to her apartment. She pressed her lips quickly to his and then glued herself onto his arm.

David wanted to pull his arm away because, within his suit, his dress shirt already felt slightly damp with perspiration. But he refrained from doing so. Their relationship had moved swiftly to intimacy at the end of their first date, even though he'd been prepared to give her a quick kiss and leave her at her doorstep. Her aggressiveness had surprised and pleased him on that night. In retrospect, he wished he'd been more circumspect. He wasn't in the military or Atlanta anymore, where casual relationships could flourish and end with little fanfare. Augusta was a small town, and Lillie was Jan's Junior League friend. The ending of this relationship required a finesse that he hadn't yet figured out. As a result, here he was going with Lillie to meet Andy and Jan at the Augusta Country Club for dinner.

David's irritation with the girl rose a notch as he opened the car door for her to get in, and she said, "How old is this car? Isn't it about time to start thinking about a new one?"

The car door groaned loudly as he slammed it shut, seeming to validate her question. Once inside, he said, "I love this car. Just had a new transmission put in last year, and the mechanic assured me it should be good for another 100,000 miles." He watched with amusement as Lillie's expression turned to dismay.

To Lillie's further annoyance, David didn't pull behind the line of luxury cars for valet parking when they reached the club. He parked instead in the first available space, which was some distance from the building. Watching Lillie take small steps in her extremely high heels made him feel guilty. He realized he should have at least dropped her off at the front of the building. As atonement, he reached out to take her hand in his, bringing a happy smile to her face.

Andy and Jan, with her slightly protruding stomach, were waiting for them inside the front doors. The girls hugged, and everyone exchanged pleasantries before Andy led them down an elegantly wallpapered hallway into a mahogany-paneled bar. The soft jazz of the piano player in the back corner was an invitation to sit down and stay a while.

"What will everyone have to drink?" Andy asked the group.

"Something cool and soft," Jan replied sweetly. "Maybe some orange juice?"

"Something warm and strong," Lillie laughed. "Just kidding. How about a glass of Merlot?"

Andy looked at David. "A Bud Light is fine for me," David said.

As Andy placed their orders, David looked around at the people sitting in small groups in various seating areas. The way the seating was arranged was nice so that you could share the room while maintaining a semblance of privacy within your own group. Since Andy wanted to put David up for membership in this club,

David tried to imagine himself sitting among these jacketed men and exquisitely thin and well-dressed women. His roving gaze paused for a moment on one of the elegantly clad women across the room— Rita Forrester. She was wearing a gold pants suit, holding a champagne glass, and motioning animatedly with the other hand to the people surrounding her. A couple sat directly across from her, and the man who sat beside her seemed entranced with what she was saying.

Almost as if Rita felt David's eyes on her, she looked up from her companions and straight across the room. David saw a look of recognition cross her face. He nodded his head toward her in response before turning to Andy to take his glass of beer. When he looked back, Rita's group was following the maître d into the dining room.

David thought no more about Rita Forrester until later that night when he was heading to the men's restroom and found himself face to face with her, coming out of the women's restroom.

"How nice to see you, Dr. Miller," Rita said in a socially-polite voice.

"Nice to see you, too," he returned in the same polite but chilly manner.

"Are you finding Augusta to be a nice change from Atlanta?"

"Augusta definitely has some positives that Atlanta doesn't have."

Rita shifted topics. "I hope your first meeting with Jessica went well."

"It was pretty standard for a first meeting," David said. "It takes a while for a therapist and patient to establish rapport."

Rita nodded in agreement. "Yes, I'm sure. Well, I'm glad you are starting her off at three days a week. I wouldn't be against her going every day." She paused. "Sometimes I wonder if she shouldn't be put into some sort of in-patient center. She is positively morose from dawn until dusk."

Medical ethics and his own feelings of discomfort forbade David from talking about a patient's mental state, especially in the hallway where people passing them by could easily hear. "Well, I'll certainly take your opinion into consideration," he said. "If you'll excuse me, I need to get back to my friends." He could tell from the expression on Rita's face that she wasn't used to having people end a conversation with her first.

"Of course," she replied haughtily. "So sorry to have detained you."

CHAPTER 10

Jessie had started sleeping in her bedroom because the den was no longer an option with her mother coming and going at all hours and frequently bringing friends home for a late night drink after dinner. On this evening, though, Jessie was reclining on the living room sofa when she saw car lights in the driveway. She switched off the television, gathered her things, and was almost up the stairs when her mother's voice said from the doorway, "Don't run away. I want to talk to you."

Jessie turned to see Rita, looking lovely in a regal gold pants suit. Jessie knew by the brilliant look in her mother's eyes that she'd been drinking champagne.

"I saw your Doctor Miller at the club tonight." Rita threw her keys carelessly into a carved wooden bowl on the coffee table.

Jessie murmured, "So, after one session, he's now *my* Doctor Miller?"

Rita seemed slightly amused by whatever she was thinking. "He was like a fish out of water at the club. Although he is attractive, I must give him that. Still, he has no manners to speak of."

Jessie said nothing, but Dr. Miller was suddenly seeming better and better to her if Rita found him unappealing.

"I was talking with Gerald about your situation tonight," Rita continued, "and he gave me the name of an in-patient treatment facility in Atlanta that has a proven record of success with cases like yours."

Fear uncurled in Jessie's stomach. "I wish you wouldn't talk about me with Gerald or anyone else. And when did Gerald become a doctor?"

Rita shrugged. "You don't have to be a doctor to diagnose your condition. Everyone knows you are depressed. And perhaps at an in-patient facility, you could get better faster."

"Mother, if you truly want me to get better, please don't talk about in-treatment facilities with your friends at the country club. The thought of that makes me feel depressed. Besides, I like Dr. Miller. I think he can help me."

Rita started walking through the den to the back part of the house where the master suite was located. As she was about to go out of sight, she stopped. "Well, I want to see results. And I want to see them soon."

CHAPTER 11

On Monday morning, Jessie entered David's office promptly at 10 o'clock, looking pale but attractive in slim black jeans and a flowing tan top. There was an air of fresh innocence about her that David found appealing, though very different from the glamorous beauty he remembered from the accident. Which woman was the real Jessica Graham?

He stood up from behind his desk and smiled. "Welcome, Jessie. Have a seat wherever you feel most comfortable. Can I get you some water, coffee, or a soft drink?"

Jessie sat down in the seat across from his desk, looking as though she'd rather be anywhere else. "No, I'm fine, thanks."

David sat down. "Okay. Today, I want to start off with an explanation of how I work. My job is to help you help yourself. I hold a mirror up so that you can see your life more clearly, and together we'll work through whatever is causing you problems. My first question to you is, do you believe you are depressed?"

David watched her think for a moment before answering somewhat reluctantly, "I guess so."

"Well, depression often occurs after traumatic brain injuries. Did your depression start after your concussion?"

David watched emotions play across her face, revealing an internal struggle. Finally, she shook her head.

"So, you've suffered from depression at other times in your life?"

She nodded. "I think so."

"I'd like for you to tell me every instance in which you think you might have been suffering from depression."

"Okay," she answered before looking blankly off into the distance. At least a minute went by before she started talking. "The first time was when I went off to boarding school in the ninth grade. I'd just lost my father and then was forced to leave everything I'd ever known behind. I had a tough time."

"Did you see a therapist?" David asked.

"I'm not sure the school counselor qualifies as a therapist, but I did have to meet with her a couple of times a week for about a month. After a while, I decided I'd rather pretend to be happy than listen to her platitudes about how to get over my father's death. Telling a fourteen-year-old girl that time heals all things is rather pointless, don't you think? Especially when time seemed to be standing still at that particular period in my life."

David smiled slightly. "I'll try to remember. No platitudes. And the rest of high school?"

"Nothing major, probably nothing more than most teenage girls have. Boarding school is very structured, and I do well with structure. I wasn't Miss Sociable, but I don't think anyone thought I was crazy." She paused. "I did pretty well until I went to the University of Georgia and had to go through sorority rush."

"Had to?" David asked. "I always thought sororities were optional activities."

She sighed. "Not for girls from Augusta who go to Georgia. You're told you won't have any friends, or dates, or life if you don't join a sorority. And I was already so different from the girls in Athens I figured it was probably true even more so for me."

"How were you different?"

"They were all so pretty and perky," Jessie said.

"You are pretty." David stated it plainly, as a matter of fact.

Jessie flushed. "Thanks. But even on my best days, I don't think anyone would ever call me perky. However, one good thing did come out of me joining a sorority. I met Wendy Scott, my best friend."

"Was she perky?" David asked, a bit tongue in cheek.

"Well... yes," Jessie admitted wistfully. "But she was also the sweetest and most genuine person I've ever met, so I forgave her perkiness. Most girls just acted that way. Wendy actually *was* that way. Besides, she single-handedly pulled me out of the dark place I went after arriving at Georgia and losing the structure I'd had at boarding school."

"What happened? What put you in that dark place?"

Jessie looked away from him. "I hated rush. It was just a bunch of lies. Sorority girls pretending to adore girls, and then blindsiding them by cutting them. I had girls in my rush group talking about dropping out of college because they didn't get a bid from the 'right' sorority."

David jotted down: *Depression when she first went to boarding school and depression when she first went to college. Change issues?*

"But you joined a sorority anyway?"

"Yes. I didn't know what else to do." She paused. "And once I met Wendy, everything seemed better."

"Tell me about Wendy."

"She was my big sister in the sorority. And she was really wonderful."

"So you didn't hold her responsible for hurting those girls in your rush group?"

Jessie looked up, surprised. "Well, no. I mean, she hated the whole process as much as I did."

"I see. So you didn't blame Wendy, but you did blame the other girls in the sorority. Seems a bit unfair, don't you think? Are you still friends with Wendy?"

A half smile. "Yes and no. We will always be friends, but Wendy married a missionary right after graduation, and she now lives in Thailand. She teaches English by day and Christianity by night. It's hard to remain close friends when you live half a world apart."

David wrote down, *Feels abandoned by best friend.* "Any other episodes of what you would call depression?"

"After I married Nick and we moved to Atlanta. My husband was starting his medical practice, and he was gone all the time. I think I was depressed then."

David assigned a name, Nick, and the profession of doctor, to his memory of the dark head slumped over the steering wheel. Knowing the name of the man in the accident made him seem more real.

Now the question that sometimes popped unexpectedly into his head would be a bit more specific. *Had he been responsible for Nick's death?*

David pulled his thoughts back to Jessie. "Why do you think so?"

"I felt useless. I didn't know anyone, and Nick didn't want me to get a job. I pretty much slept all day." Jessie moved around restlessly in her chair. "You mind if I ask you something now?"

"Of course not."

"I understand you ran into my mother at the country club on Saturday night."

"Yes, I did. Let me reiterate what I said on Thursday. You are my patient, not your mother. I would never talk to your mother about you or your treatment."

David saw her smile a smile that didn't reach her eyes. "I believe you," she said. "And I think my mother believes that as well. She's starting not to like you very much. She likes to be in control, and you don't seem willing to give her the control she wants. She's mentioned that I might receive better treatment at an in-patient facility in Atlanta. But I think the truth is she can't wait to take off for the south of France or wherever for her next great adventure."

"Why would your treatment affect her travels?" David asked.

Jessie sighed. "My mother likes to do what she wants to do, but she also likes to maintain a certain level of respect in this town. And evidently it has been communicated to her by a number of people that a mother's place is with her daughter when that daughter is cracking up, or whatever it is I am doing now. You see, as long as I'm in Augusta, people will know if she has abandoned me. If she could ship me off to Atlanta, no one would know, would they?"

"I see," David replied. He wrote down, *definitely abandonment issues.* "Okay, I think we've probably done enough digging today. You need to know a few other things about how I operate. I'm a behavioral therapist, which means basically that I want you to fake it until you make it."

"What does that mean?"

"It means I'm going to start giving you some homework assignments to get you back to participating in ordinary life again. Are you an honest person?"

"Certainly," Jessie said indignantly.

David looked her straight in the eye. "I hope so. If you truly want to get well, then you will do these homework assignments, and you will report back to me honestly about how you did, and in particular, if you don't do them. If you aren't honest with me about how things are going, we won't make progress, and you won't get better. The discipline involved in doing these tasks and the honesty required from you about the tasks is very important."

"I promise I'll do my best," she said solemnly.

"Good, that's what I want to hear. Your first homework assignment is for you to go to the mall for an hour today and tomorrow. Window shop, observe people, and engage in conversation when it's appropriate. Pretend you're a mystery shopper doing observational research—that is, observing people in their natural habitat."

"But I hate the mall," Jessie protested. "Can't I go somewhere else?"

"Not today and tomorrow," David said. "You will survive an hour in the mall for a couple of days."

CHAPTER 12

Jessie drove straight from the doctor's office to the mall. She couldn't remember the last time she had visited the Augusta Mall, as she didn't consider shopping to be a recreational sport as her mother did. But Dr. Miller hadn't told her she had to shop. All she had to do was put in an hour watching people. She looked at her cellphone as she pulled into a parking place outside the Apple Store. It was 12:00, and she had promised to stay for one hour. Could she, in all fairness, start her time now before she'd even opened the door to her car? Probably not.

A young couple in jeans came out of the store, holding hands. They looked comfortable with each other and very much in love. Jessie envied them. Nick had never been the touchy feely type. Not in private, and definitely not in public. At least not with her.

She got out of the car and walked to the mall entrance, wondering how best to observe people without looking like a potential shoplifter. She stopped outside a restaurant inside the mall entrance and pretended to read the menu. Remembering that it was lunchtime, she decided she could go to the food court and get something to eat. There, she could sit and observe people without anyone ever noticing her.

At the food court, people swarmed like clumps of bees in front of each food vendor. Jessie's stomach growled, and she remembered that all she had eaten for breakfast that day was a banana. The Chinese food smelled good, but the line was shorter at the chicken place. She decided to settle for a chicken sandwich and moved into one of several lines to wait.

In front of her, a woman was bent over a double baby carriage. One of the two very small babies was sleeping, the other was squalling, and the mother was attempting to quiet him with a pacifier. Jessie had a sudden thought. She might have had a baby about the age of these babies if it hadn't been for the accident. A feeling of disorientation swept over her just as the crying baby quieted, and the woman straightened and turned around. With a shock of recognition, Jessie stood face to face with Mary Jane Brinkman, better known as MJ to all of Augusta. Jessie watched as MJ's eyes opened wide with surprise.

An awkward pause, and then a slow, Southern drawl. "Jessie Forrester as I live and breathe." MJ's face crinkled into an attractive smile of happiness.

Jessie found her voice. "Hello, MJ." She felt her chest tighten as she looked from MJ down to the twins. And then she forced out a light-hearted, "How can you be old enough to be a mother? And a mother of twins at that."

MJ shook her head and laughed. "To tell you the truth, I ask myself the same thing every day. Doesn't seem that long ago we were playing tether ball at recess."

Jessie smiled slightly. "Yeah, we had some cutthroat games at the Day School, didn't we?" MJ had been Jessie's best friend all through elementary and middle school. Conveniently, they had lived down the street from each other, and Jessie had spent a fair amount of her childhood at their house.

MJ had reached the front of the line. Before she turned to place her order, she asked, "Won't you join me for lunch? I can't promise that it will be peaceful. But as this is my first journey out alone, I'd sure love your company, and maybe even some help."

For a second Jessie toyed with the idea of getting her food to go. She felt almost nauseated. But she knew her hour wasn't up, and she had promised Dr. Miller. "Sure."

Within five minutes, they were settled at a table for two in a corner big enough to park the double stroller.

"It's really good to see you," MJ said as she unwrapped her sandwich. "I'm sorry I've been unable to get by to visit with you since you've been home. I was bedridden the last few months of my pregnancy, and this really is the first time I've been brave enough to go out alone since the babies were born. What are you doing these days?"

Jessie rolled her eyes. "I'm trying to survive living back home with Mother," she said. Then she figured she might as well give MJ something to report back to her mother, who had, after all, been the one to call Rita in New York and tell her the stories she had heard about Jessie's inability to function in everyday society. "And I've just started therapy with a new doctor here, a Dr. David Miller. Have you heard of him?"

MJ looked suddenly animated. "Heard of him? He's Augusta's most eligible bachelor! Is he as good looking as I've heard? And is he a good therapist?"

Jessie was surprised to realize she hadn't even thought about Dr. Miller as a person. She had been so self-absorbed that she hadn't considered whether he was good looking, or married, or anything else. But now that she was thinking about it, she supposed he was handsome. She said, "Yeah, I suppose he is good looking, but the verdict is still out on how good a therapist he is as I've only had two sessions. He does seem nice, though."

M.J. smiled. "I've heard he's been dating a nurse at University Hospital, but that won't slow down all the single women in this town who still have their eyes on him."

Jessie took a bite of her sandwich as she mulled over this new information. The Hill section of Augusta had always been a very small fishbowl, so she wasn't surprised to hear that people were speculating about Dr. Miller's love life. She decided to move to a different subject.

"What about Allison and Frankie? What are they doing these days?" she asked. They had been a close-knit group back in their younger days. As hard as it had been for Jessie to leave her best friend when she had gone to boarding school, it had been even harder to return at Christmas and realize that she was now the odd man out in their group. While she'd been away, MJ, Allison, and Frankie had shared three months of experiences that Jessie hadn't been a part of.

"Allison is in Ireland getting her doctorate in medieval history," MJ said. "However, I think she's more interested in some Irish guy she met over there than in medieval history. And Frankie is a kindergarten teacher in Columbia, South Carolina. She's engaged to be married in the fall. To another teacher at her elementary school, how about that?"

One of the babies began to make a whimpering sound that soon turned into a full-blown cry. MJ bent to pick up the infant. "I think my leisurely lunch is over." The other baby began stirring around. "Yes, definitely over."

"Can I help you?" Jessie asked tentatively.

"Sure. Hold Sammy while I ready their bottles."

Jessie gingerly picked up the baby and held him close to her, smelling the unmistakable baby powder aroma. She inhaled deeply. "I haven't held a baby this small in forever. It's wonderful."

MJ was pouring water into two small bottles filled with a powdery substance. "Feel free to drop by any time and get your baby fix," she said. She screwed the top on one bottle and began to shake it. "Everyone keeps telling me that twins are easy after a couple of years because they'll play with each other. But now, two years sounds like an eternity." She handed the bottle to Jessie. "Want to feed him?"

Jessie took the extended bottle automatically and placed it in the baby's mouth. Immediately he started sucking.

"I just realized you've hardly eaten any of your lunch," MJ observed. "Let me do that so you can eat."

"No, no." Jessie replied. "I wasn't that hungry. I'd rather do this." Surprisingly, she realized she was being honest with MJ.

"All right, then. I'll feed Jeremy." MJ picked up the other baby, who still wasn't quite awake, and nudged him with the nipple of the second bottle. "Sammy is always ready to eat. Jeremy, not so much. But I try to keep them on the same schedule."

Jessie felt an ache in her heart as she looked down into the blue, trusting eyes of baby Sammy. She could feel tears beginning to well in her eyes, and she wanted to leave before she started sobbing over the loss of a baby that she'd known existed for only a couple of weeks.

At last she pulled the empty bottle out of the baby's mouth. "I think he's done with this, and I've just remembered an appointment I have shortly."

MJ, struggling to keep the bottle in Jeremy's mouth, looked disappointed. "Put

Sammy here in the buggy," she said. "I'm really glad that we bumped into each other today." She shifted Jeremy a little higher on her arm before continuing. "I know you've been through a difficult time, and I'd like you to know that I meant what I said about you dropping by any time. With the twins, it's hard to get out much, but I'd really love for us to reconnect. With you back in Augusta, let's make it happen."

Jessie placed little Sammy carefully in the blankets and gathered the remains of her lunch. "Okay," she said. Then as she rose from the table she added vaguely, "I'll give you a call." She glanced at her watch. It was 1:45. She'd completed her homework. She could leave.

The next day, Jessie rose early. She dressed in her exercise clothes and sneakers and was at the mall at 8 a.m. to walk with the geriatrics before the stores opened. She figured that by putting herself in that location at that hour, she could do her homework without running into any of her contemporaries.

By 9:15, she'd done what was required of her. She'd observed sweet elderly couples plodding along, and energetic gray-haired women power walking. She'd forced smiles in response to their cheerful hellos. She had even managed some friendly banter with an eighty or so year-old man who flirted with her. "I hope we'll see you again," he said as she started to leave, "It's so nice to share the company of a young, beautiful girl." The happy smile on his face when she'd replied, "Yes" brought a bit of lightness to her otherwise dreary day.

CHAPTER 13

David had added two more patients—an eighteen-year-old angry, rebellious male and a middle-aged woman undergoing a painful divorce. He had to make himself focus on their situations as he set up their files because his mind tended to drift back to Jessie Graham whenever he let it.

He had dreamt of the accident the previous night. Waked up shaken after feeling the warmth of her body in his arms and seeing the blood slowly redden her white-blonde hair. The dream had been very true to life, with one exception. Instead of handing her off to the EMTs as had happened in reality, in the dream he had dropped her on the ground. She had fallen with a sickening thud, opened her startlingly blue eyes, and asked him one word, *Why?*

He had lain awake until the morning light gleamed through the windows. He wondered what his subconscious was trying to tell him. Why was the girl in his office so different from the one in the accident? Why hadn't he told Jessie the truth immediately after realizing who she was? And why did he feel so strongly that he was the only one who could help her?

To shake off his mental fuzziness from lack of sleep, David poured himself another cup of strong, black coffee in the break room. He looked over to the door when he heard voices and saw Jessie being escorted by Cindy to his office. Jessie was unaware of him watching her. Unlike the vivid blonde in his dream, this Jessie had caramel-colored hair that had been left free today to fall in soft waves. It gave her an earthy look, particularly when combined with the blue jeans and gauzy orange top she was wearing.

Jessie was standing, looking out of the window when he came in. She turned with a blank look on her face.

"Anything interesting out there?" David asked lightly. He walked behind her to take a quick glance out the window and caught a whiff of her shampoo or scent that reminded him of the outdoors. "Nothing but the same old pine trees as far as I can see. I just made some coffee. May I get some for you?"

"No, I'm good, thanks." She turned from the window.

"Okay, let's get started." David sat down behind his desk and motioned for Jessie to sit in front of him. "How've you been doing the past couple of days?"

"I've been okay. I did my homework."

"And what else?" David asked. "How much have you been sleeping?"

"I've probably slept a little less than usual."

"Which is?" David prodded.

"I don't know. Maybe 15 or so hours a day."

David wrote that down. "What activities other than your homework have you done?"

Jessie looked surprised at the question. "Just the usual. Don't you want to know about my trips to the mall?

"Yes, and we'll get to that at the end of our session. Tell me, what is your usual? How do you fill your days?"

"I guess I watch a lot of television. Sometimes I run errands for our housekeeper, Maggie."

"Nothing else?"

Jessie shook her head.

David decided to change direction. Sometimes he got more honest answers when the patient wasn't prepared for the question. "Okay," he said. "How about we talk about your father for a bit? What was he like as a dad?"

Jessie shifted and leaned slightly forward in her seat. "He was the best dad ever."

"Why?" David wished he could decipher the expressions that flickered over her face.

Finally, she said, "I was important to him. He loved doing stuff with me."

"What kind of stuff?"

"He always tried to have breakfast with me. And if he was home, he read to me before I went to bed. Just simple stuff."

"Did your mother share these times with the two of you?"

"No. My mother liked to stay up late and sleep in. And she hated staying home at night. She was twenty-five years younger than my father, and reading Harry Potter bedtime stories wasn't her idea of fun."

"What was your mother's idea of fun?"

Jessie shifted again in her chair. "She enjoyed going out to dinner and parties and movies with friends. Anything other than being at home." Jessie leaned back in her seat. "If you don't mind, I'll take some of that coffee now."

"Sure, come on. I'll show you where the break room is. Feel free to help yourself at any time during our sessions."

CHAPTER 14

Five minutes later, Jessie was back in Dr. Miller's office, slowly sipping her coffee and remembering MJ's statement about him being Augusta's most eligible bachelor. Now that she was looking at him from MJ's perspective, she could clearly see how handsome he was—probably in his late thirties, with the rugged look that was so popular these days. And he had those brown eyes that seemed larger than an average man's eyes.

"Are you ready to talk about your homework now?" Dr. Miller interrupted her thoughts. "I'd like to hear about your trip to the mall on Monday. What'd you do? Who'd you observe?"

Jessie had been anticipating more talk about her mother, so she felt a bit disoriented by his sudden shift in subjects. "Well, I left here and went straight to the mall. Since it was lunchtime, I thought I'd go to the food court and get something to eat. While waiting in a food line, I ran into an old Augusta friend, MJ. She and I ate lunch together. By the time that was done, my hour was up."

Jessie noticed Dr. Miller making a note. She wished she could see what he was writing about her. "So tell me about this old friend, MJ? You've led me to believe that you have no friends here in Augusta."

Jessie sighed. "I meant no current friends. MJ was a childhood friend. Our mothers were, I mean, still are friends. You know the kind, tennis and Bloody Mary lunch friends. And MJ and I sort of grew up together."

"How come you and MJ didn't remain friends?"

"I went to boarding school for high school. She stayed here. We lost touch." She shifted some more in her chair.

"How long after your father died did you start boarding school?"

"Two months."

"How long after you went off to school would you say that you and MJ remained friends?"

Jessie thought for a moment. "I suppose our really close friendship was pretty much done by the time I came home for Christmas break. I realized that things were different between us. I mean, everything in MJ's life was the same. And everything in my life was different. We didn't have much in common anymore."

Dr. Miller made a more few notes. "Other than the obvious, that you'd lost your father and were going to a boarding school in Virginia, what else was different in your life than in MJ's?"

Jessie felt unexpectedly irritated, "Well, there was the fact that MJ still had both of her parents, and I, for all practical purposes, had lost both of mine. That was a pretty big difference."

"So you felt like you'd lost your mother as well?" he asked.

"How else could I feel? I was fourteen years old, terribly homesick in a totally foreign place. I called home to beg my mother to come get me, ready to promise her anything if she would just bring me home. But to my surprise, Maggie told me that she was in Europe for an indefinite stay. And my mother had never mentioned to me that she was going. Yeah. I felt like I had lost my mother, too."

Jessie watched Dr. Miller's face, but there was no sign of what he might be thinking. "Did you feel any connection to MJ the other day?" he asked.

Jessie was again surprised at his swift change in the conversation's direction, and just when she was ready to really blast her mother, "Yes," she admitted honestly. "MJ had these twin babies, and she needed my help. And surprisingly, I really wanted to help her."

"Did you?"

"Yes. I fed one of the babies a bottle."

"Did you like feeding the baby?"

Jessie recalled how perfectly the baby had fit in her arms. "Yes."

Jessie noticed Dr. Miller looking at his watch. "I guess you'd better tell me about your experience on Tuesday before we run out of time."

"I went to the mall on Tuesday before it opened and walked for an hour. And before you fuss at me, there were plenty of people for me to observe, and I even interacted with some of them."

He halfway smiled. "Monday was more the kind of experience I was hoping you would have."

Jessie countered, "You never said the mall had to be open."

"You got me there." After a pause, he said, "Exercise is also good. Your homework for the next couple of weeks is the same, but it doesn't have to be the mall. I'd like for you to get out in public somewhere for an hour each day where you are interacting with people. You can continue your early morning mall walking one day of the week, but I'd prefer for you to see more of a mix of people on other days. Maybe go for a walk in a park or go to an exercise facility. Just get out among different groups of people."

Jessie asked, "Do you use this sort of treatment plan on all of your patients?"

Dr. Miller nodded. "I'm a behavioral therapist, remember? I believe that people can learn new behaviors. I also believe that people can't empathize with others, or with themselves, if they are never around other people. Human beings weren't designed to spend all of their time alone." He looked directly into her eyes. "You do want to get well, don't you, Jessie?"

Jessie thought for a moment. "I don't really know what *well* means. But I'm tired of feeling the way I feel."

"I think that's a good start." He stood up from behind the desk. "And that's it for today. I'll look forward to hearing about your further adventures on Friday."

When Jessie arrived home, she smelled her mother's perfume before she saw her in the kitchen. Rita and Maggie were standing in front of a stack of cookbooks, and Jessie felt herself tense, ready to do battle.

"There you are," her mother said. "Did you accomplish anything today?"

"Yes. Dr. Miller said I was cured."

Rita turned to Maggie, "Have you ever heard such a rude daughter?" Turning back to Jessie, she said firmly, "I just want to know if this doctor, whom we really know nothing about, is doing you any good."

"Things are going fine." Jessie was suddenly incredibly weary. She wanted nothing more than to escape her mother's gaze. "Can I go upstairs now?"

"Sure, go rest, because we're having company for dinner tonight. I've invited Phoebe and MJ and their husbands, and I expect you to dine with us."

Surprised, Jessie stopped mid-stride. "It would have been nice if you had checked with me first before inviting over people whom I'm expected to help entertain."

"I think we both know that would have been futile," Rita countered. "But since Phoebe said that you and MJ had such a nice visit with each other at the mall on Monday, I thought certainly you would enjoy seeing her again. Whether you appreciate it or not, I'm doing this for you."

"Of course you are, Mother." Jessie felt anger rise quick and sharp. "Just like you were only thinking of me when you sent me off to boarding school. And that semester abroad that I didn't want to take was all for my benefit too, wasn't it? And, oh yes, you were only thinking of me when you encouraged me to marry Nick. It had nothing to do with how wonderful you thought it might look to have a doctor for a son-in-law."

Jessie saw Maggie shoot her a warning look. Thinking she might have a rare last word, she turned to leave the room.

But, no. Her mother would always have the last word. "Am I always going to be responsible for everything that's gone wrong in your life?" Rita demanded. "You might want to talk on Friday with Dr. Miller about taking personal responsibility for your own life."

Lying on her pristine bed, with the drapes closed tightly to darken the room, Jessie took solace in the fact that the dinner party could probably count as her homework for the night, so she didn't have to go out again later in the day. She stared at the ceiling blankly until, blissfully, sleep finally overtook her.

CHAPTER 15

David called Amelia to see if it might be a good weekend for him to visit since he hadn't seen his nephews in several weeks. He was always amazed by how much they changed between visits.

"Of course!" Amelia said. "You are welcome anytime, and Mike's thinking about finally getting started on that back deck. I'm sure he'd love your help."

"Hey, I want to spend time with my nephews, not work on a deck," David complained.

"Okay, I'll help Mike with the deck and you can babysit."

David laughed. "I'll see you late Friday afternoon. One good thing about not having very many patients is that I can always leave early on Fridays. Not much money coming in, but I have lots of time to visit my family."

He decided to go for a run just as a text came in from Lillie, wanting to know if he was interested in dinner. He decided he'd text her after he finished his run. After all, if the message had come in one minute later, he would have missed it.

Within minutes, sweat was dripping into his eyes. Somehow it seemed hotter in Augusta than in Atlanta, even if the two cities were only two hours apart and in a perfectly straight line from each other on the map. However, the beauty of the area helped to make up for the heat. He was renting a small cottage behind a grand old house in the heart of The Hill area. The towering oaks and majestic magnolias that lined the street where he lived were spectacular. Although he wasn't much of an expert on plants, he realized that the multitudes of azalea bushes filling almost every yard would be beautiful to behold come spring.

He stopped to let a car go by in front of one of the most intriguing houses on his running route. The white mansion, which occupied almost a full city block, could have been lifted from the pages of *Gone with the Wind*. Four white columns on the front and a circular driveway provided those passing by with a hint of the elegant grandeur that must lie inside. Even the white brick mailbox contributed to the perfect picture, with ivy growing tastefully around and through its wrought iron pedestal. For the first time, he noticed that the name in the wrought iron read, "Forrester."

Could this possibly be Rita Forrester's house? A woman like that would live in a house like this. He imagined Jessie as a child growing up in such a massive mansion. One might hide and never be found in a place as large as this.

Then, as he started to run again, he thought to himself, *That's just what Jessie's doing now. She's gone into hiding in that house, and no one has even bothered to look for her.*

CHAPTER 16

Jessie sensed Maggie's presence but kept her eyes closed because she knew what was coming next. Sure enough, Jessie felt Maggie's light touch stroking her back in a half scratch, half rub that was the way Maggie had always awakened her for as far back as Jessie could remember. The pressure increased until Jessie opened her eyes.

"Come on, baby girl," Maggie urged her. "You need to get up and get dressed for Ms. Rita's dinner party."

Jessie groaned and rolled over to face Maggie. "I really don't want to do this."

"I know, I know," Maggie said soothingly. "But you know Ms. Rita's got her mind made up. You can either go along with her the easy way or deal with her the hard way. And look, I've already picked out one of those new outfits Ms. Rita brought you from New York."

Jessie flipped back to her stomach and put the pillow over her head. "Oh, Maggie, I don't want to wear those clothes."

"I know. But it will make Ms. Rita happy for you to wear one of them. So do it."

"Only because she can then tell everyone how she spent all of her time in New York shopping for me. Just more evidence of what a thoughtful mother she is."

Maggie's voice changed from cajoling to firm. "Baby girl, you get yourself into that shower, right now. The guests will be here in a little over an hour, and I've got to get downstairs and put the final touches on dinner."

Jessie sat up in the bed. "Okay, okay, I'm up. Tell my mother I'll be down by 7:00."

Maggie shook her finger at Jessie. "I'm not telling her any such thing because you will be downstairs by 6:30, or I'll send that MJ up here to help you finish dressing."

Jessie realized when she was beat. She swung her feet over the side of the bed to the floor and stood up. For just a second she felt the room swirl, a not uncommon occurrence when she changed positions rapidly. Maggie could tell that something was wrong and reached for her arm. "Slowly, Jessie, slowly. You okay now."

The room stilled. "Yeah, I'm okay," Jessie said softly. "Go on. You've got to finish dinner."

A little over an hour later, Jessie had showered, applied a thin layer of makeup, and put on the outfit that Maggie had laid out for her—slim tan slacks, a shimmery navy blue top, and silver loop earrings. She heard the voices of her mother and her friend Gerald, ever so distantly in the den as she walked slowly down the steps.

"Jessica!" Gerald exclaimed when she walked into the den. "You look absolutely gorgeous. That outfit your mother and I picked out is stunning on you. Come sit here and catch me up on how you're doing."

Jessie pasted a smile on her face and went to sit next to Gerald on the blue sofa. She glanced up at her father's face over the mantel and wondered for a moment what he might have thought about her mother's best friend. Gerald was an attractive, slightly gray-haired man with a commanding presence. He was equally at ease in her mother's closet helping her coordinate an outfit or at the most formal affairs as her mother's escort. Since he made no secret that he preferred men to women, no one ever gossiped about Rita Forrester when she took Gerald with her to New York or Europe. If anything, most of Rita's friends were jealous of Rita's relationship with Gerald. Who wouldn't want to have a handsome man around who shared their interests in flowers and fashion and never expected more than a peck on the cheek at the end of the night?

"Your mother's been so worried about you," Gerald said conspiratorially in a fake whisper.

Jessie was saved from replying by the chime of the doorbell and by Rita's swift movement toward the front door. Gerald, the quintessential Southern gentleman, rose and followed her. Jessie made a silent vow to put on her best act tonight. As Dr. Miller had said, she needed to 'fake it until she could make it.' And that's what she vowed to do.

Rita led Will, Phoebe, and Tom through the archway into the den, and Gerald brought up the rear.

"What can I get you to drink?" asked Gerald. "Phoebe, a glass of merlot? Something stronger for the gentlemen?"

Jessie was confused to see Tom by himself. "Where's MJ?" she asked no one in particular.

Tom turned from Gerald to Jessie. He was fairly short for a man, with a receding hairline that seemed more appropriate for a forty-something-year-old than the thirty-two- year-old he was. "One of the twins might be running a fever, and she decided she'd better stay home tonight than leave them with a strange babysitter," he said.

Phoebe stepped into their conversation. "It's Rita's fault. She invited MJ and her most trusted babysitters to the same dinner party!" She sat down next to Jessie and gave her a hug. She had cropped white hair and a classic air of sophistication.

"I saw the twins the other day at the mall," Jessie began. "You must be very proud of your grandchildren and of MJ. She seems like a wonderful mother."

Phoebe beamed with pride. 'Yes," she said in the Southern drawl upon which MJ's voice had obviously been patterned, "MJ was disappointed that she couldn't come tonight. But I don't think she would have enjoyed herself while worrying about little Sammy all night."

Jessie noticed that Tom didn't seem to be having a problem enjoying himself as he accepted a dry martini with three olives and laughed heartily at something Gerald was saying. Tom might have stayed home with poor little Sammy and let his wife have a night out with her family's friends.

Gerald handed Phoebe her wine. "Anything for you, Jessie? Wine? Soda? Water?"

"Nothing, thanks."

"How are you doing, dear girl?" Phoebe asked.

Phoebe's Southern tones stirred long-dormant memories for Jessie. She decorated sugar cookies at their house and had her hair French braided with ribbons by Phoebe. "I think I'm doing better," she answered honestly.

Phoebe gave her another quick hug as she said, "I'm so happy to hear that!"

Maggie came in with a tray of appetizers and set it down on the coffee table in front of Phoebe and Jessie. Rita sat down in the chair on Phoebe's right and skewered a shrimp with a toothpick.

"Imagine my surprise," she said, her eyes pointedly on Jessie, "when I ran into Phoebe yesterday at tennis, and she told me that you and MJ had a lovely lunch at the mall—your least favorite place in the whole world." Rita smiled grimly. "I really wish you had told me you were going, and I would have gone with you."

Jessie could easily have explained that having lunch at the mall had only been part of her therapy. But she preferred to let her mother think whatever she wanted to think. Perhaps her mother would be encouraged to believe that Jessie was on her way to psychological wellness because she had suddenly discovered a love for the mall.

Phoebe, the perfect guest, sensed the tension between mother and daughter and changed the subject. "You still haven't told me about your trip to New York, Rita," she said. "I can't imagine anything worse than New York in the summer."

"The weather was ghastly hot, but we saw three plays, and the shopping was spectacular. As a matter of fact, Jessie is wearing the Stella McCartney slacks and Nicole Miller top I bought her in New York."

Phoebe looked at Jessie again. "I do love your outfit, and you look so pretty now that you've let your hair go natural again. You never seemed quite right as a platinum-blonde. Looking at you now, I think you look just like your dad."

Jessie watched Rita squirm uncomfortably. After all, Rita had suggested Jessie's makeover after Nick's interest in her had seemed to fade soon after the wedding. "It's a woman's responsibility to make herself appealing to her husband," Rita had instructed Jessie. Obediently, Jessie had followed Rita to New York where specialists had given her facials and dyed her blondish brown hair to a white blonde. Then Rita had scoured the best stores and bought her a new wardrobe. Jessie had returned to Atlanta a different woman on the outside, and her new appearance had seemed to garner Nick's attention again, at least for a while.

"Dinner is ready," Maggie said from the doorway.

Rita rose gracefully and motioned to the men. "Will you escort us into the dining room?"

Gerald moved toward Rita and offered his arm. Will followed suit with Phoebe, which left Tom and Jessie staring awkwardly at each other. They had not liked each other from the moment they'd met in college at Georgia. Jessie knew Tom considered her to be odd, and as far as she was concerned, he was a pompous ass. *Fake it until you make it,* Jessie reminded herself. She pasted on another false smile and asked pleasantly, "Shall we go into the dining room?" He nodded, and they walked silently, side by side without touching, where unfortunately Jessie found Tom seated at her right-hand side at the dining room table. Luckily, Phoebe was on her left.

During dinner, conversations swirled around Jessie like eddies on a beach without her having to bother to stick her toe into the water. Only occasionally did a conversational wave break over her, forcing her to get wet.

Two hours later, wiping the rarely-worn makeup from her face, she felt exhausted. If it hadn't been for Phoebe's sincere efforts to make the night go smoothly, Jessie never could have endured the evening. *Why couldn't her mother be more like Phoebe?*

CHAPTER 17

After almost a month of the three-times-a-week sessions with Jessie, David was frustrated. He had not done such intensive therapy since medical school. In the military, critical patients were sent off to in-patient facilities. The others had to make do with what treatment they could get, which was nothing like the treatment Jessie was receiving.

However, even if he hadn't practiced intensive therapy for a while, he knew that successful treatment required an intimacy between patient and therapist that had failed so far to materialize between him and Jessie. She'd remained frustratingly distant as they'd explored her nonexistent relationship with her mother and her deeply rooted love for her father. She'd answered his questions about Nick without ever shedding a tear or really exhibiting any kind of emotion. He had been waiting for a bond to form between he and Jessie before telling her about his role in her accident. Now he was beginning to think that maybe he should tell her in the hope that the truth might shake her out of her malaise.

Andy certainly would be happy if David told Jessie his secret. Andy stopped by with an expectant look on his face after each of David's sessions with Jessie. Then he issued dire warnings after discovering David had failed to reveal the truth once again. In a way, David was surprised that Andy hadn't already taken matters into his own hands and told Jessie the truth. It was past time.

Jessie arrived promptly as always for her appointment, which David took as a positive sign. Severely depressed people were frequently late or canceled appointments at the last minute with inane excuses.

She hadn't pulled her hair back again today, and it fell softly around a face that appeared largely devoid of makeup. Again, he contrasted this naturally pretty girl with the stunningly beautiful woman from the accident. Whether it was a result of her depression or a part of her natural state of being, the girl in his office seemed to have very little interest in her outward appearance.

David wanted to transition gradually to his confession rather than jump into it. "Today, I thought we'd talk about your husband a bit more," he began after Jessie was settled in her chair. He watched her nod, a strained look on her face. "Did you consider him to be a good doctor?"

"I suppose so," she said quietly. "He was at the top of his graduating class and he was offered a position right out of residency with a very sought-after practice in Atlanta."

David looked down at his notes. "You said earlier that Nick was gone a lot when you moved to Atlanta and that his absence made you feel depressed." Jessie nodded. "What was your relationship like with him at that time?"

Jessie began hesitantly. "I guess you might say that marriage wasn't exactly what I had expected it to be."

"Which was...?"

Jessie shrugged. "You know. Happily ever after and all that stuff."

"Can you be more explicit?" David asked.

"Once we were married," she said calmly, "I realized that surgery was my husband's first love. He was never too tired for a date with an appendectomy, but was always too tired for dinner or a movie out with me."

David imagined the dark-headed Nick from the accident being so committed to his job of saving people's lives that he worked all the time. His death had been a real loss in many ways. "How did you meet your husband?"

"Do you remember me telling you about my sorority sister, Wendy?"

David nodded.

"I met Nick because Wendy went a little wild one night." Jessie gave a half-hearted laugh. "My naïve and sweet little friend had an argument with the guy who is now her husband, and she decided to show him that she didn't need him anymore. So we went to a fraternity band party, and my friend, who never drank much, got herself drunk on cheap red wine. Nick had come with another medical resident who was visiting his brother. Nick helped me take care of Wendy that night. By the time Wendy was well enough to go running back to Lloyd, Nick had sort of swept me off my feet."

David felt a pang of guilt, thinking about all that Jessie had lost in the car accident. "Go, on."

Jessie stood up and walked to the window. "Nick was very handsome, and he could be charming when he wanted to be." The unexpected pain in her expression made David realize suddenly that Nick often hadn't been charming.

"When did things start to change?"

"As soon as the honeymoon was over, really," Jessie said honestly. "We moved to Atlanta, and from the very beginning things were different. I began to feel as if everything I did irritated him."

"Can you give me an example?"

Jessie walked back to her chair. "I was pretty clueless around the house. All of my life I'd eaten in restaurants or had someone cook for me. I didn't know how to do the laundry or clean the house because the boarding school I went to included maid service. And when I went to Georgia, my mother sent our housekeeper, Maggie, to Athens every Saturday to clean up and wash my clothes."

David found it interesting that she said these things so matter-of-factly, as though it weren't uncommon for a woman in college to have maid service and to graduate from college without basic life skills. Did she have any idea how pampered she'd been?

Then Jessie added, "But I tried to learn how to do those things after we were married." She made an attempt at a laugh. "I had some spectacular failures. Did you know that 'tsp' means teaspoon and not tablespoon? Let me tell you, it makes a big difference when you're making chicken tortilla soup."

David made a couple of notes while keeping his face expressionless.

Jessie's face went tight and grim as she continued. "About a year after we were married, I discovered Nick was seeing a woman he had known before our marriage."

"How'd you find out about it?" Something that felt very much like anger hit David, a feeling that was unexpectedly strong.

"Clarisse, that was the other woman's name, believed Nick when he told her that he was going to leave me for her. I suppose she thought that telling me about their long, passionate love affair would make me leave him and speed things along." Jessie paused and then continued without expression. "Her telling me about their wonderful sex life almost worked."

"What made you stay?"

"Nick begged me to stay. He agreed to go to marriage counseling and declared his undying love for me, and I, like a fool, believed him."

David watched her face struggling with emotions, "Why do you say like a fool?" He thought they might finally be on the verge of a breakthrough, but then her mask snapped back into place. She put her hand to her head and rubbed her forehead with her fingers. "I'm really starting to get a headache. Do you think we might call it a day?"

David looked at his watch. They still had about thirty minutes, plenty of time for him to share his secret with her. "How about I get you a cup of coffee and some Advil? You can relax for a few minutes. There's something I want to tell you."

She nodded in agreement, a resigned expression on her face.

While David was getting her coffee, he rehearsed what he was about to say and imagined Jessie's possible reactions to his confession. Regardless of what was going to happen, it was past time for him to tell her the truth.

He returned with her coffee and Advil. After she accepted the pill and had sipped on her coffee for a minute, David said carefully, "I need to tell you something about myself. Honestly, I probably should have told you this when we first started counseling. It was just that... I didn't know quite how to tell you."

He sat down and watched her looking at him with curiosity, or was that suspicion? He wasn't sure. He took a deep breath and hoped for the best. "As you know, I lived in Atlanta before moving here."

"No," she said hesitantly. "I don't remember you saying that you lived in Atlanta."

"Well, I did, at least sort of Atlanta. I was based out of Fort McPherson." David knew he was stalling. "On the night of April 2nd of last year, I was involved in an accident on Riverside Drive."

Jessie's eyes widened with confusion. "What? Why, that's the night of my accident."

"I know." David took another deep breath. "Jessie, I was the one who called 911 that night. I was the one who pulled you from your Mercedes."

"I don't understand." Her blue eyes looked as wide as saucers in her pale face.

David tried again. "You were in a red Mercedes. It crashed into a tree on Nick's side of the car. You had long, white-blonde hair and wore a silver dress."

Her eyes widened even more as the truth finally hit her. "Oh, my God! You were there. How? Why?" Her voice trailed off as she seemed to lose her train of thought.

David forged ahead. "Why didn't I tell you when you first walked into my office?"

Jessie nodded, her face telling him nothing.

"I honestly didn't recognize you the first day. I never knew your name before you walked in, and you look much different now than you did that night."

Jessie stared blankly at him. "But when I told you about the accident, you knew then."

"Yes," David agreed. "I don't know why I didn't say something immediately except that I was stunned by the incredible coincidence. And you seemed so fragile that day. I was afraid you would run, not walk, out of this office. I honestly thought it might turn you away from therapy, which you really seemed to need. So I decided it was in your best interests to tell you when you were stronger."

CHAPTER 18

Jessie was unsure of what she was feeling or what she should be feeling. She looked at the man sitting in front of her, her doctor whom she'd come to think of as sort of a friend, and he'd turned into a total stranger. Finally, she said, "You pulled me out of the car that night?"

"Yes," he replied.

"You saw Nick?"

"Yes."

In a ragged voice, she said, "I can't really remember that night. I remember lights, and I have a vague memory of being held." Jessie looked down at Dr. Miller's hands and suddenly realized that the hands that had held her that night had been his. They weren't like Nick's hands, which had been soft and pink. Dr. Miller's hands were tanned and calloused with a Band-Aid showing on his wrist near the edge of his shirt sleeve. Knowing that those hands had held her made her feel shaky, unbalanced, as though everything in her world had shifted and now was slightly off kilter.

Although he seemed to be waiting for her to say something, she couldn't think of anything to say. Finally he said, "I understand if you want to change doctors. However, I believe that I can help you better than another doctor because I know what you went through that night."

Still unable to process everything, Jessie asked, "You were in the car that came around the corner?"

"Yes."

Jessie was suddenly back in the car with Nick in the darkness and then the sudden bright lights of another car. She looked up at Dr. Miller, the person behind those lights, who was now in front of her. "What happened that night?"

Jessie watched him move restlessly in his chair. "It had been raining. There were standing puddles of water on the road. I think Nick hit one going too fast."

"No, I mean...tell me what you were doing that night. Why were you on Riverside Drive?"

"Do you remember I told you I have twin nephews?"

"Yes."

"They were born that night. I was on my way to a date when my brother-in-law called to tell me the news about the babies' birth. It was sprinkling rain and dark, and I came around a corner. I was blinded for a second or two by the lights of your car. Then I watched as your car spun in a circle and went off the edge of the road. I parked, called 911, slid down the hill to where I saw you hanging upside down inside the car, and then got you out of the car."

"Was Nick dead when you got to the car?" Jessie asked grimly.

"I think so. I couldn't find a pulse."

Jessie processed the information for a minute or two, her heart beating so hard that she thought it might explode in her chest. She finally said, "I know I should say something, but I can't think right now."

"Of course. I know this has been a shock. But nothing's really changed. This is still a safe place for you. And I promise you can trust me."

"Can I?" Jessie asked. "I thought you said it took honesty for therapy to work. Well, you certainly haven't been honest with me." She was quiet for a moment. "I'm going to go now."

"But you'll be back on Monday, right?"

She nodded slightly.

David wondered if he could trust that head nod.

CHAPTER 19

After Jessie left, David walked over to Andy's office. He was relieved to see that his partner's door was open, indicating that Andy was between patients.

"Got a sec?" he asked Andy, who was typing furiously on his computer, indicating that he really didn't have a second. Nevertheless, he stopped typing and swiveled around in his chair.

David leaned against the door frame. "I finally came clean with Jessie."

Andy's eyes grew big with surprise and, perhaps, relief. "How'd it go?"

"About as well as it could have gone, I guess. She seemed shocked, confused, and uncertain. I may have just lost us my best client."

"I'm okay with you losing a patient. I just don't want a lawsuit."

"I know," David admitted.

"What's next?"

"She's going to let me know on Monday."

"You and Lillie want to come over for dinner tonight, and we can talk some more? My next patient is already in the waiting room."

"Thanks, but I'm going to the mountains for the weekend." David started to leave but then turned around. "I'm sure Jan already knows this, but Lillie and I aren't dating anymore."

Andy shook his head in disbelief. "You may have set a new record for dating a girl seriously and then breaking up. It's hard to know someone after such a short time."

"Believe me. I knew she wasn't the one for me, so I didn't want to string her along."

"Well, I hope you are just as confident about what you are doing with Jessie Graham. Then, maybe her mother won't try to ruin us."

CHAPTER 20

After leaving the doctor's office, Jessie was driving to the one place where she knew she could sit and think in peace.

In the spring, the meandering road through the cemetery was a showcase for the dogwoods and azaleas that lined both of its sides, offering a tranquil peacefulness to those traveling on it. But today, the azaleas looked brown and parched from the unusually dry summer. Today Jessie found the twisting road through the cemetery to her dad's gravesite devoid of anything resembling beauty or peace.

She pulled her car over, parked, and got out. Her father's black and grey marble headstone was substantial but not ostentatious, just like him. There were two gravestones located to the right of her father's headstone. One was for Lucinda Caldwell Forrester, his first wife, and the other was for Rosalyn, his first daughter, who had been stillborn. Jessie said a little prayer for all three, and then, as she had done often in the past, went to sit on a concrete bench under a magnolia tree.

The heat was a physical force that lay heavily on her. This day was very different from the last time she had come to the cemetery, when it had been bone-chillingly cold. It was the day after a cocktail party given in honor of her upcoming marriage to Nick. The party had been stressful from its inception. She had asked her mother for a small event, but the final guest count had been close to 150. Nick had been on call the night before the party and hadn't gotten much sleep. On the night of the party, he was exhausted and irritable, and he was drinking much more than he was eating.

Recognizing the early signs of trouble in his behavior and pulling him to a back bedroom to talk privately, Jessie had offered to get him a glass of water.

"Waterrrrrr?" he had said loudly, slurring the "r." Waterrrr isn't what adults drink at parrrrrties. That's what little girrrrrls like you drink."

Insulted, Jessie had left him alone and returned to the party. Later, when she found him snoring loudly in that same back bedroom, she made no effort to wake him. She'd explained to the party hostesses that he had been up all of the previous night, which was true. She also said that he'd been feeling ill earlier in the evening, which wasn't true. The sympathetic owners of the house had insisted that he stay there and sleep undisturbed for the rest of the night.

So she'd left him, but had gotten up early the next morning to go to the cemetery to think, seriously considering calling off the wedding. It wasn't the first time Nick had embarrassed her when he'd been drinking, as he wasn't a nice drunk. But he was a really good apologizer after the damage was done.

"Please forgive me," he'd begged later when he'd come to talk to her. He'd looked about as bad as he professed to feel about his actions the night before. "It's been a difficult week at the hospital, and I've had very little sleep." Then playing off her own frustrations with the party, he'd added, "There were so many people I didn't know, and so many important people that I'd like to know. I think I drank too much because I was nervous about the party in the first place."

Jessie's resolve weakened. She understood completely his need for support to get through one of her mother's parties.

"If you want me to," he continued, "I'll stop drinking. I can lose the alcohol, but I can't lose you!"

He'd looked so desperately unhappy and so adorably handsome pleading his case that Jessie's hardened heart had softened. She was wary of certain parts of Nick. But when he'd taken one step forward and wrapped her in his arms, his embrace had felt just right. And when he'd begun to kiss her, she wondered why she'd ever doubted that being anywhere but in his arms was where she was supposed to be.

Sitting on the concrete bench in the cemetery now, contemplating the disastrous years since that earlier day, Jessie vowed to make better life choices. She wouldn't ignore warning signs when they were right in front of her. And wasn't Dr. Miller's lack of honesty with her a red flag if there ever was one? He had been preaching about the need for complete honesty for therapy to work, when he wasn't being honest with her about the accident.

She supposed she could understand his initial shock when he discovered who she was. What she couldn't understand was why he hadn't told her about the connection between them the next day or any of the other days of her therapy. While he'd been probing her most intimate thoughts and experiences, his delay in revealing the truth about her accident seemed unethical. She wondered if the best thing to do would be to call his office and say she wasn't coming back anymore.

If she were being totally honest with herself, however, she knew that he'd already begun to help her. She recalled that first day leaving his office and feeling as though there was nothing in her life to look forward to. Her feelings had been scary, making her think life itself was pointless. Now she had begun to look forward to their sessions. The thought of not having those sessions was unsettling, as was the thought that, if Rita found out what Jessie had learned today, she'd likely bring up that treatment facility in Atlanta again.

The heat was becoming unbearable, so Jessie stood up to leave. "Daddy," she whispered, "I remember you telling me that I could do anything when I put my mind to it. If only you'd been around a little longer, maybe I would have started believing you."

CHAPTER 21

As David drove to Amelia's house, his thoughts returned again and again to Jessie. He worried about the blank expression on her face as she left his office. He wondered if he shouldn't have insisted that she stay for a while longer and talk to him. Yet how could he have forced her to stay? He wondered about Rita's reaction if Jessie chose to tell her about his lack of honesty. He imagined that things could go badly really fast for him and, unfortunately, also for Andy. He never should have put Andy in this situation.

As the mountains appeared like a blue line in the distance, David's thoughts shifted. Tomorrow would be the 30-year anniversary of his mother's death. He'd gotten good at blocking out the painful memories over the years, but he never forgot. Would his sister remember? After all, she'd been only a two-year-old at the time, and their dad hadn't made remembering their mother a priority when he remarried within six months of her death.

In medical school, David had diagnosed their mother's condition as a neurosis with significant postpartum depression. Attaching a label to her behaviors had helped him to step back and analyze her objectively rather than emotionally. She had been sick. Still, sometimes he longed for his mother as a young boy might and felt white-hot anger toward his father, who had never tried to get his mother the help she needed. Perhaps in a different situation, with a more loving and generous husband and with the proper treatment, his mother might have been different, might even still be alive.

As he went up the unpaved driveway, he felt more peaceful just looking at the log cabin home Amelia and Mike had made their own. The scattered flowerbeds, fruit trees, and vegetable garden screamed practicality rather than landscape design. Still, David found a beauty in the haphazard arrangement of their front yard that he never saw in perfectly manicured lawns.

When he got out of his car and smelled the welcoming charcoal aroma of the grill, his peaceful feelings expanded. He walked around to the back of the house where his brother-in-law stood with a barbecue fork in one hand and a beer in the other. The lid of the grill, which sat on the partly-completed back deck, was open.

"Smells good." David grinned when Mike's head whipped around in his direction.

"Hope so," Mike replied casually as though he hadn't just been startled. "I've been cooking these ribs for a couple of hours already." He poked one with the fork. "I think we're getting close."

"Good man. What's on our agenda for the weekend?"

"Getting the deck railings up. Amelia says you can't leave until we get these railings installed."

"Speaking of whom," David said, "let me go tell her I'm here."

He opened the kitchen door quietly to see Amelia putting food on the trays of the boys' high chairs. He was always amazed at how his nephews changed between each of his visits. They looked like such little boys now, sitting in their high chairs and eating by themselves.

Amelia's dark hair was pulled back in a loose braid, and David gave it a playful yank before jumping back quickly as she whirled around with a spoon in her hand.

"Ouch! You! Just wait 'til the boys get a little bigger. They'll beat you up for something like that."

David smiled knowingly. "Not when Uncle David is the one who brings them treats and spoils them rotten." He leaned in and gave Amelia a kiss on the cheek before turning to greet his nephews.

Later they ate their meal, taking turns stopping the boys' mischief. On one of his turns at twin-intervention, David noticed that Amelia had finished the painting of the lake behind their house, a canvas that she had been working on for several months. The picture was framed and displayed on an easel in what had been a dining room but was now Amelia's art studio. David admired the blues, pinks, and purples captured perfectly in the dappled light of a sunset.

"You finished the lake painting. Congratulations," he said, once back in the kitchen. "It's spectacular."

"I'm glad you like it. The painting is your birthday present."

"Wait! My birthday isn't until March."

"Well, it's sort of a combination late present 'cause I didn't get it finished in time for your birthday last year, as well as an early present for this year."

David felt a rush of warmth for his sister's thoughtfulness. "As beautiful as it is, it definitely should cover a lot of birthdays." Then with concern he added, "Are you sure you want to give this to me? A painting like this would command a large commission."

"Oh, hush, and say thank you, Mel."

"Thank you, Mel!"

When David left for home on Sunday night, he and Mike had finished putting up the railings. The physical labor had been just what he needed to keep his mind from drifting into places where he didn't want it to go. He'd had no time to think about the anniversary of his mother's death or about what might happen with Jessie on Monday. But he knew it wasn't just the physical labor that made him feel more relaxed. Being around Amelia and her family at their home in the mountains always made him feel better. And when he loaded Amelia's painting of the lake into his car, he felt as if he were taking a little bit of that peace with him.

He decided to hang his new painting in his office on Monday morning and was just finishing the task when Jessie was ushered in. The blank look was back on her face, so reminiscent of her first days of therapy.

Damn it, she'd withdrawn back into that hole again because of him.

"Jessie, I'm so glad to see you." He figured it had been about fifty/fifty that she'd even show this morning.

She didn't respond. She went to her usual chair and sat down. "I've done a lot of thinking over the past couple of days. And the bottom line is that I guess I want to continue our sessions."

A sense of relief swept over him. "I'm glad."

She looked at him directly. "However, I'm sick and tired of people not being honest with me and thinking they know better than I do what's best for me. My mother, Nick, and now you."

He felt each word like a punch in the stomach. He started to defend himself but wasn't sure what he could say.

"And my mother must never know what you've told me. She'd be more than happy to ship me off to that treatment facility in Atlanta, given any excuse."

"You're an adult, Jessie," David felt compelled to explain. "Your mother can't commit you to an in-patient facility without your permission."

"I know. But I'm afraid I'd end up doing it. She always gets her way. Plus, I have nowhere to go if she throws me out."

"Like she'd do that to you."

"You don't know my mother as well as I do."

"Okay," David said, "but I don't want you continuing to work with me out of fear of your mother. If you're not comfortable continuing our sessions, Andy says he has some time now and can work you into his schedule. Of, if you prefer, I can recommend someone else you could see for therapy."

David watched Jessie weigh the options carefully. At last she said, "I don't understand why you waited to tell me such important information, but I'm going to give you the benefit of the doubt. I'm going to believe that you believed you were doing what you thought was best for me. So, no, I don't want to change doctors. But I do insist on getting what you promised me that first day in your office. Honesty!"

Regret sluiced over David. He wanted to explain why he had done what he had done, which was hard because he couldn't even explain it to himself. He had been acting on a feeling, a gut instinct, rather than on reason and logic. The best he could do was to speak from the heart.

"You walking into my office a few weeks ago seemed like a sign or something," he said. "In some weird way, I believe I'm meant to help you."

Jessie remained expressionless, her hands folded in her lap. When his words didn't seem to elicit any reaction from her, David decided it'd be best to get back to business. "Are you ready to get started today?"

"I guess so," she said dully.

"Where do you want to start?"

"How about the night of the accident?"

David wasn't surprised by her choice of topic. In fact, he had anticipated this reaction. "Sure," he said. Then he dove in. "One thing that has been bugging me since I realized who you are is that you look quite different now. You had really blonde, almost white hair before."

Her blank look was firmly in place, but when she spoke, her voice was filled with emotion. "Maybe I should ask you as a man what this blond thing is all about. I mean, don't men prefer blondes?"

David was taken aback by her sudden attack. "Personally, I don't pick my girlfriends by their hair color. But did Nick prefer blondes? Was the woman he had an affair with a blonde?"

He noticed that she seemed to be looking behind him at Amelia's painting. Finally she brought her attention back to him and said, "I don't know. Coloring my hair was part of a desperate attempt to bring my husband's attention back to me after his affair."

"Did it work?" he asked.

"For a while, maybe."

"Was he seeing someone else at the time of the accident?" David asked as anger began to simmer just under the surface of his words.

"I think so. The signs were all there. He was working a lot of extra hours and was extremely irritable with me when he was at home." She was looking over his shoulder again. "I really like your new artwork. The way the sunlight dances on the water is mesmerizing."

David was surprised at the hard feelings he was experiencing toward Nick for being unfaithful to Jessie. He felt almost relieved that Jessie changed the subject. "My sister surprised me this weekend with this gift of her painting. It's of the lake behind her house."

"She's very good."

"I think so." David got up and went to his desk, opened a drawer, and pulled out one of Amelia's business cards, which he handed to Jessie. "Here's her website if you want to look at some of her other work." He looked at his watch. Her hour was half way over. "How was your homework this weekend?"

"I actually didn't do anything this weekend except lie in my bed and try to decide whether I was going to continue these sessions with you. Doing your homework assignment seemed pointless if I wasn't sure you were even going to be my doctor."

David nodded in agreement. "I was thinking it was time to step up your homework, anyway. I would like you to start interacting with people on a more intimate level."

"What does that mean?" Jessie asked sharply.

"I want you to reach out to someone." He looked down at his notes. "What about your old friend, MJ? What about setting up something with her? Maybe lunch or coffee?"

Jessie shook her head. "She doesn't get out much with her new babies."

"Well, you met her at the mall before, so she must get out some. Or you could go to her house."

When Jessie's face remained closed, he decided to change tactics. "Okay, it doesn't have to be MJ, but what I want, Jessie, is for you to do something different than you do every day. Something that requires you to put yourself in a new situation and stretch those emotional boundaries you've set up for yourself."

"I really don't like MJ's husband," Jessie said.

"I bet he's not around during the day," David said. "Or ask her to meet you for dinner one night when her husband could keep the babies."

"I don't think he keeps the babies by himself yet."

David suspected Jessie was trying to irritate him. "Look, you can come up with a hundred different reasons why getting together with MJ won't work. However, you won't know whether it *will* work unless you call her and try to get together with her."

"Okay, I'll call her."

David smiled. "Great. Let me know how it turns out."

After Jessie left, David sat down to record his notes. He felt discouraged because the session seemed like starting all over again. He felt angry with himself because he was the one responsible for Jessie's setback.

Andy appeared in the doorway. "I saw Jessie Graham leaving," he said. "How'd it go?"

David sighed, "I don't think you have to worry about being sued because she doesn't want her mother to know about my connection to the wreck."

"But she's okay continuing to see you?"

"Apparently. But all trust between us is gone."

"You surprised by that?"

David shook his head. "I guess not. But, Andy, you know as well as I do that sometimes when you are treating a patient, you just go with your gut. That's what I did."

"Yeah. Well, look on the bright side," Andy said with a sudden smile. "You've still got those three times a week billable sessions for the foreseeable future. Good job, partner!"

CHAPTER 22

The next day, Jessie stood on MJ's doorstep feeling dreadfully tired and slightly headachy. She wished she were home in bed. She had hoped that by giving MJ such short notice, she would already have plans for the next day. But no, MJ had been ecstatic about getting together with Jessie.

The door opened to reveal MJ, who was wearing a look of exhaustion and a pink, slightly stained bathrobe. "I think the boys are teething," she groaned. "They were up all night and just went down for their morning naps."

"Do you want me to come back another time?" Jessie asked.

"NO!" MJ exclaimed. "I just wanted to explain why I'm still in my pajamas. I've been counting down the minutes until you got here."

Jessie carried the large bag of Chinese food from PF Chang into the house. MJ had asked if she would pick up food rather than trying to go out for lunch with the babies. Bottles in various stages of emptiness covered the kitchen counter, and a mountain of clean baby clothes was piled high on the kitchen table, waiting to be folded.

"I apologize for the mess," MJ said. "I had planned on getting up this morning and straightening this disaster, but the boys have been real pills, and...well, you can see how it's been."

Jessie studied MJ's pale face—totally devoid of makeup—and suddenly recalled the two of them in middle school, practicing putting on lipstick. MJ could certainly use some lipstick right now. Jessie felt a wave of pity for her friend.

"Why don't you go take a shower and get dressed?" she said. "I'll listen for the boys and set up for lunch."

"That would be a dream. The monitor's there. But they've been fed and changed. If you hear them crying, there's really nothing else to do but try to comfort them with the pacifier."

Jessie folded the baby clothes into neat piles and then set about emptying and rinsing the baby bottles. She placed the

Chinese food containers on the table and found plates and forks. The boys were still sleeping contentedly when MJ reappeared in jeans and makeup, looking nothing like the strung out madwoman of earlier.

"You are a life saver," MJ said. "I really thought I was going to lose it this morning when the twins were being so fussy." Noticing the folded clothes, she said, "Ah, you didn't have to fold those."

"No problem. Why don't you call your mom when you have nights like last night? I'm sure she loves helping with her grandbabies."

"Yeah, she does," MJ agreed. "But she and Dad are out of town until Sunday."

"What about Tom? Can't he come home for an hour or so and spell you for a bit?"

MJ shook her head. "He's always so busy, and besides he wouldn't want to take a chance on one of the babies messing up his suit."

Jessie started to suggest that a big apron might give him all the protection he needed, but held her tongue and started opening containers.

"Food looks great. I haven't had Chinese in a while," MJ said.

"Me either."

"How's therapy with Dr. Miller going?"

A slight tremor danced unexpectedly through Jessie's stomach at the reference to Dr. Miller. "Pretty good." She imagined telling MJ that Dr. Miller had been the one to pull her from the crushed car or even that she was only visiting MJ because he had assigned the visit as homework. Instead she said, "It's been interesting."

MJ smiled brightly. "And he's not too hard on the eyes either, right?"

Jessie felt her face redden. "Well, no, I guess not." Then in an effort to steer the conversation away from Dr. Miller's looks, she said, "Did you know he has a sister who is an artist? He has one of her paintings in his office, and I think it's really good." Jessie remembered the card he'd given her and made a mental note to look at the sister's website later.

"No, I didn't know that, but I do know that he dumped that nurse he'd been dating, and apparently he left a string of broken hearts all over Atlanta."

"Really?" Jessie, usually skeptical of gossip, felt somewhat inclined to believe what MJ was saying. If he'd lie about one thing to her, why not other things to other women?

MJ gave a flick of her ponytail. "Yes. A friend of mine, Donna, is in the Junior League with Lillie—that's the nurse he was dating—and she said that Lillie said everything with them was going great. Then he just ended it with no warning. She's absolutely devastated! Wouldn't you think that, with him being a psychiatrist and everything, he'd be a bit more considerate of how she felt?"

"Yes, I would," Jessie said. MJ's words seemed like more evidence against Dr. Miller. But as lunch went on and she felt herself relaxing and actually enjoying being with MJ, Jessie had to admit that his suggestion to reconnect with MJ had been a good idea. Besides, what he did outside the office was really none of her business. All she wanted from him was honesty about her therapy so that she could continue to get better.

Back at home, Jessie was relieved to find that Rita had yet to come home from a board meeting at the Augusta Bank. She pulled up the website of Dr. Miller's sister on her iPad and immediately recognized the real life version of the lake pictured in the website's banner headline. The woman in the thumbnail-size picture looked warm and friendly, with little physical resemblance to Dr. Miller.

Jessie clicked on the artwork tab to view the paintings the artist had for sale and felt an immediate connection with all of her artwork. Each painting was riveting, with thick globs of bold and brilliant color. One, in particular—a startling red bird sitting in the bare branches of a tree, surrounded by a barren snowy landscape—caught Jessie's attention. Jessie felt a visceral connection to both the loneliness of the bird's surroundings and the vibrancy of life the red bird seemed to represent. Before she stopped to think, she clicked on the email button and wrote a quick note expressing her interest in purchasing the painting.

And in the north Georgia mountains, Amelia—the sister of David Miller—heard the ping of an email arriving and rushed to the computer to respond to a potential new client.

CHAPTER 23

"I can't believe you've done it again," Jan chided him. The flickering candles on the wrought iron table between them created shadows that danced over her face while Andy worked diligently at the gas grill in the corner of the patio.

David took a slow sip of his whiskey before answering, "Done what?"

"Don't be coy with me. You know what! Dumped another perfectly nice girl before you've really given yourself a chance to get to know her."

"Jan, Lillie may be nice, but she's just not right for me."

"What are you looking for?"

"I don't know," he answered honestly.

"Well, then, how do you know Lillie isn't it?"

"Okay, I was trying to avoid this because I know she's your friend. But she talks too much, and she became serious too fast. And most of all, she didn't like my car!"

Jan started laughing. "Well, if she doesn't like that beat up old piece of junk, there's no hope for her. I guess I'll start looking for another prospect, perhaps one who collects old cars."

"Why is it that married people always want single people to be married?" David asked Andy as he walked up with a plate of steaks.

"Haven't you heard? Misery loves company," Andy said. But the quick kiss he placed on Jan's head made it clear that he was anything but miserable.

CHAPTER 24

Jessie was surprised when she checked her email an hour later to see that Dr. Miller's sister had already responded to her inquiry.

Dear Jessie,

Thank you for your interest in Redbird Waiting. *I saw the bird last March after a late spring snowstorm. The crimson red against the pure white snow caught my eye, but even more important to me was that the bird's appearance after a rather brutal winter gave me hope that spring was close. The framed painting is $1,200. If you want only the unframed painting, it's $1,000.*

Please let me know if you are interested, and we can make arrangements for shipping. Or, if you live in the area, you can pick the painting up and avoid the shipping costs.

Take care,

Amelia

Jessie liked the friendly tone of the message and the promptness with which Amelia had responded. Now that she knew the story behind the painting, she wanted it even more. However, did she even have $1,200 of her own money to spend on a painting? And if she could afford to buy it, where would she put a painting like that? Its bold primary colors and rough wood frame certainly wouldn't fit into her French provincial showroom of a bedroom. She supposed that buying the painting didn't make a whole lot of sense. Still, for the first time in a really long time, Jessie felt a desire for something building within her.

The next morning Jessie was sitting at the kitchen table with a cup of coffee and a white legal pad full of questions when her mother walked into the room. Jessie had stayed up half the night thinking about her current life—the purgatory in which she currently lived and possible reasons why she had allowed things to drift for as long as she had.

"Mother, I want to ask you some questions."

"Can I have at least one cup of coffee first?" Rita wearily opened the cabinet where the coffee cups were stored. For once she didn't look perfectly put together. Her hair was sticking out in odd places where she had slept on it. Without makeup, her mother looked every bit of her sixty years.

Armed with a cup of hot coffee, Rita looked somewhat more awake. "So, what do you want to know?"

"Where's Nick buried?"

Rita frowned slightly. "His parents came to Atlanta and took his body while you were still in the coma. They buried him down there where they live, in Tifton, right? They called a few times to see how you were doing, but I haven't heard anything from them in six or seven months."

"I never really knew them," Jessie said, "but I suppose the right thing to do would be to give them a call sometime. Did he have life insurance?"

"Not any personal life insurance that I was able to find. I stayed at your house while you were in the hospital, and I went through all of his office files." Rita paused for a sip of coffee, and Jessie imagined how Nick would have reacted to her mother going through his personal things.

"All I found were bills," Rita continued, "and the life insurance policy his partnership took out on him. But those benefits were payable to the partnership, not to you."

"And the house?"

"The house was in both of your names, so you shouldn't have any legal problems selling it. Of course, it was purchased just before the real estate market crashed. So I doubt you'll get as much for it now as you paid for it."

"How much do we owe?"

"You owe about $200,000. I've checked with several realtors in that area, and I think you could probably sell it for maybe $400,000. So you do have a little equity in it."

"And how much do I owe you for paying the mortgage and whatever else since the accident?"

"Roughly—$20,000."

"So if I can sell the house for $400,000 and sell all of the contents in the house for maybe another $5,000, I'd have about $175,000 left over after paying you back, right?"

Rita nodded. "Of course, that's an optimistic scenario. You may get less for the house."

"I know. I'm just trying to get a ballpark figure here."

"What are you thinking about doing?"

Jessie didn't answer for a moment. Then she replied as honestly as she could. "I don't know. Just trying to get a rough handle on my financials."

Rita nodded approvingly. "I guess that Dr. Miller must be helping you after all."

"I guess so," Jessie said cryptically.

CHAPTER 25

On Monday morning, David checked the time once again. Jessie was only five minutes late. If she had been any other patient, he probably wouldn't even have noticed. But Jessie wasn't just any other patient, and she was never late. Had she perhaps decided to quit therapy after all?

When she walked into the room a couple of minutes later, relief washed over him. She looked pale, almost ethereal, in white jeans and a soft, white shirt, and yet there was an edge about her that hadn't been there before. Her eyes warned him that he was on probation and should be very careful.

"It's unlike you to be late. I was actually getting worried," David said honestly.

"Worried that I'd changed my mind about coming?" she asked bluntly as she stood near the doorway.

"Yes.".

"I would have called."

"Good to know."

"We Southerners may lose our minds, but never our manners," she said bitterly.

"Maybe you should," David said, making an attempt at humor, "That is, lose your manners. You might find it quite liberating."

"But dangerous," Jessie countered quickly. "You never know once you loosen those social restraints just how far out of control you might let yourself go."

David decided to give up the verbal sparring and get back to business. "Why don't you have a seat and let's get started. Where would you like to begin today?"

"I've been thinking a lot about wanting to get out of my mother's house."

"Great. So, what's the first step?"

"Figuring out my finances."

"Sounds reasonable. How do you propose to do that?" David made a note.

"I think I need to start by selling the house in Atlanta."

"You don't have any desire to live there again?"

"No. As a matter of fact, I haven't even been back to that house since my accident. My mother had me transferred from the hospital in Atlanta to a rehab place here in Augusta."

"Really? Not even to get any of your personal stuff?"

Jessie shook her head.

"Let's talk about your house for a bit. What do you feel when you think about the house?"

"Failure."

"Can you elaborate?"

"I was a failure at everything I did in that house," she said slowly, as if each word caused her pain.

"Why do you think so?" he probed.

A spark appeared suddenly in Jessie's eyes. "You tell me how you would feel if you'd spent all day cooking a gourmet meal, only to have the person you'd cooked it for take a few bites and say, 'I ate a late lunch today so I'm not very hungry.' Or, when you've spent the whole day cleaning, and it's not even noticed."

"I see your point. And you've said before that you didn't feel that Nick was attracted to you."

Jessie looked at David as if she suddenly hated him. "The bottom line is that Nick never loved me."

"I find that hard to believe," David countered. "If he didn't love you, why would he beg you not to leave him after you found out about his affair?"

She smiled grimly, and for the very first time David thought he saw a resemblance to Rita in her face. "For one reason, and one reason only. Money."

"But he was a surgeon," David said. "He made a lot of money on his own. Why would he need your mother's money?"

"He did make a lot of money," Jessie said. "But he also liked to gamble, and he had very expensive tastes. And," she paused for a second, "he never liked waiting for anything."

"I think you're selling yourself short." David felt a sudden spurt of anger at the asshole of a husband and the bitch of a mother who had made Jessie feel this way about herself.

"Really? I found proof." She paused for a second before continuing in a ragged but determined tone. "I came across a letter from my mother in Nick's desk when I was straightening his office. I immediately recognized her stationery and her handwriting on the envelope, which was addressed to his office. I know I shouldn't have, but I couldn't keep myself from reading it."

She was silent for maybe a count of ten. David watched as her lips trembled with barely repressed fury. Finally she continued quietly, "The letter was basically a financial statement listing what my mother had paid to Nick upon our marriage. She'd paid off his student loans and given him a sizeable amount for a car and a down payment on our house. The letter also mentioned another amount that would be payable to Nick upon the birth of our first child. And the letter closed with a veiled threat. My mother said she would never expect her son-in-law to repay this personal loan. However, should he ever stop being her son-in-law, she would demand immediate repayment."

Jessie straightened in her chair. "The letter was dated two days after I found out about his affair. So, you see, it's no wonder my husband fought so hard to keep me. He would be forfeiting a small fortune if I left him."

David noted how calmly Jessie spoke, how emotionless she sounded. He knew she had to be roiling inside with emotions, so why couldn't she show them? "How did you feel after reading the letter?" he asked.

Jessie looked up abruptly with anger in her eyes. "How do you think I felt? My mother had, in essence, bought a husband for me and was paying him to stay around!"

"You didn't have to stay with him after finding the letter. Why did you?" David asked bluntly.

Jessie seemed to wilt in her chair. Then she said softly, "That very morning, I had discovered I was pregnant."

David felt as though a bombshell had fallen in the room, and he must walk very carefully or trigger its explosion. He realized that not one but two deaths had likely come from their car crash.

"I don't want to talk any more today. I'm exhausted," Jessie said, her strained face lending credence to her words.

David hated to stop when she seemed so close to a real break-through. "How about just a few more minutes?" he asked. "We still need to talk about your homework." Then realizing just how pale she was, he quickly added. "Never mind. Your time is almost up anyway."

He reached across his desk and placed his hand on her hand in a gesture of comfort. Her hand was cold, and he had a strong desire to pick it up and rub some warmth into it. Instead, he moved his hand away quickly and said, "Therapy can be very painful because you have to revisit things you'd rather ignore. But it's the only way forward. Go home and get some rest, Jessie. We'll pick up here on Wednesday."

CHAPTER 26

Jessie left her session feeling very unsettled as well as physically sick to her stomach. She had only once before talked honestly about Nick and his lack of interest in her, and that had been with her mother. It had been a conversation that had ended by making her feel worse, as though somehow she had been at fault for everything that had gone wrong in her marriage. She'd never talked about the baby to anyone. When she awakened from the coma, she hadn't been pregnant. There'd seemed to be no reason to talk about it.

As she was pulling into the driveway, a red bird flew in front of her car, and she remembered Dr. Miller's sister saying that the redbird had given her hope at the end of a brutal winter. Jessie felt strangely comforted by this bird's unexpected appearance in front of her car. Not knowing much about birds, she had done research the night before and found that the painting she wanted was actually of a male cardinal with its signature black face. Native Americans associated the cardinal with good luck, which Jessie certainly could use a bit of right now. There had even been a sweet Indian legend in which the cardinal acted as a matchmaker between a lonely Indian brave and a maiden. Jessie's initial whim to have the painting of the redbird had grown into an intense need.

But how could she come up with the money to buy the painting? Her mother had given her a MasterCard to use when she bought groceries for the house or other necessities. Such a large purchase, however, would need her mother's approval. She could imagine her mother ridiculing her for wanting to buy a painting by an unknown artist. Rita would also be suspicious of the artist because she was Dr. Miller's sister.

Jessie had her own bank cards in her wallet. Who knew? Maybe she still had some money in her checking account. Maybe she could use her own credit card. A trip to an ATM seemed to be in order. Jessie put the car in reverse. Miraculously, she still remembered her pin number.

At the ATM, she put her debit card in and discovered she had only a couple of hundred dollars in her checking account.

Darn it! She wasn't sure if she could check
the balance on her credit card at an ATM,
but she put the card into the machine
anyway. Unfortunately, the ATM debit
card pin number wasn't the correct pin
number for the credit card, and the card
shot back out without revealing its secrets.
She'd have to go into the bank, a tricky
maneuver because her mother was a part
owner.

Jessie parked the Range Rover and
thought about what she should do. After a
moment, she had a plan. Inside the bank,
she told the middle-aged, tired-looking
teller that she hadn't received her credit
card statement in the mail the month
before and was wondering if she could get a
copy of it. Within minutes, Jessie saw that
she had a zero balance due and a full
$10,000 available to spend in any way she
wanted!

Receiving that information was like
getting a shot of adrenaline. Jessie could
buy the painting, and then who knew what
else she might be able to do on her own?

Rita and Maggie were in the kitchen
when she entered. "How was therapy
today?" Rita asked.

"A ton of fun," Jessie answered
flippantly, not slowing down until she got

to her bedroom, where she turned on her iPad and opened her email.

When she pulled up the email from Amelia, her heart was beating fast. Spending $1,200 on a painting just now wasn't practical. But before she could talk herself out of it, she typed a quick message saying she would like to purchase the painting and would pick it up rather than have it shipped. Jessie wasn't sure what she was going to do with the painting once she got it. All she knew was that she wanted to buy it before someone else did.

She waited and checked her email every few minutes. Fifteen minutes later, an excited response thanked her for her purchase, gave her driving directions, and said that she could come almost any time to pick it up. Jessie replied that she'd try for Saturday.

CHAPTER 27

On Tuesday night, David dreamt of the accident again and woke in a sweaty panic. This time the accident occurred as if in slow motion, and he was startled when the car spinning in front of him revealed his mother sitting in the driver's seat instead of Nick. Both his mother and Jessie were covered in blood. Then there was a loud noise, like a car backfiring, or perhaps a gunshot, just before the car slid out of sight.

David didn't do dream analysis. But he knew that the combination of Jessie and his mother was some sort of message from his subconscious. Consciously, he had never felt guilty for what had happened to either one of them. He had been only seven years old when his mother died, too young to have affected the outcome. And Jessie's car had hydroplaned, hadn't it? Their accident would have happened with or without him being there that night. He'd just happened to witness it. Yet now he lay awake, pondering different possibilities until the morning light crept softly into his room.

Jessie arrived for her appointment as casually dressed as David had ever seen her. She was wearing ragged blue jeans and a blue t-shirt that made her appear very young. In stark contrast, her body language was anything but relaxed. She sat with one crossed leg swinging to an incessant internal rhythm and one finger twirling a lock of her hair continuously and thoughtlessly. He wished he could say or do something to calm her, but he knew it would be best just to go ahead and dive in.

"Shall we pick up where we left off?" he asked.

"I guess so," she said without looking at his eyes.

"You'd just told me you learned you were pregnant."

Jessie left her chair and walked to the window and looked out. David wondered if she was trying to get as far away from him as possible before beginning to talk.

"Take your time, Jessie," he said, "I know this is hard."

She looked back at him, her eyes glittering with unshed tears, "You're the first person, besides Nick, to know that I was pregnant." She drew a ragged breath and then looked back to the window as if fascinated by whatever was out there in the parking lot. "I had taken a pregnancy test that morning before finding my mother's letter on Nick's desk. I was so happy when the test was positive. I thought a baby might help us develop a real marriage.

"But finding that letter shattered my happiness. All I could think about was that my mother had offered Nick money to marry me, and more to stay with me. And she would be paying him even more money in exchange for the baby I carried. I suddenly realized why he had been so eager for us to have a child, and I wondered if he had ever wanted a baby at all."

Jessie walked back across the room to her chair and rubbed its back absentmindedly. "For three days, I contemplated leaving him. But where could I go? I loathed my mother and what she had done. I certainly didn't want to go home to her. The only person I could have gone to for help was my best friend, Wendy. However, Thailand was a bit far to go, particularly without any money."

Her voice took on a harsh quality. "Somehow everything always comes down to money, doesn't it? Nick gave me an allowance for the household expenses, but there was never much left over each month.

I had no savings of my own. Without any place to go, or any money of my own, I couldn't think of how I could leave him."

Jessie returned to the window and looked out, hollow-eyed, before starting to speak in a flat tone. "I also kept thinking about how our baby deserved a family—a mother *and* a father." She looked back at David as if daring him to disagree with her, "Nick had his good side you know. He was a great doctor, and his patients loved him. He might have been a wonderful father. I mean, who knows? Maybe that baby would have caused him to change and become a better husband."

David schooled his face to remain blank even though inside his emotions were churning. He knew, as she probably did, that babies rarely turned bad marriages into good ones. "Maybe," he finally said.

"I decided I was going to make my marriage work," she continued. "His new partner's wedding was a couple of weeks away. A wedding seemed like a good time for us to make a new beginning. I went shopping. I bought an expensive new dress and shoes in the styles he liked me to wear. I had my hair and nails done and spent hours that day doing my makeup and getting ready so that everything would be perfect. I had the whole night planned. I imagined that he would love the way I looked in my new dress. Then I would announce my pregnancy, he would be ecstatic, and we would dedicate ourselves to building a new life and really working on our marriage."

Anger surged through David, *Why hadn't this man appreciated the natural beauty of Jessie as she was?* But carefully and unemotionally, he asked, "How did your plan work out?"

Jessie put one hand up against the glass pane and then laid her forehead on her hand. "Nothing went according to plan. I could have been wearing a gunny sack for all he cared. I was angered by his complete lack of attention after all my hard work, so I said nothing about the baby before we left to go to the wedding. Then, at the reception, there was a woman who seemed very familiar with Nick. After we left the wedding, we were arguing about her in the car. Then, right before the accident, I blurted out that I was pregnant."

Jessie turned around to David. There were tears coursing down her face for the first time ever in his office. "And here I am today. No husband, no baby, and really, no reason to be living."

David felt shaken by the resignation in her voice. Before he knew it, he was across the room and his arms were around her. She shuddered before grabbing onto him as though she were drowning. And like someone drowning, she took great gulps of air until sobs finally erupted from a deep primal well within her. David held her shaking body and stroked her hair with his free hand in an effort to calm her. But now that the dam had broken within her, she was weeping inconsolably.

"Let it out, Jessie. You've held it in too long," David murmured against her head. Somewhere inside him, an alarm bell went off. It would be so easy to tilt her face up and taste the tears on her face, to assuage her pain with a kiss. *She's your patient*, he reminded himself. *Tread very carefully here.*

After one particularly long sob, she gasped against his shoulder so softly that he could barely hear her. "And the worst thing is….that I think…I'm responsible for the accident." *Deep sobs for a minute.* "He was looking at me and not at the road. Maybe if I hadn't blurted out my news like that, he'd still be alive. Maybe I'd have a son or a daughter. Maybe I'm to blame for everything that's happened!" Her sobs took over again.

David knew exactly how she felt, as he'd been wondering just hours earlier if he hadn't inadvertently crossed the yellow line on Riverside Drive while talking on his cell phone. If he had, he might have caused the very same accident. He started to reassure Jessie, as he had reassured himself, that Nick's car had hydroplaned and that if the accident was anybody's fault, it was Nick's fault for driving too fast in those conditions.

But David knew logic wasn't what she needed right then. He remained silent, stroking her hair and enjoying the way she fit comfortably into his arms, damn too comfortably. He knew he ought to pull away from her, but he couldn't, not while she was still so needful of a human touch.

Finally Jessie did pull away from him to stand a few feet away. Her eyes were swollen, and her face was splotched with red where she had rubbed her face against his shirt. David admired her Herculean efforts to pull herself together.

"I'm sorry," she said tonelessly, having spent all of her emotions in her outburst.

David wanted to wrap her in his arms again. Instead, he said as professionally as possible, "I've thought for the past several weeks that your therapy wasn't going very well because you have been so unemotional. Today, I'm encouraged. I think we can make real progress now toward getting you better."

One lonely tear leaked out from her eye, and Jessie wiped it off with the back of her hand. "What is better?"

David thought for a moment before speaking, wanting to say just the right thing, "Better is facing reality even when you know it's going to be hard. It's trying to handle difficulties instead of avoiding them. You are getting better, Jessie, I see it in you. Now you must see it in yourself."

CHAPTER 28

Feeling drained and anxious to go to her bedroom and lie down, Jessie was thankful that the house was quiet when she walked in. Only the recessed lights were on in the kitchen, indicating that Maggie had left early for the day. Jessie made her way to the den, where, much to her surprise, Rita sat, iridescent in a circle of light with a magazine in her lap and a glass of iced tea on the table beside her. She looked up as Jessie entered, her two raised eyebrows showing 'barely contained anger.'

Jessie wanted to keep walking, but having just had a lecture about facing difficulties, she decided to stop and face whatever had enraged her mother. "Hello, Mother."

Rita continued staring at Jessie for another heartbeat. "It would be nice if I heard about what you are doing from you, rather than from my friends or the bank employees."

Ah, her trip to the bank had been brought to Rita's attention. "It would be nice," Jessie countered, "if bank employees provided their customers with a little privacy. I told you the other day I wanted to start figuring out my financial situation."

"So, rather than ask me for your bank statements and other financial information, you'd prefer to go to the bank and lie about not receiving your statements? Are you that afraid of me? Oh, and by the way, the bank teller was concerned that maybe someone had been taking your bank statements from the mailbox." Rita gave an uncharacteristic snort. "She was concerned that you might have been a victim of identity theft. As if you have an identity that could be stolen!"

Jessie flinched at her mother's harsh words. "I thought you'd be happy that I was finally taking the initiative."

The silence stretched out between them like a rubber band.

"You've never been very good at lying, Jessica," Rita snapped. "I can tell something else is going on here."

"Mother," Jessie said, frustrated, "I just wanted to know if I had any money in my checking account and if my credit card worked."

"Why?"

"None of your business."

"Everything you do is my business. Does this have anything to do with that Dr. Miller? Is he asking you for money? It must be so, since he's the only thing new in your life. What does he want from you?"

Jessie knew she should end this nonsense and tell her mother about the painting she wanted to buy. But her mother's statement insinuating that Dr. Miller wanted money from her made Jessie angry.

"Answer me!" her mother said sternly, as close to raising her voice as Rita Forrester ever got.

"You're being ridiculous," Jessie said. "Dr. Miller has nothing to do with my trip to the bank."

Rita was ominously quiet for a moment. At last she said, "If you are going to live in my house, you are going to abide by my rules."

"I don't remember any rule about not going to the bank and asking for copies of my bank statements."

Rita's eyebrows now read full-fledged furious. "From now on, I'd like for you to do me the courtesy of letting me know what you're doing before you do it, so that I don't have to hear about it on the street. Do we understand each other?"

Jessie couldn't help herself from asking, "Or what?"

Rita paused for a moment, picked up her glass, and took a sip of tea. "Or you are on your own." She took another sip. "You can't have it both ways, darling. If you want 'mummy' to take care of you financially, you must do what mummy says."

Jessie's temper flared. "Why must it always be about money with you, Mother?"

Rita smiled contemptuously. "It's easy for those who've always had money to discount the importance of it. Live without it for a while, and then we'll talk about how important it is."

Jessie tossed and turned in bed that night, unable for once to reach the nothingness of sleep that usually came easily to her. The emotional session with Dr. Miller that had ended with him holding her in his arms, followed by the difficult encounter with her mother, ran like a continuous loop in her head until she thought her head might explode. It had felt good to be in his arms, and those feelings scared her. She needed him to be her therapist, someone she could trust. She didn't want anything more from him. Or did she?

The revulsion she'd felt for her mother after finding her letter to Nick had returned in full force. Although Dr. Miller had told her she must face difficulties rather than avoid them, at this moment she wanted nothing more than to pick up her painting on Saturday and keep driving to wherever the road might lead her. *Why not do it?* Jessie thought. After all, she'd have a little over $8,000 in credit still available on her credit card. Surely, that was enough to hold her over somewhere until she could sell the house in Atlanta.

Entering Dr. Miller's office after her breakdown, Jessie felt nervous. She hadn't slept much since their last session, and she knew the feelings she'd dredged up were still hovering right below the surface. With little provocation, those feelings could erupt into another tearful scene, though she was determined there'd be no repeats today.

Dr. Miller was typing on his computer. He looked up as she walked in and said, "This will just take a sec. Have a seat."

She watched his fingers moving rapidly over the keys and remembered how those fingers had felt stroking her hair. Was her scalp tingling at the mere memory? She had become more acutely aware of him after finding out his connection to her accident. Now the vivid memory of him holding her seemed to have taken that awareness to an entirely different level.

She had to admit to herself that she was attracted to him, and the admission scared her. Perhaps, she mused cynically, he held and comforted all of his women patients. Or perhaps only the younger ones. Perhaps the comforting was all part of some sick game he played. Had she come to a point where she didn't trust anyone anymore?

She shook off her suspicious thoughts and tried to focus on his sister's painting of the lake over the sofa. There was a peaceful quality about the painting that soothed her. Then she felt a twinge of excitement, knowing that soon she'd be seeing the real lake that had inspired the painting. Now that she had opened up her emotional playbook, feelings like excitement and desire seemed to be continually coming at her, hard and fast. Was this a sign that she was better or worse?

"You really like my sister's work, don't you?" He must have noticed her staring at the painting.

She turned back to look at him. "So much so, I'm buying one of her paintings tomorrow."

"Really?" Dr. Miller's voice registered surprise.

Jessie nodded. "After you gave me her card, I went to her website and fell in love with a painting of a redbird."

"And you're getting it tomorrow?"

"That's my plan."

"I'm going up next weekend. If you want to wait a week, I'll be glad to bring it back to you," he offered.

"Thanks. But I'd really like to see the lake and it's been a while since I've gone anywhere. I'm actually looking forward to a trip outside Augusta."

CHAPTER 29

The prospect of Jessie's meeting with Amelia and Mike and his nephews was unsettling to David, and he wasn't sure why. His sister sold paintings to all kinds of people all the time. Why shouldn't she sell one of her works to one of his patients?

"And your mother? What does she think about all this?" David noticed that Jessie looked slightly uncomfortable.

"She doesn't know. I'm thinking about not telling her where I'm going or about buying the painting. I thought maybe I'd make up some story about driving to Atlanta for the day and checking on the house, and maybe just 'finding' the painting in the attic."

"Because?" David asked.

"Because I'm tired of her micromanaging my life," Jessie said adamantly. "I went to the bank the other day to see if I had enough room on my credit card to buy the painting, and one of the bank employees called Mother and reported what I'd done. I'd like to get my mother out of my life."

"Wait. You're going to purchase the painting on a credit card?"

"Yes."

"And how are you going to pay the credit card when it comes due?"

"I'm going to sell the house in Atlanta."

"That may take a while."

David could tell she was processing things by the look of concentration on her face. Finally she said, "I do have an English degree from Georgia. I'm sure I can get a job doing something."

David was surprised at her naivety. A 27 year-old woman with an English degree and absolutely no work experience was going to have a tough time finding a job unless someone with connections, like her mother, put in a good word for her. But he didn't want to discourage this spark of independence.

"I think a job would be a great," he said. "But you might be rushing things by charging something on credit before you have a way to make the payments. If you really want one of Amelia's paintings, why don't you ask your mother to give it to you as a birthday or Christmas present?"

He could tell from the look on Jessie's face that what he had said was not what she wanted to hear.

"My mother's presents always come with strings attached," she said defiantly.

David decided it was time to give Jessie a little tough love. "If you put that painting on your charge card without any way of paying it off, you are being disingenuous. Your mother will ultimately end up paying the credit card bill, right?"

A stain of embarrassment colored Jessie's cheeks.

"I think if you truly want to be independent of your mother, you should wait to buy an expensive painting until you have your own money to pay for it."

"I know you're right," Jessie said despondently. "But I really want *this* painting, and I'm afraid your sister will sell it before I can get the money to buy it."

Finally realizing how much the painting meant to Jessie, David made a snap decision. "She won't," he said, "I know my sister. She'll want you to have her painting because it means so much to you. She's funny about her paintings that way. They're sort of like her children, and she wants them to go to good homes." Although what he said was somewhat true, David didn't add that he was going to buy the painting and let Amelia pay him back when Jessie paid her for the painting.

"Are you sure? That doesn't sound like any way to run a business."

David laughed. "Once you meet my sister, you'll understand. She has a lot of wonderful qualities, but astute business sense isn't one of them."

Jessie sat quietly for a few moments. At last she said, "I was really looking forward to seeing the lake in the painting."

David surprised himself even more. "Then why don't you go with me next weekend?" he asked. "My sister would love to have another woman's company. I'll be helping my brother-in-law stain a deck, so it will be almost like I'm not there."

CHAPTER 30

Jessie was stunned by Dr. Miller's offer. Wasn't he crossing some doctor-patient line that shouldn't be crossed? Her heart was suddenly pounding in her chest so loudly that she was sure he must be able to hear it.

"I don't know," she answered hesitantly.

"Listen, if you don't feel comfortable going with me to my sister's house for the weekend, that's fine."

Jessie figured he was rapidly retreating from his just-issued invitation—but not for long. "I only thought a weekend in the mountains might be therapeutic for you," he said. "The area really is beautiful."

His casual explanation did little to quiet the staccato beating of her heart. Unable to think clearly, she finally said, "I appreciate the offer, and a weekend in the mountains sounds wonderful. Can I let you know Monday?"

"Sure."

Jessie thought about the painting she was supposed to buy the next day. "What should I tell your sister? She's expecting me to pick up the painting tomorrow."

"Just call and tell her that you can't come tomorrow, but that you still want the painting very badly. Don't worry. I'll explain to her how much you love her painting, and I'm sure she'll hold it for you until you're able to afford it."

On the way home after her session, Jessie imagined telling her mother that she was going away for the weekend to the mountains with Dr. Miller. To see her mother's face after she delivered that announcement was almost enough of a reason to go with him. Almost, but not quite. His offer made her uncomfortable even if he was sincere in only wanting her to have a relaxing weekend. No, she thought, muddying the waters of their doctor/patient relationship any more than they already had wasn't a good idea.

At home, Jessie found things in an uproar. Maggie was coming out of the laundry room with a stack of freshly pressed slacks while Rita was calling impatiently for Maggie from her bedroom.

"What's up?" Jessie asked curiously.

"One of her New York friends died," Maggie whispered. "The funeral is Tuesday and Miss Rita's flight is at three o'clock this afternoon. I don't know why she's got to pull practically everything out of her closet before she can figure out what to take."

Jessie walked back into her mother's bedroom where, as Maggie had said, mounds of clothes and boxes of shoes were piled everywhere. Rita was holding a black dress up in front of the mirror.

"What do you think?" she asked, eyes never leaving the mirror.

"Who died?"

"Marlene. So tragic and unexpected. It was a stroke or maybe an aneurism." Rita put one dress down and picked up another one. "What about this one?"

"You'll look great in either one. I'm sorry about your friend. Did I know her?"

"She was a Reynolds—a tobacco heiress," Rita answered as if that was everything Jessie might need to know about the woman. "As long as I'm going to be in New York, I thought I'd stay a few days and do some shopping. You could come with me."

"Mother, I appreciate the offer, but you know New York and shopping are two of my least favorite things." She didn't add that being with her mother was at the top of her list of least favorite things.

Rita looked at her, seemingly baffled. "I was hoping therapy might have helped you by now."

"We haven't gotten around to my New York and shopping issues yet," Jessie said as she left the room.

In her bedroom, Jessie pulled up Amelia's website and looked at the picture of the lake and at what she already considered to be her painting. She felt a strange yearning to see both and hated having to wait until some indefinite time in the future. How ironic that she was surrounded by only the best of everything—furniture, clothes, and jewelry—yet she had only $200 to her name.

Then she had a sudden thought. Jewelry! She owned some very valuable pieces of jewelry that she hadn't worn in years! Did she dare sell some of what her mother had given her? The pieces had all been gifts, so didn't they belong to Jessie now? Shouldn't she be able to do whatever she wanted with her own jewelry? But how did one sell jewelry? A small, nagging whisper in the back of her mind added that it would certainly be nice if her mother never found out.

Turning her jewelry into cash ended up being very simple. She went to her iPhone and asked Suri for the addresses of several pawn shops near her. She found one whose website picture looked fairly respectable. Then she went through her jewelry box and chose a silver and pearl David Yurman necklace. She'd never liked the combination of hard silver and soft pearls and had worn it only once or twice. But the thick rope of silver was probably worth a lot. Was it worth $1,000 or $1,200 dollars, though?

Later, as Jessie drove her mother to the airport, Rita talked nonstop on her cell phone to Gerald. She had no clue that her daughter was about to hock one of her Christmas presents.

Within minutes after dropping Rita off at the front door of the airport, Jessie was standing nervously at the counter of a pawnshop that looked somewhat less respectable than it had on its website. The proprietor was friendly, though, and soon Jessie held $1,500 in cash in her hand. She put the money in her wallet and left the pawn shop, feeling empowered for the first time in too long.

At home, she plugged Amelia's address into her phone and realized that she would have a long drive to the mountains, about four hours each way. Still, if she left early in the morning, she could be home around dark. Excitedly, she emailed Amelia to tell her that she should be there around lunchtime the next day.

Jessie told Maggie that she was going to visit a friend in the mountains for the day and that she didn't want her mother to know because it was someone Rita didn't like. When Maggie told her she couldn't go off driving to the mountains by herself, Jessie reminded Maggie that everyone had been nagging her for months to get out of the house more.

"Why aren't you happy?" Jessie demanded. "I'll be out of the house for an entire day?"

At last, Maggie gave in.

As Jessie pulled the Range Rover onto Interstate 20 early the next morning, the sun was a ball of orange in her rear view mirror and the sky a dull shade of gray. Within minutes, the orange light transformed the grayness into the most beautiful blue sky she'd ever seen. She was awestruck by the miracle of the sunrise, and a sense of hopefulness suddenly filled her.

CHAPTER 31

After Jessie's reaction to his invitation, David knew she wasn't going with him to Amelia's house in the mountains. And honestly, he was relieved. As soon as the words had come out of his mouth, he'd wondered where they had come from. What had possessed him to invite her like that? He'd always made it a rule never to mingle with patients outside the office.

However, his self-analysis would have to wait as he was playing in the Augusta Country Club member/guest golf tournament that weekend, and he had a lot to do to get ready. What had made him agree to be Andy's partner in this golf tournament? He hadn't played golf in years, as anyone who looked at the state of his golf bag would realize. Before the kick-off party that night, he needed to clean the outside of the bag and make sure all of his golf clubs were accounted for. He supposed he could pick up some balls at the pro shop in the morning before their tee time.

In the club lounge that night, he was enjoying the last of many beers when Andy turned to him jovially and said, "Oh I forgot to tell you. I talked with Rita Forrester the other day."

David didn't give a damn what Rita Forrester had to say, and he was just about to inform Andy of that fact when Andy said, "And I guess you must have known what you were doing with her daughter after all because Rita said she can see some real improvements."

David had had just enough alcohol to loosen his tongue, "So glad I'm able to clean up the mess she made out of her daughter. What a narcissistic bitch!"

"Whoa there, partner. Like I've told you before. Rita Forrester is not someone you want to be on the wrong side of."

"Does she have a good side?" David asked bluntly. "I've never been very skilled at kissing ass, you know."

"You don't have to kiss her ass, but please don't wave a red flag in front of her. Come on, let's call Uber. I think it's time for you to go home."

Talking about Rita reminded David that he hadn't called Amelia about Jessie's painting. Oh, well, it was too late, and he'd had too many beers to call tonight.

The Augusta Country Club golf course was immaculately manicured and as green as only a course with an automatic and liberal watering system could be at the end of a brutally dry Augusta summer. Even with a pounding head from too many beers the night before, David was able to appreciate the beauty surrounding him. After the first nine holes, he took a break and called Amelia. He'd been trying to come up with a concise explanation for why he wanted to buy a painting for one of his patients and have Amelia pretend to the patient that he hadn't done so. So far, none of his proposed explanations made sense, even to him. Still, he needed to call Amelia.

She answered on the first ring.

"Hey, Mel. What ya doing?"

"I'm trying to bake bread while chasing the kids and waiting for a client to come pick up a painting. It's a great time for Mike to be away making a furniture delivery, right?"

"Which painting did you sell?" he asked, suddenly anxious.

"*Redbird Waiting.*"

Damn! David's heart dropped. Why had he forgotten to call Amelia yesterday?

"That's great," he finally said, wondering if perhaps the buyer might be willing to reconsider. "Do you know the buyer? Is it one of your regulars?"

"No, I've never had any contact with her before. She's from Augusta. Her name's Jessie Graham."

David felt a rush of emotions. "Shit!"

"Do you know her?"

"Ah, yeah. She's one of my patients."

"You sound upset that she's buying one of my paintings. What's wrong?"

"No, it's not that at all. I just wanted her to wait until she can afford it."

"Are you sure she can't afford it?" Amelia asked. "I think she's coming up the driveway now, and it looks like she's driving a Range Rover."

"It's complicated," he said.

"What do you want me to do?"

"Tell her your credit card machine is down."

"And if she gives me a check?"

"She won't. She can't. She doesn't have any money."

"Okay," Amelia said. "I gotta go."

CHAPTER 32

When Jessie first saw Amelia standing on the porch of the large log cabin, her first thought was of a tiny but sturdy Amish woman. Amelia was young, probably about the same age as Jessie, and had a thick braid of dark hair over one shoulder. She wore a big white shirt over denim jeans. The shirt sleeves were rolled to reveal slender but strong-looking arms that held a chubby-faced toddler on each hip. Jessie looked for hints of Dr. Miller in his sister's face but didn't see any.

"You must be Jessie," Amelia said warmly. "Your trip okay?"

Jessie thought about the panic she'd felt each time she drove around a sharp curve on the last twenty miles of winding two-lane road, but all she said was, "It was fine, thanks." One of the boys smiled and reached out for Jessie to take him. "He's a cutie," she added.

Amelia smiled. "And has yet to meet a stranger. Come on in, and let's have some tea."

Without waiting for Jessie's response, Amelia opened the door and motioned her in, not an easy feat with a child on each hip. She guided Jessie through a front room where toys dotted the floor like land mines. They moved into what had been designed as a dining room, but was currently an artist studio. Drawings and paintings in various stages of completion were attached to paint-splattered easels, and a floor lamp with no shade stood in the middle of the room. Beneath the windows, an assortment of plants created a vibrant green border that decorated that side of the room.

When they entered the kitchen, a bright explosion of color hit Jessie's eyes—a potpourri of cheerful yellow, warm orange, and cool turquoise, with splashes of pink thrown in here and there. It was a kitchen more reminiscent of a Caribbean island than the mountains.

With her senses overloaded, Jessie took in the scene as best she could. In the spacious kitchen, two high chairs sat at the end of a large farmhouse table. Amelia placed each of the boys into one of the chairs before distributing cinnamon oatmeal cookies to their outstretched hands. A wooden board, just out of reach of the children, held four long, fat strips of bread dough. A light dusting of flour covered the board and everything else nearby.

"Have a seat there." Amelia pointed to a bench on the side of the table. "Oh, wait," she said and handed Jessie a tea towel to dust off the bench, "Better use this first. I can't make bread without the flour going everywhere." Then she looked down at the bread and added, "Would you mind if I get this bread into some pans to rise before I fix our tea?"

"Of course not. Can I help you?"

Amelia smiled warmly. "No, thanks. It'll take me just a minute." Amelia's movements were sure and deft as she pounded each piece of dough and then gently placed each strip into a greased pan. Then she placed the pans on the windowsill to rise and covered them carefully with white cheesecloth.

At last she reached for the tea kettle. "I've already fed the boys, but I haven't had lunch yet. Would you like to join me?"

"I don't want to intrude. The tea is plenty."

"You're not intruding. We don't get much company up here, so you'd really be doing me a favor. Would egg salad be okay?"

"Well, in that case, sure. I love egg salad."

Jessie looked at the two cherubs in the highchairs getting as much cookie on the floor as into their mouths. "Your boys are adorable," she said. "I wish a friend of mine in Augusta who just had twin boys could see your boys sitting there so happily. She's a little overwhelmed right now with two infants."

"It can be overwhelming at first," Amelia agreed. "But now that the boys are fifteen months old, it's a lot easier. I'm actually beginning to feel sad that they are growing up so fast." She unwrapped a loaf of dark rye bread and pulled a large, blue ceramic bowl from the refrigerator. As she put the bowl on the table, she said, "I was talking to my brother when you arrived, and he mentioned that you are a patient of his."

Jessie felt her face redden slightly as she imagined Dr. Miller's surprise when Amelia told him she was there. Why should she feel guilty?

Amelia misunderstood her reaction. "Hey, I didn't mean to embarrass you or anything about being his patient. Listen, he's been analyzing me all of my life."

Jessie smiled as she imagined a child version of Dr. Miller conducting therapy like Lucy in the Peanuts cartoon. "I guess he always wanted to be a therapist."

Amelia's laugh sounded like glass tinkling. "Or maybe he's always thought he knows what's best for everyone. How's my brother adjusting to life in Augusta?"

"I really don't know him that well," Jessie admitted.

Amelia laughed again. "I'm sorry. What was I thinking? He always keeps his professional life completely separate from his personal life."

Jessie thought about the many personal things she and Dr. Miller had shared and supposed that sometimes his professional and personal lives did coincide. However, she didn't want to contradict this magical woman, who could paint incredible pictures of redbirds and create a cocoon of warmth within a room by filling it with bright colors and the tantalizing smells of cinnamon oatmeal cookies and bread rising.

"I'll slice the bread," Amelia said. "How 'bout you spread the egg salad?"

"Okay."

They had just finished making the sandwiches when one of the boys demanded release from his highchair. The other boy followed suit. Unperturbed, Amelia wiped each child's mouth and hands before placing both boys on the floor.

"Look, boys," she said, opening a cabinet door. With squeals of delight, the boys ran to the cabinet as if it held their greatest treasures.

"What's so exciting?" Jessie asked.

"Tupperware," Amelia explained matter-of-factly. "Best toys ever made. Should give us at least fifteen minutes to eat our lunch."

Amelia sat down across from Jessie and asked, "How'd you find *Redbird Waiting?* And what do you like about it?*"

"I loved your brother's painting of the lake so much that he gave me your card with your website address," Jessie replied. "From the moment I saw the painting of the redbird, I was enchanted by the confidence and hope expressed in the bird's eyes. The contrast between the stark white snow and the bird's red color is truly amazing. You are so talented!"

"Thank you," Amelia said excitedly. "That was just what I was trying for. I love it when people understand my paintings." The room erupted with noise as one of the boys had clobbered the other one with a wooden spoon. "I think it is nap time. Let me put the boys down for their naps, and then we'll walk next door to where the painting is hanging."

A little later when they walked out through the back door, Jessie saw first hand the lake scene in Dr. Miller's painting. The view was stunning. "It's so pretty here," she said.

"As long as you don't look at the deck disaster," Amelia responded lightly. "Don't know why men can't clean up as they go along. Yeah, we are lucky to have this view. And you should see the mountains when they have snow on them, I've tried painting them several times but haven't been able to do them justice yet."

"I wish I were as talented as you are. Your paintings are remarkable. And those cookies, your bread, the egg salad— everything is just perfect."

Amelia smiled. "Thank you. I'll let you in on a little secret about the food. Everything tastes great because it's all fresh. The eggs in the egg salad were laid this morning by those hens," she said, pointing to some chickens pecking happily at the edge of the forest. "We grow as much of our own food as we can and then put it up for the winter. And there's really nothing that compares to home-baked bread."

Jessie couldn't even imagine all the work involved with what Amelia was talking about. "How do you manage to find the time to do all of that, and paint, and take care of the twins? I'm in awe."

Amelia's laughter tinkled again. "Please don't be. People always find the time to do what they really want to do. Living a sustainable and healthy life here with our children is really important to both Mike and to me. I'm lucky that Mike is willing to help with everything, but as he says, it's not work if you enjoy doing it."

Amelia slid open the door of what appeared to have been a horse barn in an earlier time. Jessie's breath caught in surprise at the furniture in front of her.

"Oh, my!" She motioned to the carved wooden bar and bar stools. "Those are works of art." Besides the furniture, the large space inside the horse barn was filled with large stacks of wood, woodworking machinery, and an assortment of tool racks.

"Mike does have a way with wood, doesn't he?" Amelia said. "His work is what pays the bills. When we bought this property three years ago, David thought we were crazy. He said it was too far from any town and that the house and barn needed too much work. But real estate prices had plunged as a result of the financial meltdown, and we knew we'd never be able to afford anything like this property again. So, we did it! Now we can't be happier. Who needs civilization?"

"How do people find your work?"

Amelia smiled. "Just like you did, on the Internet. At first, we went to a lot of craft shows and festivals to get the word out. But Mike's gotten so busy with his furniture that we don't do much in the way of promotion anymore. Sometimes he even has to hire part-time help." Amelia walked to the back of the barn where horse stalls had been converted into individual display rooms. "Here's the redbird. She's still waiting."

Jessie walked into the horse stall and felt a rush of emotion. The painting was even more beautiful in real life. From this close, she could see how Amelia's bold strokes of color were slashed through with muted variations of the same color family. Somehow the painting managed to be both vibrant and peaceful. Hanging in the horse stall, the painting looked perfect in its roughhewn frame as though it had been designed specifically for that spot. Oh, how she wanted the painting for her own!

"I'm speechless," she finally said. Then she noticed a photograph of the bird tacked up on the wall. "Is this what you used for the painting?

Amelia nodded. "I like to show potential purchasers my inspiration."

Jessie stepped closer to the photograph and felt moved by its stark simplicity. "I like this almost as much as your painting."

"Thanks. When I first started painting, I thought painters who used photographs were cheating. I would spend many hours sketching and working on a design before ever picking up a paint brush. But as I matured in my craft, I learned that taking a really good picture is an art in itself, and having the picture allows me to get to the painting part a lot faster."

Jessie looked back and forth from the painting to the photograph. "Of course, you've added emotion to the bird's eyes. That's something that doesn't really come through in the photograph. But the contrasting colors are just as brilliant in both."

"You have a good eye, Jessie," Amelia said. "Are you an artist?"

Jessie laughed, "Me, no. I mean, I've always liked art, but nothing more."

"You could have fooled me," Amelia said. "Oh, I forgot to tell you that my credit card machine isn't working. I hope it's not a problem for you to write a check."

"That's okay," Jessie answered without hesitation.

"Are you sure? 'Cause I'd be glad to hold the painting for you if you don't have the money now."

Jessie smiled slightly, remembering that Dr. Miller had said that's what his sister would do. "That's okay," Jessie repeated as she pulled the envelope stuffed full of money from her purse. "I was going to pay you in cash anyway."

As she made the long trek back to Augusta, the curves in the road didn't seem quite as sharp as they had on her journey there. Jessie glanced occasionally at the photograph of the red bird that was riding shotgun beside her on the passenger seat. When she had asked if Amelia would keep the painting for her for a little while, Amelia had insisted on giving Jessie the photograph to take home. Now Jessie found the photograph appealing, but in a different way from the painting. Amelia's camera had captured a moment in time. It was real, not Amelia's interpretation of reality. To view the picture was to be there *with* the bird, surrounded by the blanket of snow.

Jessie knew she could never be a painter, someone who added a bit of herself to each scene. But could she possibly capture the reality of a moment in a photograph? Just considering the possibility sent a small shiver of excitement through her.

CHAPTER 33

After his phone conversation with Amelia, David had to work hard to find any sort of rhythm on the back nine. Why did Jessie's decision to buy the painting on credit bother him so much? Patients often did the opposite of what they said they were going to do in therapy. Such dissimulation was part of their illness. He thought he'd gotten over feeling disappointed when they lied to him. But Jessie's apparent lack of honesty was definitely bothering him. Still, he had to admit that Jessie's newfound confidence in overriding his advice and her ability to make the trip to the mountains alone showed just how far she had progressed in her therapy.

Although he and Andy weren't last in the final golf rankings, David's lack of practice and inability to focus on the game after talking with Amelia put them toward the end, which was quite a feat with Andy being a scratch golfer.

"Not your best game, buddy," Andy said as they walked into the clubhouse.

"Sorry. I told you I hadn't been playing for a while when you invited me."

Andy laughed. "I guess I was counting on that natural athleticism of yours. Next time I'll take you seriously."

On his way home from the golf course, David phoned Amelia again. "How did it go? Did you sell her the painting?"

"Yes."

"Amelia! After I asked you not to? Why?"

"Listen here," Amelia said defensively. "You asked me not to let her buy it on a credit card, and I didn't. She had cash. Lots of it."

David felt confused. "Just a few days ago she said she had only a few hundred dollars to her name. I wonder if she ended up borrowing from her mother after all."

"I don't think so,' Amelia said, confusing him even more. "She asked me to keep the painting for a while because she didn't want her mother knowing anything about it yet."

"That's strange," David said, pondering this new information.

"David, what's going on between you and Jessie?"

"I told you. She's a patient of mine."

"Yeah, I know. But I've never known you to take such a personal interest in a patient before."

"Kind of hard to do that in the military," David hedged.

"Don't lie to me."

"It's complicated, Mel. Look, I'll be up there next weekend. We'll talk then. Right now, I've got to shower and get back to Andy's club for the closing party."

On Monday, David looked at his watch for probably the tenth time, wishing the minutes would hurry along. When Jessie arrived for her appointment, she looked more alive than he'd ever seen her. She practically bounced into the room before landing in the seat across from him and placing a backpack carefully on the floor beside her.

Then, still filled with energy, she launched immediately into the conversation, "I guess you heard that I bought the painting," she said. "My mother went to New York unexpectedly. It was the perfect opportunity for me to get away."

"Well, well," he began. "Maybe my sister is the real therapist in the family. One day with her seems to have worked wonders."

"She is incredible."

"I've always thought so," David agreed. He waited no longer to get to the point. "How did you pay for the painting, Jessie?"

Jessie preened with pride. "I pawned a piece of jewelry."

David was taken aback. "That was certainly resourceful of you."

"Thanks. And although I appreciated your offer to take me next weekend, I think it was good for me to go by myself."

"No doubt about it." Professionally, David had to agree with her. So why was he feeling slightly deflated?

"And," Jessie went on as she lifted a backpack, "I'm starting something new." She unzipped the top of the backpack and pulled out a camera. "Amelia has inspired me to take up photography."

"Really?" David asked. "How'd that happen?"

"I had a little money left over after purchasing the painting, so I spent the rest of the money on a camera."

"Oh. And how did you go from buying her painting, to being inspired to take up photography?"

Jessie unzipped a small pocket in the backpack and pulled out Amelia's photograph of the redbird, which she placed on David's desk. "She gave me this."

David looked down at the picture. It was a good one. "Have you ever done photography before?"

"No. But I've always been attracted to color and light. And since Saturday, I've started noticing things in ways I've never noticed them before. Like this bee hovering over a flower," she said, opening a folder and spreading photos across the front of his desk. "Or this lizard sunning himself on a green leaf on the patio. It's crazy how much more I'm already able to see."

David picked up the lizard photo and analyzed it critically. It was good, a real study in greens and yellows. He flipped through all of the photos, making a mental note of which ones seemed particularly well done. Jessie did have a knack for photography, for seeing design, for choosing colorful combinations and contrasts. He wished he had picked up on this artistic side of her himself.

Finally he said, "These are great! Have you thought about taking a class or joining a group?"

For the first time she paused. "I'd like to explore photography on my own for a while. I bought a couple of books, and Amelia said she taught herself."

"Amelia did go to art school," David reminded her.

"Oh." Jessie's excitement dimmed for a moment. "Well, I'll see how it goes. I'm having so much fun taking pictures in my back yard that the thought of sitting in a class doesn't seem very appealing."

David smiled, pleased with her excitement. "Do you see this as a hobby or as something more? Maybe a way to make a living?"

A slight frown flickered on her face. David hated to have been the one to put it there. Still, reality was something she had to start facing.

"At this point, who knows?" she said. "Making a career out of photography is probably a long shot."

David liked her reasonable and well-thought out response. "You know, my dad refused to help Amelia with art school. He thought her painting was a hobby and said he would only help pay for a 'real' college degree."

"How did she manage?"

"She waited tables, she babysat, basically did anything she could to support herself while she was in art school. And in between, she painted."

"I'm even more in awe of her now."

"My point is, if you want something badly enough, you'll figure out how to make it work." David paused and looked at his watch. "I'm really proud of you, but we are almost out of time. How about taking your camera out of the back yard for your next homework assignment? Let's see how you do somewhere else, where there might be some people around to interact with." He felt gratified to see sparkles of excitement come back into her eyes.

"You got it," Jessie said as she gathered her photographs and camera and put everything carefully into her backpack. "I will have much more fun photographing people than walking with the senior citizens at the mall."

"That was your choice, not mine," David reminded her.

Jessie just smiled jauntily and left his office.

CHAPTER 34

Jessie woke to the sound of thunder, a relentless rain on the rooftop, and a sense of deep disappointment. She'd planned to go early to Pendleton King Dog Park and photograph dogs and their owners before the day got too hot. What now?

She was lying in bed considering other possibilities when the memory of David holding her in his office popped unexpectedly into her mind. Funny how she'd started thinking of him as David since being with Amelia. And funny how much she had looked forward to her appointment with him the day before. She'd had full-blown butterflies in her stomach as she walked up the sidewalk to his office. But how could she have any kind of romantic feelings for him when she didn't even trust him completely?

Jessie suddenly remembered that MJ had called her the day before to see about when they might get together again. Perhaps she and her boys could be Jessie's homework assignment for the day.

"No," MJ said firmly when Jessie called and asked about photographing the boys. She went on to politely explain that the boys weren't dressed for pictures, and they were still teething and were quite fussy. In a word, it wasn't a good time for pictures.

"I'm just trying to learn how to use my camera," Jessie explained. "If you want any of the pictures, I'll give them to you. Otherwise, I'll throw them away. And didn't you say I could stop by any time for a visit? Just consider this a visit. You won't even notice that I'm taking pictures while we talk."

MJ laughed. "Now, you sound like the Jessie I remember from when we were kids. Okay, come on over. But I swear, if you show anybody pictures of me or my babies looking like we look right now, I'll, I'll... make you wish you hadn't," she finished lamely.

Jessie dressed hurriedly in exercise clothes and then ate sparingly of the oatmeal Maggie placed in front of her. "You know you don't have to cook breakfast for me, Maggie. I can fix my own breakfast, and I'd just as soon eat a piece of fruit or a breakfast bar."

"Ummmph," Maggie muttered as Jessie stood up, "You need to eat more than that."

"Not today. I'm too excited. I'm going to photograph MJ and her twins."

Maggie looked at her curiously. "Why are you going to take pictures of those Jacksons? Don't they have their own camera?"

Jessie felt laughter bubbling up inside. "Of course, silly. I *want* to take their pictures to practice using my new camera. I want to be a photographer."

"A photographer, huh? Well, when you get really good, I'll let you take my picture."

After putting her dishes in the dishwasher, Jessie gave Maggie a quick hug and said, "When I get really good, you'll be begging me to take your picture."

"Oh, you go on and get out of here," Maggie said gruffly.

Jessie wouldn't let MJ look at the pictures as she was taking them. She wasn't happy with the color composition, so she switched to black and white and found that by focusing only on their faces, she could capture some interesting shots. There was one of MJ looking at the boys and one of the boys looking at each other that she found riveting. *If I were doing a show, I'd call these "Expressions of Love in Black and White"* she thought giddily as she drove home.

When Jessie saw Gerald's car in the circular driveway in front of Rita's house, her heart dropped. How peaceful things had been for her and Maggie while her mother was in New York. But if Gerald's car was there, her mother must be back. Should she leave the camera in the car? Would the heat hurt the camera? Before she finished her musings, the front door opened, and Gerald and her mother came out. Since they were headed in her direction. Jessie decided she might as well take charge of the situation and carry the backpack with the camera inside.

"Welcome back, Mother," Jessie said. Her mother presented to her another composition in black and white—perfectly creased black slacks, a starched white blouse, and a black diamond choker around her neck. Jessie fought a compulsion to pull out her camera and start snapping pictures. "I didn't realize you were coming in today. I would have picked you up at the airport if I'd known."

"Oh, I wanted to pick her up," Gerald said cheerfully. "You are looking well, Jessie."

"Thanks." Jessie turned to her mother. "How was your trip?"

Rita's eyebrows were idling in neutral, a good sign. "Fine. Glad I went. I picked up a few pairs of shorts for you. End of summer prices were too good to pass up."

Jessie thought about all of the unworn shorts she already had in her room. "Thanks."

"Well, I've got to go," Gerald said as he turned to Rita and fake kissed her on each cheek. "Bye, darling. Missed you lots. So glad you're home."

As they started back to the house, her mother said, "Maggie told us you went to photograph MJ's babies. What's that all about?"

"I've become interested in photography."

"Interesting." One eyebrow lifted quizzically as Rita stopped in the foyer. "Where'd you get your camera?"

Heart pounding, Jessie quickly considered several different explanations, including the truth that she'd pawned her jewelry. "I borrowed it from Dr. Miller," she finally lied.

"Is this part of his therapy? Providing you with a hobby or extracurricular activities?"

"Yeah, I guess so. I don't know. You need to ask him."

"He might have suggested something more suitable for your background."

"What would you suggest, Mother?"

"Perhaps going back to school? Getting a master's degree or a teaching certificate?"

"I've never wanted to be a teacher."

"And you've always had a passion for photography?" Rita's eyebrows mocked her. "Oh, well, I suppose I'm happy that this photography is getting you out of the house." Rita stretched her arms in front of her. "I'm really exhausted from the flight. Even flying first class these days isn't very relaxing. I'm going to lie down for a bit."

Jessie went to her room, considering how the secrets she was keeping from her mother were beginning to pile up. Her lies were allowing her to have some control over her life, which was a good thing, right? But the lies didn't exactly coincide with David's theory about facing reality.

CHAPTER 35

The lake's water glittered in the autumn sun. The newly finished deck provided David with the perfect platform for viewing nature's tableaux—stately red and yellow hardwoods interspersed liberally with green pines against the curve of blue water. The day couldn't have been more perfect. And with Mike on a walk with the boys, Amelia was savoring a rare moment of peace. She was stretched out on the deck chair next to David with her eyes closed, but David knew she wasn't asleep, merely biding her time.

"What's up with you and Jessie?" she finally asked, eyes still closed.

"It's complicated."

"That's what you said on the phone. Twice. Care to elaborate?" Amelia stretched her arms overhead and then placed them under her head.

"You know I can't talk about my patients." David closed his eyes, hoping that maybe Amelia would take a hint and let the conversation end.

"My sisterly intuition tells me that she's more than a patient to you. So why don't you tell me about the non-patient part of your relationship?"

"It's not what you're thinking."

"What am I thinking?"

"I'm not romantically involved with her."

Amelia opened her eyes and rolled over onto her side to look directly at David. "Okay, so what gives? What else is going on if not anything romantic?"

David decided he might as well be blunt. "She's the girl from the car accident that I was involved in the night the boys were born."

Amelia sat straight up. "What?! The girl you pulled from the car?"

"Yep. She's from Augusta, and her mother brought her home after the accident for rehabilitation. You can imagine how surprised I was when she walked into my office."

"Did she come to you because you were involved in her accident?"

"Oh, no. She never knew anything about me. It was just one of those strange coincidences you don't believe can happen unless it happens to you."

"But she knows now, right?"

"Right."

"Whew, good. I was starting to get worried." Amelia reclined against the chair again. "You know she's about my age, but she seems much younger."

"Yes. She's led a very sheltered life, went to boarding school, and has a very controlling mother who probably isn't even capable of real love."

Amelia's voice became soft. "Mothers often leave a lot of wreckage in their wake, don't they?"

David knew Amelia wasn't referring only to Rita Forrester. "It's not just mothers, you know," David said, jumping to their mother's defense. "Fathers do their fair share of damage as well."

Amelia was quiet for a minute or two, thinking. "Tell me something about our mother. You never want to talk about her."

"She was creative like you are."

"Do you think I'm like her?"

"You certainly got her creativity."

"Tell me a good memory."

David considered carefully what to say, "She baked this cake one time, and for some reason the layers didn't rise. They looked like spongy pancakes in the pans when she took them out of the oven. Instead of getting upset, she placed the cake circles on plates, mixed up different colors of icing, and told me to paint them. It was so much fun, and I thought they tasted great."

Amelia smiled. "I like that story and the idea. I'll have to try painting cake layers sometime with the boys." Then she shifted back to her original train of conversation. "I like Jessie, too."

"She likes you as well. As a matter of fact, she's taken up photography because of that picture you gave her."

"She has a good eye."

"She's shown me some of the pictures she's taken, and I think so, too. However, regardless of whether she's any good or not, having an interest in something is good for her. I'd love to think that photography might be a way for her to gain some financial independence from her mother, but that's a very, very long shot."

"You sound just like Dad when you said it would be a long shot."

David was offended. "Thanks, Mel. I'm just stating the facts. If her mother cuts her off, Jessie needs to know that she can support herself."

Amelia looked thoughtfully at the lake. "Regardless of whether her mother cuts her off or not, Jessie needs to know that she can support herself."

"When did *you* get your psychology degree?"

Amelia smiled. "Women's intuition is better than any degree. Which, by the way, is telling me that you're still not being totally honest with me about Jessie."

David started to deny once again that Jessie was special to him. Then, taking a deep breath, he tried to be as honest with his sister as he was being with himself.

"Our lives literally collided one night, so yes, I suppose my relationship with her is different from the usual doctor-patient relationship. I held her in my arms when she was hurt and bleeding and unconscious, and I can still remember how slight she feels. Jessie came to for a moment that night and asked me to help her. And that's what I've been trying my best to do, to help her, since she walked into my office in Augusta. So if you think I've got romantic feelings for Jessie Graham, then you are sadly mistaken. She's my patient, and that's it!"

CHAPTER 36

Fall was David's favorite time of year. He'd enjoyed watching the distinctive fan-shaped leaves on the ginkgo tree outside his cottage turn a brilliant yellow before falling into decorative piles on his lawn. One day he'd returned home from work to find that the yard service had hauled them away. Now he thought the bare green lawn looked naked and sad. He much preferred his yellow snow.

On Thanksgiving, he had much to be thankful for. His practice was continuing to grow, and he was feeling more and more as though Augusta might be a place he could put down roots. Andy and Jan had become like family. They had him over to eat as often as he would come, saying that they would get their payback in the spring after the baby arrived. Although Jan still tried occasionally to play matchmaker, he was trying to convince her that he wanted to take a break from dating for a while. Instead he had become one of the regulars at O'Leery's Pub, and his casual flirtation with the bartender continued although she made it clear that she now had a serious boyfriend.

Now it would soon be Christmas. David stood at the window in his office, waiting for Jessie to arrive. Although it was mid-morning, gray fog hung heavily on the street outside, and only the Christmas lights twinkling on the businesses and houses along Central Avenue managed to bring a little cheer to what would otherwise have been a dismally dark, dreary day.

"Must be something really interesting out there," Jessie said brightly as she joined him at the window, "cause you sure are lost in thought."

David felt a quickening of his pulse as she came to stand next to him, and he caught a whiff of the clean, natural smell that he'd recognize anywhere as being Jessie's smell. "You're like a cat. You come in so quietly! I'm just admiring the Christmas lights. It's hard to believe that Christmas is next week."

"I know," she said. "Seems like only yesterday I was suffering through Thanksgiving with Gerald and my mother at the Augusta Country Club, and here I am already dreading the open house Rita's having on Christmas Eve." Jessie rolled her eyes dramatically. "Can you imagine anything more horrible than having strangers drop by your house all evening on Christmas Eve? And this is what my mother considers fun." Then she grinned at him and added, "You are going to be so proud of me today."

David smiled at her cheery demeanor. "Prouder than I was when you won first place in photography at the Westobou Arts Festival for your series of baby pictures?"

Jessie shrugged. "Well, it's not *that* exciting. But I am finally taking the first step toward independence. I've been talking with a realtor in Atlanta, and I'm putting the house on the market right after Christmas."

David felt that his job was to always be the Devil's advocate. "How about going back to the house before you sell it?" he asked. He'd been encouraging Jessie to face this aspect of her past for the last few weeks. Yet there never seemed to be a good time to visit the house, as far as Jessie was concerned.

Jessie turned away from the window and walked to her chair. "I know, I know. I have to tie up this last loose end."

David felt a slight jolt at her mention of the last loose end. She had been doing so well lately that they'd been talking about decreasing her sessions. But now maybe she was thinking about quitting therapy altogether. Was that why he'd felt so melancholy lately?

Jessie looked pensive as she continued, "I know it's past time I went back to the house, and I'm determined to start the New Year off right. So I'm going to Atlanta now and see what needs to be done to the house before it goes on the market in January."

"Who's going with you?"

"No one. I did think about taking Maggie, our housekeeper, but she'd have to ask Mother for the time off, and with Mother's party and everything, I don't think that's possible. Plus, I'd rather not involve Mother in this house-selling venture."

She looked earnestly at David, "Mother would just take over, and before I knew it, the house would be sold and the money invested securely, and I'd never get my hands on it."

"Is that all you're worried about? The money? I'm much more worried about the emotional upheaval you're going to feel by returning to your old house. I think this is going to be much more difficult than you anticipate."

David studied Jessie for a moment before he continued. "Going back into your old house with all of its memories for the first time is going to be extremely painful."

"It scares me to death to think about it," Jessie said.

"I don't think it's a good idea for you to go alone."

"I agree, but I'm telling you, there's no one I can ask without involving Mother, and I don't want to do that."

Ignoring every warning bell clanging loudly within him, David asked, "What about me?"

CHAPTER 37

David's question hung in the air between them as Jessie stared at him in surprise. For several months, her relationship with David had returned to what she considered to be an appropriate professional one. Now his offer to go with her to Atlanta seemed once again like crossing a professional line.

After what seemed like a minute, he continued matter-of-factly. "Our office will be closed all next week for the Christmas holidays. I'm going to Amelia and Mike's on Christmas Eve but was planning to spend a few days in Atlanta, visiting some buddies first. It wouldn't be that big a deal to meet you at your house one day. We'll count it as therapy, and I'll bill your mother," he added with a smile.

Jessie felt relieved by his explanation but not amused by his attempt at humor. It only served to remind her that she hadn't added the cost of her therapy to the list of expenses she already owed her mother. She floundered helplessly for a moment or two, trying to come up with an appropriate answer.

Finally David saved her by saying unequivocally, "I'm not giving you a choice here. As your doctor, my opinion is that it's not in your best interest for you to go back into your old house alone. Either you find someone who can go with you, or I'll meet you at your Atlanta house one day next week."

Jessie nodded her head like a puppet, even while her mind was racing in a thousand directions. Her first thought was strangely of MJ. What would MJ say if she heard that Jessie and Augusta's most eligible bachelor had been together in Atlanta? And Jessie couldn't even imagine her Mother's reaction. And wasn't David worried about how his actions might affect his practice?

Jessie could feel her chest beginning to tighten like the faint beginnings of a panic attack that she hadn't felt for a long time. Why was his offer to help upsetting her so much?

"Are you okay?" David asked in a concerned tone.

Jessie needed to leave, get away from David, and sort through her feelings, "I'm fine. I'll call you tomorrow or the next day and let you know what I've figured out."

"What about our session today?"

"I've got to go now," she said, feeling it hard to breathe. "I'll let you know."

CHAPTER 38

Two days had gone by, and David had yet to hear from Jessie. Every time his cell phone rang, he looked to see who was calling with equal parts excitement and dread. He realized that he had become overly involved with this woman, but he wasn't sure what to do about it. The smart thing for him to do would be to tell her that something had come up and that he could no longer meet her in Atlanta. But then he would think about how vulnerable she was, and he couldn't imagine that she could walk back into that house alone after all of this time had passed and be perfectly all right.

He was dripping with sweat from the run he'd just gone on when Jessie finally did call. He pushed the answer button on his cell phone and said lightly, "I was beginning to think you'd forgotten to call me."

"Hello," she said hesitantly, and then in a stronger voice," I'm going to Atlanta on Monday."

"Okay. What's your plan? Did you find someone to go with you?" he asked.

"No, but I've decided to go against your medical opinion and do it by myself." Jessie sighed. "I need to figure out who I am and what I'm made of, and surely you can support me in that, can't you?"

David felt a wave of relief followed by a wave of concern. "Will you promise to call me if you change your mind, or if you get there and it's too much for you? I'll be in Atlanta anyway, so I can come if you need me."

Another long pause, and then Jessie said, "I hope I don't need to do that, but if I do, I promise I'll call you."

"Have you told your mother what you're doing?"

"No. I don't want her to take over and start managing everything. I can see her giving me a detailed plan with step-by-step instructions. I'm going to call her from Atlanta once I get there."

David could visualize Rita doing exactly what Jessie had described. However, her intervention might not be such a bad thing, Jessie really was an innocent in many ways. He didn't want a realtor taking advantage of her. "Rita won't like that, I'm sure."

Jessie forced an empty laugh that held no amusement. "Since she likes very little of what I do anyway, I'm trying to learn not to worry about what she likes or doesn't like anymore."

Although David admired this new bravado that Jessie had found, he feared that it might shatter like glass and break her into pieces along with it.

"Okay, Jessie," he finally said after the silence continued for too long. "Remember, I'll be close by in Atlanta if you need me."

CHAPTER 39

The house on Park Avenue was buzzing with action in the last steps of preparation for the Christmas Eve open house. In fact, Rita had been so busy that she had barely noticed Jessie for the last couple of days. Having her mother ignore her had been perfect as far as Jessie was concerned.

Planning for her trip had kept Jessie focused, and there had been a lot more to consider than she had originally realized. Where had her mother put the keys to Jessie's house? What about the keys to Jessie's car in Atlanta? Was the house security code the same? Should she take her mother's car to Atlanta or rent a car so she wouldn't have two cars there at one time?

When her mother left with Gerald to go shopping for a few additional wreaths and topiaries, Jessie took that opportunity to search her mother's desk. There she found a box with the Atlanta house address on it, and inside was everything Jessie needed. She emptied the box and put it back exactly where she'd found it.

Then she reserved a rental car from a company that advertised "We'll pick you up." She took a chance and made a reservation for mid-morning, a time when both Maggie and Rita were typically busy. How to sneak a suitcase out was more problematic. Finally Jessie decided to stow a few essentials in her largest purse. After all, she didn't need much for an overnight stay.

Surprisingly, she slept well on Sunday night. She rose on Monday, dressed casually in jeans, and went down to gauge what was going on.

"Where's Mother?" she asked after she caught Maggie's attention.

Maggie frowned. "I'm not sure, but she is on the warpath. If I were you, I'd stay out of her way."

"Just what I was thinking," Jessie said as she walked over to Maggie and gave her a big hug.

"What's that for?" Maggie asked suspiciously.

"'Cause I love you," Jessie answered.

"What do you want from me?" Maggie said gruffly, but Jessie saw that her soft eyes were in direct contrast to her words.

In the end, her escape was very easy. Jessie walked out of the house at 10 o'clock in the morning carrying her purse, and neither Maggie nor Rita seemed to notice her. Or, if they did, neither stopped long enough to wonder where she was going. The man from the car rental agency had parked the Ford Taurus down the block just as she'd asked him to. "Do you want to drive us back to the rental office?" the man asked from the window as she approached the car.

"No," she replied, quickly opening the passenger door before the man could get out and open it for her. "Let's go."

Only later, as Jessie was cruising west on Interstate 20 toward Atlanta, did the panic surface once again. She'd never had a job, and she'd never done anything like buy or sell a house. What made her think she was capable of taking those actions now?

For about twenty miles, she fought against turning the car around and heading back to her Mother and the safety that Rita represented. But then she thought about how empty her life was living with her mother, and she remembered David's advice to her when she'd started therapy, "fake it until you make it."

She wanted a new life. She wanted her own life. She'd have to fake it until she could actually make it happen. So she kept driving, mile after mile away from Augusta, and before she knew it, she was turning into her old neighborhood off Roswell Road.

CHAPTER 40

David was drinking a cold beer with a couple of friends at Taco Mac in the Virginia Highlands section of Atlanta and listening to them give him a hard time for having left Atlanta.

"Man, I can't believe you gave up all this. Are you crazy?" Without waiting for an answer, the larger of the two guys, Tom, threw back most of the beer in his mug in one gulp and then burped loudly.

"I never knew you guys were so attached to me," David commented dryly.

"It's Dis-Augusta, Georgia, for heaven's sakes. I mean, the only thing of any interest in Augusta is the Masters Tournament, and that's just one week a year!" The slightly built and bearded Harry shook his head questioningly and asked, "What do you do there the other fifty-one weeks of the year?"

David smiled. "You guys sure are taking this personally."

"It's like this," Harry began with mock seriousness. "If you'd left us for New York or Los Angeles or really anywhere else, we could have said, 'Our best bud, Dave, got this great job in the Big Apple, or he's schmoozing with the stars out in LA. But instead, all we can say is he moved a couple of hours down the road to nowheresville."

"It's really a nice town," David said. If you'd only come visit me sometime, you'd find out how nice it is. I mean not sitting in traffic for half of your day alone makes it wonderful." He finished his beer and looked around. "I don't know where our waitress disappeared to. I'm going to see if I can order another round of beer at the bar."

The bartender was an attractive, slender blonde who reminded David of Jessie. He wondered if Jessie had made it to Atlanta. The odds were at least 50/50 that she had changed her mind. He wanted to call and find out. After all, if she were still in Augusta, he could stop thinking about her every few minutes and relax.

While trying to catch the bartender's attention, David considered how he felt about being back in Atlanta and realized that he had been honest with his friends. Augusta was a nice place to live, and there wasn't much about Atlanta that he was missing.

CHAPTER 41

For at least fifteen minutes, Jessie had been sitting in the rental car in the driveway of her Atlanta house. A thousand bittersweet memories had paralyzed her. She felt incapable of taking the next step and actually opening the car door. How foolish she'd been to think she could do this on her own! Should she call David? Should she just drive back to Augusta?

Her cell phone rang. She hit the answer button. "Jessica," her mother's voice filled the car, strident and sharp.

Jessie felt her backbone stiffen in response. "Yes, Mother."

"All day long, Maggie and I thought you were upstairs in your room because the Range Rover was here. Imagine our surprise when Maggie went up to check on you just now, and we discovered that you had left without telling us that you were going anywhere."

"Does it really matter?" asked Jessie.

"Jessica, where are you?" Rita demanded.

"I'm at my house in Atlanta. I decided to check things out before finalizing the arrangements with a realtor here."

"Might have been nice if I had been consulted since I've been the one taking care of things there." Rita's voice was a cross between anger and disbelief. "Did you go into my desk and take the keys?"

"Yes, Mother, I did. I needed to do this on my own, without your help. Besides, you've been so busy with the Christmas Eve open house that you haven't had any spare time."

Jessica heard nothing but her mother's breathing for a few seconds. Then Rita said, "Jessica, do you remember what I told you about keeping me informed about what you're doing?"

"Not really," Jessie replied honestly.

"You don't remember what I said would happen the next time you did something without letting me know?"

For a second Jessie was confused, but then she remembered her mother's threat after she had gone to the bank teller instead of asking her mother for her bank statements. "You said I would be on my own."

"That's right. And since that seems to be what you want as well, I guess you won't care that I'm cutting off your bank cards and your phone first thing tomorrow. There won't be any more payments going to the Atlanta house mortgage, either. That is, unless you want to come home now and apologize to both me and Maggie for causing us to worry." The cell phone clicked in Jessie's ear and went silent.

Jessie sat in shock, absorbing what her mother's words meant. As of tomorrow, she would have no more access to her mother's money. Luckily, before leaving Augusta, she'd withdrawn the $200 from her checking account. And she still had $10,000 credit available on her personal credit card. Still, how long could she survive? How was she to pay the mortgage on the house, and everything else until the house sold? What was she to do?

She was stuffing her cell phone into her purse when a tapping on the car window startled her. "Ma'm," a young boy of maybe ten, dressed in long sweat pants and a jacket, said politely, "You must be at the wrong house, 'cause nobody's lived here for a really long time."

Jessie realized how strange she must look to the young boy. "I know. I used to live in this house," she answered.

His mouth formed a perfectly shaped "O" before he said, "Are you moving back?"

"Maybe. For a little while," she said. Then, since her only other choice seemed to be to drive back to Augusta, she gathered her courage and opened the car door.

The boy was watching her as she approached the door of her house. Somehow knowing that he was observing her gave her the strength to slip the key into the lock and open the door with one fluid motion. The alarm system beeped, and Jessie stepped in to enter the security code. The boy stepped up behind her so that he could peer in curiously. Jessie found the boy's nosiness strangely comforting.

She turned to him. "Would you like to come in with me?"

The boy hesitated. "I'm not supposed to go anywhere with a stranger."

"Of course," she replied. Then she added conspiratorially, "I'll leave the door open in case you want to look in from a distance."

Jessie took a couple of faltering steps further into the foyer, finding that with each step it was harder and harder to breathe. She was face to face with the spiral staircase. She saw herself again on the night of the accident, all decked out in her silver dress, floating down that staircase, anxiously anticipating Nick's reaction.

She turned toward the den and saw the leather sofa where Nick had been sitting, watching television and waiting for her to come down. How odd that nothing had changed, and yet everything had changed. Jessie felt dizzy. As the room started to swirl around her, she reached out for the stair railing and held on as she crumpled to the floor. *I need to call David* was her last thought before darkness overtook her.

When Jessie opened her eyes, the boy and an older woman stood beside her.

"Is she dead?" the boy was asking somewhat wistfully.

"Don't be silly," the woman said in a no-nonsense voice, "She just fainted." Noticing that Jessie's eyes were open, the woman said, "Welcome back."

Jessie started to sit up, and the room teetered just a bit.

"Whoa there," the woman said. "Let me help you."

The woman reached behind Jessie and gently helped her to a sitting position.

"Thank you," Jessie said simply.

"I'm glad to help. I'm Madeleine Merriweather and this is Robbie. We live across the street."

"I'm Jessie Graham," Jessie began, but then wasn't sure what else to say. Should she blurt out her whole sad story while sitting in the middle of her foyer floor?

"Robbie said you used to live here, right?" Madeleine asked.

Jessie could tell from the woman's expression that she had already heard her whole sad story from someone else, maybe another neighbor. She nodded.

"Is this your first time back?"

Jessie nodded again.

"Is there anyone you want me to call?"

Jessie nodded a third time, before adding, "If you'll hand me my purse over there, I'll make the call."

CHAPTER 42

Taco Mac had grown more crowded as the afternoon went on, and the noise level had gone up several decibels. A close college football bowl game was in its final minute, and the entire restaurant was in the middle of a touchdown cheer when David felt his cell phone vibrate.

"Jessie?"

"I've changed my mind. Do you think you could come now?"

"What's the address?"

"127 Stonehaven Trail, Roswell."

"I'll be there as soon as I can."

"Thanks, David," she said realizing she'd just used his first name. "It's not an emergency, so no need to rush."

"See you soon."

The door of the traditional brick house was opened by a towheaded boy who reminded David of Dennis the Menace. "You the doctor?" the boy asked solemnly.

"Yes."

The boy motioned for David to follow him and led him back to the kitchen. Jessie sat at a table, looking pale and fragile. A dark haired, very tan woman stood next to Jessie, holding a cup. Jessie looked up as he came into the room.

"What happened?" David asked of no one in particular.

"She fainted," the woman said. "We live across the street. Robbie was being his typical self, poking his nose where he shouldn't be, but in this case, I'm glad he was."

"Oh, Mom," the boy said, exasperated. "She," he pointed to Jessie, "left the door open, and I saw her do like this." The boy illustrated what Jessie had done by crumpling to the floor in front of David.

"Hi, Madeleine, Robbie. I'm Dr. David Miller." David picked up Jessie's wrist to take her pulse. It'd been a while since he'd performed a medical doctor's activities, but he supposed, like riding bike, you never forgot how to do some things. Jessie's heartbeat was a bit fast but not at a rate to be concerned about.

He looked closely at Jessie. "How are you feeling?"

Jessie looked him straight in the eye. "My head hurts a little, and I feel like I might throw up."

"Perhaps a concussion?" Madeleine asked David.

"I didn't hit my head," Jessie replied immediately.

"I'll run home and get some Coca-Colas and crackers," Madeleine said. "Maybe those will help. I always think everything gets better with Coke. I'll be right back. Come along, Robbie." Robbie's face registered immediate disappointment.

As soon as the front door closed behind them, David asked, "What's going on, Jessie?

Jessie closed her eyes and then opened them wearily, "My good intentions," she said, "didn't get me very far—only as far as the front door."

David felt his heart tighten at the hopelessness in her demeanor. "Don't get discouraged. Just a short time ago, you wouldn't have considered even attempting something like this on your own. You've really come a long way."

David heard the front door open, and then Madeleine, without Robbie, came through the kitchen doorway with a full grocery bag. "I brought the Cokes and crackers and a few other things."

"Thank you so much for everything you've done," Jessie said.

"It's not much," Madeleine replied. "I've got to take Robbie to soccer practice, but if there's anything else you need, I've written my cell number on a piece of paper in the bag."

David walked Madeleine to the front door. "I think she's fine," he said. "It's the first time she's been back to the house since her husband was killed, so it's a difficult time for her right now."

Madeleine nodded in agreement, a look of concern on her face. "I'm sure it is. Listen, if there's anything she needs, please let me know."

"Will do."

As David went to close the door after Madeleine, he noticed the white car in the driveway. "Whose car is outside?" he asked Jessie.

A look of sudden concern crossed her face, "Oh, no, we've got to take that car back to the rental agency before they close at 6 p.m."

"Hey, you're in no condition to be driving right now. We can take it tomorrow."

Jessie stood up. "No, we have to take it today because tomorrow I'll have to pay for another day's rental, and Mother's cutting off my use of her credit card."

"What do you mean?" asked David.

"I mean, if I take it back today, I can put it on my mother's credit card. Tomorrow, I'll have to pay for that rental car out of my not very large funds."

"Your mother cut you off because you came to Atlanta?" David guessed.

Jessie smiled slightly. "Well, not exactly. She had warned me after I did a couple of things without telling her what I was doing, that if I ever did such a thing again, I was on my own. I think this is her version of tough love."

"Why didn't you just tell her you were coming to Atlanta?"

"My mother would have insisted that I wait until she could come with me."

David frowned. "How much money do you have?"

"About $200 in cash, and $10,000 I can access on a credit card."

"Maybe you should consider calling your mother," David said.

Jessie looked offended, "Not if I want to get out from under her control."

"It's just that I think you need to transition a bit slower into complete independence, that's all."

Jessie looked up at him defiantly. "I'm going to sell everything in this house in one of those estate sale things, and then I'm going to sell this house as fast as I can."

"And then what? Although you may think you'll have a large sum of money after selling the house, it really won't last long."

"I'm going to teach English and be a photographer In Thailand."

David was stunned. "*Thailand!* What do you mean, Thailand?"

"Remember my best friend, Wendy, who lives in Thailand? We've been emailing, and she said she can get me a job teaching English while I work on my photography."

"Don't you think that plan is a bit extreme for someone who not too long ago had difficulties going to the Augusta Mall?"

Jessie deflated right before his eyes. "Maybe. But, right now it's the only idea I have. Hey, I was serious about needing to take the rental car back. Do you mind following me in your car? If you don't want to, then I suppose the rental people can give me a ride back here."

"Walk around the room a few times, and let me see how steady you are on your feet before you get behind the wheel of a car."

She stood and strode back and forth without any obvious dizziness.

"Okay," David said. "I guess you are steady enough. Let's go."

While David was following Jessie to the rental car agency, he thought about how desperate she must feel even to consider selling everything she owned and starting her life over again in Thailand. His cell phone rang. "What's up, Amelia?"

"Are you still planning on coming Thursday? I was thinking maybe you could come a day or two earlier. Mike needs to deliver some furniture, and I'd really love for him to do it when you are here to help me."

"Let me get back to you about Thursday. Something has come up here in Atlanta." David suddenly felt inspired, "Hey, Amelia, you remember Jessie?

"Of course."

"What would you think about Jessie staying with you for a while until she figures out some things? She could help you with the kids in exchange for a place to stay."

"I'd say, how soon can she get here?"

David smiled to himself. "That's what I thought you'd say. I haven't talked with her about this yet, so I don't know what she'll think. But it would be a lot better than what she's been planning to do. And if she agrees, both of us will be there tomorrow."

"Well, let me know as soon as things are settled."

When Jessie struggled to open the passenger door of his old Camry, David felt slightly embarrassed. He tried to imagine what someone who had been riding around in a Range Rover might think about his mode of transportation. "Everything go okay?" he asked her as she settled in the seat and searched for the seat belt.

She nodded.

"Maybe your mom is just bluffing about cutting off the credit card."

"You don't know my mother," Jessie said adamantly. "She never bluffs."

David looked at her pale face and wondered how long it had been since she had eaten.

"Are you hungry?" he asked.

"I guess I could eat something. I ate some nuts driving over. That's all I've had all day."

"How about that deli across the street?"

"Fine."

And then there was silence as David pulled into the deli parking lot, and the silence continued as they walked into the restaurant. It was a bit early for the dinner crowd, so they were seated immediately. A young, tattooed waitress hovered eagerly, waiting for their order, until Jessie decided on matzo ball soup and a bagel. David wasn't really hungry after all of the wings he had eaten at Taco Mac, but he ordered the same. Then they glanced awkwardly across the table, each uncertain how to proceed.

Finally David said, "I've been thinking about Thailand, and I think you going there is a really bad idea."

Jessie sighed. "Believe me, if I had a Plan B, I would take it. As both you and my mother have reminded me, I have no job experience, no money, and no other options."

David took a deep breath. "Well, I have a suggestion for a Plan B. I just talked to Amelia, and she would love to have some help with the twins. Mike has a room above his workshop that they use as a guest room. You could stay there for as long as you want to in exchange for helping her around the house, and with the kids."

Jessie's eyes widened in surprise. "You've already talked to her?" she asked hesitantly.

"She called me while I was following you to the rental place."

The waitress interrupted them by setting their food on the table. "Can I bring you anything else?"

Perhaps a good stiff drink? David thought. What in the hell was he doing?

"No, we're good, thanks," he replied, reaching for his bagel.

CHAPTER 43

As she picked up her spoon and took a taste of the soup, Jessie felt touched by the look of genuine concern in David's eyes. However, his invitation to live with his sister had stunned her. Still she had to admit that she could more easily imagine helping Amelia with her children than she could imagine teaching English to Thai children halfway around the world. She looked around the restaurant as if the two Asian women sitting nearby might provide her with assistance in formulating a response. Finally, she said the only thing that she could say. "I appreciate your offer, and as much as I'd like to accept, it's not a good idea."

"Why?"

Jessie wasn't exactly sure why, but instinctively she felt that David's offer might not be a good idea. She mused for a few minutes while rubbing her finger along the rim of her glass. Then she said, "It's probably too close to my mother. Going to the other side of the world is likely the only way that I can make a clean break with her."

A look of exasperation crossed David's face. "Then your mother is still controlling your life."

"Is that your professional or personal view?" Jessie snapped. She'd suddenly remembered MJ's comments about his womanizing. "Do you give all of your patients such personal treatment? Or just the young, female ones?"

David's face reddened. "What the hell? Listen, if you go live with Amelia, you won't be my patient anymore." Then he said in a calmer, more controlled voice, "I promise you, I'm only trying to help you. I have no ulterior motives here."

Jessie leaned back in her seat, considering this last statement. Every fiber of her being wanted to accept his offer, but still she held back. "My mother can make things very unpleasant for you in Augusta."

"Why would your mother care about you living with my sister? You've said that if you were out of Augusta, she could get back to living her own life without any gossip."

"That part is true." Jessie looked for words to explain the apprehension she was feeling. "But my mother will find it hard to explain to people in Augusta that I'm working for my therapist's sister as a nanny in North Georgia. She'd have a much easier time saying that I'd gone abroad to be a missionary in Thailand or to visit a sorority sister. And she doesn't like you very much, so she'll naturally be suspicious of your intentions." Jessie could feel the heat rising in her face after those last words.

David sat back in his seat and said coolly, "Just like you?"

Jessie felt her face reddening even more while she scrambled to think of a reply.

"Never mind answering," David said quietly. He picked up his glass of water and took a couple of sips. Then he said, "I did step over professional boundaries when I asked you to my sister's place before, but I promise it wasn't with the intention of seducing you. I honestly thought that the trip might help you progress in your therapy, sort of like a class field trip. And it did help. You've made more progress toward independence since visiting with Amelia than in all the time before."

With each word he spoke, Jessie felt worse and worse. Of course he had only been thinking of her in a professional manner. Why had she let MJ's gossip infiltrate her thoughts like that? Or was she perhaps hoping that he would suddenly say he did have more personal feelings for her? Otherwise, how else could she explain her sudden sadness after his denial of any personal feelings for her?

"I'm sorry," she said in a strained voice. "I don't have a good track record of reading people's intentions."

David was looking at her sternly. "Trust me, Jessie. All I want is for you to be healthy and whole." He pushed his uneaten bowl of soup aside. "If I thought going to Thailand was the best course for you to take, I would support you fully and help you get there. But I don't. You don't adjust well to change, and moving there would entail a lot of changes at one time."

Jessie leaned toward him to interrupt, but David put up his hand for her to listen. "Also," he continued, "how will you live in Atlanta until your house sells? Even if you find the money for food, gas, and so on, can you imagine how difficult living in your house will be? Go live with Amelia and Mike now, at least until the house sells, and give yourself a chance to get your finances in order. Then go to Thailand if you decide that's what you want to do. But not now, in desperation because you think you have no other options."

Jessie had to admit that everything he said made perfect sense. When she had conceived her plan to go to Thailand, she hadn't anticipated her mother cutting her money off before the house was sold. Still, she hesitated. "I don't want to be a bother to Amelia and her husband."

"Jessie, Amelia needs help. You would be doing them a favor."

"I don't have a lot of experience caring for children or, as you know, with helping around the house."

David gave a half smile. "I'm sure Amelia can give you lots of on-the-job training."

Jessie shifted her thinking from being a burden to Amelia to being a helper. Somehow thinking about David's offer in that way made it easier for her to accept. "Okay," she said, finding the courage to look him directly in his appealing brown eyes.

David smiled at her approvingly. "Good. I think you are making the right decision."

David reached for his wallet and paid for their dinner, all the while chatting casually about the twins' latest accomplishments and about how excited Amelia would be to have Jessie staying with them for a while. Jessie appreciated David's attempt at normal conversation, but her ugly accusation against him seemed to hang in the air between them like an invisible barrier. Worse, Jessie was feeling increasingly anxious as she thought about staying at her house that night.

David must have been having similar thoughts for he said, "How about we find you a nice Hampton Inn or Holiday Inn Express? We could look for one near where I'm staying with friends. I don't think going back to your house tonight is a great idea."

Jessie looked at him gratefully for understanding exactly how she felt. Then she thought about her limited funds. "Seems like a waste of money to get a hotel room with that house just sitting there."

David looked surprised by her thriftiness. "I thought Rita wasn't cutting off your funds until tomorrow. Just add it to her account today. What's one more thing?"

Jessie smiled a genuine smile for the first time since she'd arrived in Atlanta. "Dr. Miller, I like the way you are thinking. You're full of great ideas today."

CHAPTER 44

After David left Jessie at a Holiday Inn Express, promising to return for her at eight o'clock the next morning, he thought of an old saying his dad often quoted—'In for a penny, in for a pound.' David was certainly 'all in' now. He was risking a lot by going further with this very unprofessional relationship with Jessie Graham. But he couldn't back down now, and even if he could, he wasn't so sure that he would. His desire to help her seemed to override everything else, including his understanding of ethical doctor-patient relationships.

He had to admit that Jessie's questioning of his motives had angered him. Okay, maybe he did have a physical attraction to the woman. When she was near, his senses were acutely aware of her. But maybe his reaction to her was only because he hadn't dated anyone since

Lillie. Their breakup had been so ugly that he had been hesitant to start another relationship with anyone else in Augusta. That was it, he was sure. His relationship with Jessie was strictly platonic.

After returning to his friends' house in Virginia-Highlands and accepting their good natured ribbing about leaving them stranded at Taco Mac, David phoned Amelia to explain the situation more fully. At the end of his explanation about what had happened with Jessie's mother, Amelia said, "Poor kid."

"You're okay then if I bring her tomorrow?" David asked.

"Sure," she replied, He could hear one of the twins suddenly crying in the background.

"Sis, have I told you lately that I love you?"

"Don't have to. It's understood."

"Well, I do."

"Me, too, you big lug. See you tomorrow."

David tossed and turned all night, considering the ramifications of what he was doing. He tried to imagine Andy's reaction when he discovered that David had not only lost his most lucrative patient, but that this patient was now living with his sister. Although David's practice had grown, he was far from contributing significantly to the partnership yet.

He also tried to imagine what Rita Forrester's reaction would be. Maybe she would be relieved to have her daughter off her hands. However, considering the woman's need to be in control of every situation, he somehow doubted that would be the case. And he wondered just how far Rita would go to get Jessie back under her control.

Jessie was sitting in the lobby, looking pensive and pale, when David arrived at her hotel. Breakfast was being served in a room off the lobby, and he could see people serving themselves from the buffet line. Jessie rose as he approached.

"How are you doing this morning?" he asked, somewhat concerned about her expressionless face.

"Fine. I have a slight headache. Maybe breakfast will help. Are you interested in eating? Breakfast is included with the room."

"I'm feeling in desperate need of some coffee," David said, "and if breakfast comes along with it, so much the better."

Jessie picked at yogurt and fruit, while David ate pancakes and bacon and liberally poured caffeine into his system. He thought that eating breakfast together seemed more intimate than lunch or dinner.

"I talked to Amelia last night," he said, "and she said for us to come on."

Jessie's luminous blue eyes looked at him thoughtfully. "I did a lot of thinking last night," she said. "Maybe I should just go home, apologize to my mother for my inconsiderate actions, and then let her help me sell the house. I mean, I don't know where to start with the sales process. And I really don't know what I was thinking by taking off alone like I did. I can declare my independence after the house sells."

Although she was only saying pretty much what David had said the day before, now he didn't feel inclined to agree. "Is that what you really want to do?"

"No. I'd rather go to Amelia's and help her with the twins."

"Then why not do that?"

Jessie shrugged her shoulders, expressionless.

David was concerned by her lack of emotion. "Jessie, don't do this."

"What?"

"Don't pull back into yourself. Don't give up before you even start to try. It would be easy to go crawling back to your mother and let her handle everything. But I think you described your situation perfectly the other day. You are never going to be truly healthy until your mother isn't running your life."

She smiled slightly. "Kind of cruel to use my own words as an argument against me." She put her yogurt spoon down beside the almost full yogurt container. "Do you know anything about selling a house?"

"Honestly, no. But I do have friends here in Atlanta who might be able to help."

David watched as her expression went from conflicted to determined, "Okay," she said. "Do you mind taking me back to the house to pick up a few things and get my car? Then I'll follow you to Amelia's."

A feeling of relief swept over David. "That's the spirit. Let's do this."

As they drove swiftly up Georgia State Route 400 toward Jessie's house, she asked, "Should I bring sheets or blankets or anything to Amelia's? I could take some from the house."

"I don't think so," David replied. "The room where you'll stay is a nice one, and it has a bathroom attached. I guess it's kind of basic—a comfortable bed, a nightstand, and a lamp. No television or clock. If you want anything else, maybe bring it."

He heard Jessie's cell phone ring in her purse, but she made no move to answer it. When she saw that he'd noticed, she said, "Mother's been calling regularly this morning since right before you arrived at the hotel. I'm not answering her calls anymore, and she doesn't leave a message."

"Don't you think you ought to answer and at least tell her that you're all right?"

Jessie shook her head negatively. "If she had a specific concern, she'd leave a message."

"You're going to tell her that you're moving to the mountains, right?"

"I really think it's got to be all or nothing," Jessie said. "Either I go back to Augusta, or I make a clean break. As a matter of fact, if you see a cell phone store, can we stop long enough for me to buy one of those pay as you go phones? I'm expecting the service to be cut off on this phone any time now."

David thought things were getting a bit melodramatic. "Jessie, Rita may not win any awards for being the mother of the year, but she's still your mother. You can't just disappear. That would be cruel, don't you think?"

"Look, I did talk to her briefly this morning," Jessie said. "I told her I was fine and that I would be in touch soon. I thought maybe when you get back to Augusta, you could tell her that I'd been in contact with you and that I was safe and wanted some time to be on my own. And for her not to worry." Jessie looked questioningly at him. "I mean, you have that whole doctor-patient confidentiality thing, right?"

Jessie's bringing up the fact that she was his patient wasn't exactly what he wanted to think about at that moment. Finally, he replied, "You're right. She can't force me to tell her where you are. But I won't lie to her. I'll tell her that you've asked me to keep your location a secret from her." David imagined how that conversation would go over really well with Rita.

"There's a cell phone store," Jessie said. "Quick, turn right."

David did as she instructed and turned into the parking lot. While Jessie went inside to buy a phone, he tried to imagine how difficult it would be to tell Rita Forrester that he knew where her daughter was and that he wasn't going to give her that information. Andy had said that Rita wasn't someone to mess with, and David believed him. Perhaps it would be best for everyone concerned if David reversed course and took Jessie back to her mother after all.

However, when Jessie came bouncing out of the store with a smile on her face for the first time that day, David knew that it was now too late to change directions.

CHAPTER 45

When they pulled up in front of her house, Jessie felt better prepared to face her memories, or perhaps having David there with her made her feel stronger. She recognized Robbie across the street, about to take off on his bike.

"Are you ready to do this?" David asked with a look of concern.

In response, Jessie pulled the house key from her purse and nodded. They walked to the door in silence.

Before she put the key in the lock, Robbie suddenly skidded his bike to a stop behind them. "Are you back for good?" he asked breathlessly.

Jessie tried to smile in spite of the butterflies in her stomach. "No, I'm just getting a few things and my car."

She thought she saw a look of disappointment on his face. "Need some help with anything?"

"Thank you, but I don't think so." Then she opened her purse and took out a five-dollar bill and offered it to Robbie. "I want to give you a little reward for helping me yesterday. If it hadn't been for you, who knows what might have happened to me?"

Robbie eyed the money eagerly but said politely, "I didn't do nothing, really."

"Well, I'd like for you to take it anyway. Please."

"Gee, thanks!" he said, taking the money and stuffing it into his jeans pocket. "I'm on my way to my friend's house. See ya later." And just as quickly as he had arrived, he was gone.

"That was nice of you," David said.

"He's a cute kid." She opened the door and walked in, with David following closely behind her. She did a quick internal check of her reaction. So far, so good. No dizziness, no panicky feelings. Next she took a close look at the slightly stale-smelling house where she'd spent several years of her life. She wondered if her mother had scheduled periodic cleanings, because it didn't feel or look like a house that had been empty for so long.

Suddenly, David's presence seemed like an intrusion. Jessie wanted to be alone with her memories. She turned to him. "Here are the keys to my car. Why don't you go through that door to the garage and see if it still starts, and maybe see about the gas level? I want to look around in here on my own."

"Of course," he said, taking the keys from her. "Just yell if you need anything."

After the door to the garage closed behind David, Jessie started her tour of the house. Shadows of Nick hovered everywhere. There he was stretched out on the den sofa, and there he was eating his breakfast standing at the kitchen bar instead of sitting on a bar stool because he was always in a hurry. She stopped at the door to his office. A strong memory of him sitting with his tennis shoes on his desk and wearing his favorite gray sweat pants reminded her of the Nick she had fallen in love with. For perhaps the first time since the accident, she felt sadness that Nick was gone. He may not have been the best husband, but he had been far too young and talented to die as he had.

She started up the stairs. Echoes of her past followed her. Truly, there weren't many good memories in this house, as their marriage had begun to deteriorate almost from the moment they moved in. But there were one or two positive notes. Jessie paused at their bedroom door, remembering the last time she had stood in this room, dressing for the wedding. She stared at the room's earth tones—the browns and beiges that Nick loved so much. She envisioned him, wet-headed and dripping water as he walked out of the bathroom. She stood frozen as memories good and bad assailed her, one after another.

"The car seems fine," David said, coming up the stairs and startling her out of her trance. Seeing her tense posture, he said quietly, "Tell me what you're feeling."

Jessie shook her head, not knowing what to say. She walked over to Nick's closet and opened the door. All his clothes were organized and aligned perfectly, just as he had left them. On top of his dresser were his hairbrush and an empty box that had held the cufflinks he wore to the wedding that night.

"I guess he's really gone," she said hollowly. "I'm not sure his death has seemed real to me until today." She turned to David. "He didn't want to go to the wedding on the night of the accident. He wanted to stay home. But I insisted. I wonder if he would still be alive if I hadn't insisted."

"Please don't do this to yourself, Jessie," David said. "His death was an accident. You aren't responsible." He took a step toward her, but Jessie stepped back. She didn't want to be comforted right now. She didn't deserve to be comforted right now.

"Maybe it was my fault."

"It wasn't your fault any more than it was my fault," he said adamantly. "We need to get out of here and get on the road before it gets any later. Let's get whatever you want and go."

"I need a suitcase from the attic because I'm going to need some more clothes."

"Point me in the direction of the attic; and you start gathering what you want to take."

CHAPTER 46

"I don't know if you should be driving by yourself," David said after they had loaded her suitcase into the back of her car. He was worried by the way Jessie had gone deep within herself while she was in the house. While she was packing her suitcase, she had answered his questions with only monosyllables.

"I'll be fine," she said, still expressionless.

He explained the general driving directions to Jessie and then programmed Amelia's address into the car's navigation system. In case they got separated, he suggested a place to stop outside Atlanta. Finally, unable to think of anything else he could do, David watched her get into her car, then went to his own car to wait for her to back out of the garage. They were off.

David watched anxiously in his rear view mirror as Jessie navigated the four lanes of traffic on Interstate 285 behind him. He'd relax once they were out of the city, but now he worried that she wasn't as aware of her surroundings as she needed to be with cars changing lanes at 75 miles per hour on both sides of her. Still, perhaps it would be good for her to have some time alone to think things through. Facing the memories in that house must have been difficult for her. He just wished that her time alone to think wasn't happening as they were cruising at high speeds.

Once they were onto Interstate 85, the traffic lessened, and David began to breathe a bit easier. He knew he had stepped into uncharted territory with Jessie. Next week, he was going to schedule some office time with Andy and tell him everything, He'd never allowed his personal life and his professional life to become so intertwined. Why was it so important to him that he save her?

When they exited the interstate, David called her new cell phone and suggested they stop for coffee. Jessie agreed, but in the restaurant she seemed as far removed from him as if she were still driving down the interstate in a separate car.

For some minutes, David let her sit there, looking out the window. When he'd waited for about as long as he felt he could, he finally said, "Where's the girl who came bouncing out of the cell phone store this morning?"

Jessie's lips curled up slightly into what was more of grimace than a smile.

"It might help to talk about it," he offered. "Tell me what you're feeling."

She looked at him with a sigh, "I know this might sound crazy, but subconsciously, I must have been thinking that Nick was in Atlanta. How else can I explain the fact that I've given him so little thought, or really no thought, since the accident? Now I'm just feeling sad, I guess. He didn't deserve for his life to be taken away so suddenly."

David thought about describing how people often block out information when it's too painful, but then decided that Jessie wasn't in need of analysis right then. "After the accident," he said, "you were in a coma. You also had a concussion, which is a significant brain injury, and other physical injuries. Cut yourself some slack if you've been a bit preoccupied."

Her eyes were pensive when she replied, "For a long time after the accident, I felt nothing. No emotions of any sort."

"It's called *flat affect*,'" David said. "And it's not uncommon after a brain injury."

Jessie sighed. "When I thought about Nick or the baby being gone, I had the same feelings that I might have had for a stranger who had died in an accident. I was sorry but not emotionally engaged." She sighed again. "Not anymore. I feel the pain of their loss acutely now. I mean, Nick might not have been the best husband, but he certainly didn't deserve what happened." Her eyes filled with tears, "And the baby...." Her voice trailed off.

"I know it's hard to feel those feelings, but it's actually good that you are starting to hurt," David said. "That means you are facing your pain, not hiding from it. Forgive me if I sound like your high school guidance counselor, but the healing process does take time. You are really only beginning that process now that you are feeling these emotions." He thought that Jessie's troubled eyes seemed to settle a bit.

David laid some coins on the table and asked, "Ready to get back on the road?"

CHAPTER 47

The moon hung low over the lake, making shadows that seemed to reach out menacingly from the house and the surrounding buildings as Jessie approached the farm in her car. For the past couple of hours, she'd been having second and third thoughts about whether coming here was the right thing to do. She'd been anticipating the warm, welcoming feeling she had experienced on her first visit here. She'd expected that once here, that feeling would affirm that what she was doing was right. Instead, she felt nothing like before. Now her head was throbbing, and she wanted only to crawl into a bed somewhere and sleep.

"You look pale," David said, concerned, as he opened her car door.

"My head hurts."

"Let me show you where you'll be sleeping, and you can rest for a while."

Jessie looked gratefully at him. "I'd love that, but don't you think I should at least say hello to Amelia and meet Mike? Seems kind of rude not to."

"They'll understand."

Jessie let him get her suitcase out of the trunk, and then she followed him to the workshop building. He slid open the door, flipped the light switch on, and led her to stairs just inside and to the left that she hadn't noticed her first time in the building. There was another door at the top of the stairs. When David opened it, Jessie saw a white iron bed with a wedding ring quilt, and over the bed her picture of the redbird was hanging. Jessie felt an immediate rush of emotions—thankfulness at Amelia's thoughtfulness and the cheery, bright, welcoming feeling she'd been anticipating. A large window on the other side of the bed looked out over the lake.

"This is beautiful," she said.

David smiled. 'I thought you'd like it. It has always felt a bit feminine for my taste."

"Where will you sleep?"

"There's an extra bedroom in the house," he said. "The only reason I slept out here was so that I didn't have to rise at the crack of dawn with the boys. But they sleep to a more reasonable time these days. And with Mike starting his work downstairs bright and early each morning, there's not a whole lot of sleeping going on regardless of where you are." He walked over to a narrow door and opened it. "Here's the bathroom. It's small, but it has everything you need."

"It's perfect," Jessie said. She walked to the window and looked out. "If you don't mind, I will take a nap. Please give Amelia and Mike my apologies."

"No apologies necessary. Just relax."

After David left, a sense of peace enveloped her. She suddenly felt confident that she was right where she needed to be. She walked to the bed and tentatively pushed down. Nice and squishy, no TempurPedic mattress here, thank goodness. She pulled back the quilt to reveal crisp, white sheets. No frills, no monograms, just soft cotton sheets on a nice, old-fashioned bed. She sat down, pulled off her shoes, and sank into the softness that was exactly right. Her last thought before sliding into nothingness was *I should have set the alarm on my cell phone to wake me up.*

CHAPTER 48

While the twins played happily on the floor with some trucks, the three adults sat around the kitchen table, and David tried to explain Jessie's situation. "She really has no money until she sells her house and no idea of what she wants to do next," he said.

"She's welcome here as long as she needs to stay," Amelia said. "Isn't that right, Mike?"

Mike laughed. "As if I have a say in anything around here. But, seriously, Amelia could use some help. I'd love for her to be able to paint more than she does."

David knew that painting was as important to his sister as food or water, so if she had cut back on her painting time, she was definitely stretched too thin. "I'm not sure how much Jessie knows about taking care of a house or children. You're probably going to have to teach her everything."

Amelia smiled. "She did pretty well helping me with the bread baking."

"She's not going to expect us to wait on her, is she?" Mike asked anxiously.

"Mike," Amelia said chidingly. "That girl jumped right in and offered to help when she was here before. She's not going to expect us to wait on her."

David picked apart a paper napkin absent-mindedly. "I know she won't expect you to wait on her, but she does sleep a lot. It's one of the symptoms of her depression."

"Doubt that will be as much of a problem here as it might be in her home," Mike laughed. "Some of my tools can really shake that building she's sleeping in."

"Do you think we need to wake her so she can have some time to settle in before dinner?" asked Amelia.

David thought for a moment. He was torn. On one hand, Jessie hadn't eaten much for lunch, so she probably would enjoy dinner. On the other hand, letting her sleep might be best for her right now. Finally he said, "Let's let her sleep."

CHAPTER 49

Jessie woke with a start, wondering where she was before reality set in. She glanced at her cell phone. It was 8 p.m. and dark in the room except for the moonlight coming through the large window. She had slept for several hours. She rose quickly, checked her hair in the bathroom mirror, and went in search of everyone else.

At the door of the house, she paused. Should she knock? Just walk in? She tried knocking, but no one came. Tentatively she opened the door and went in. If the house had been charming in the fall, it was even more special decorated for Christmas. Pine swags looped their way up the banister, their pungent aroma welcoming her into the house. The pine scent was mingled with the earthy smell of smoke from the blazing fireplace in the den, and from somewhere in the house, Jessie could hear "Deck the Halls" playing softly on a radio or MP3 player. Through the doorway in the front room, she watched everyone seated around the farmhouse table in the kitchen. It was a Norman Rockwell Christmas painting—the perfect American family dinner scene.

Then the painting came to life. David saw her and motioned for her to come into the kitchen. "Hello, sleeping beauty," he quipped.

Jessie felt her face flush as she started forward. "I apologize for taking such a long nap."

Amelia rose from beside the boys in their high chairs and gave her a big hug. "I'm so happy to see you again."

"Thank you for letting me stay here," Jessie said earnestly.

"Are you kidding me?" Amelia asked with a huge smile. "I'm so excited I can't stand it. Finally, another woman to help even the score against all these males. Three against one has been too much. Speaking of males, this is Mike. And you remember the twins—Michael and Davey?"

Jessie held out her hand to the tall lumberjack of a man seated at the end of the table and noted that the twins had grown significantly since her last visit.

"Sit down here next to me," Amelia said, "and help yourself to the pasta and salad. We were about to have coffee and dessert, but we'll wait until you finish. Do you want a glass of wine?"

"No wine, and please don't wait for me. I'll feel better eating if you are eating something, too."

One of the boys threw a piece of tomato that landed with a splat in front of his dad. "I guess Michael's finished eating," Mike laughed. "I think you are out of range, Jessie."

After dinner, David volunteered to do the dishes so that Mike and Amelia could put the boys to bed. Jessie quickly offered to help David. They started clearing the dishes from the table as Mike scooped up a twin in each arm before they could run away.

"I'll wash, you dry," David offered after his sister and brother-in-law departed.

"Sure." Jessie noticed how his brown hair was slightly mussed from roughhousing with the twins. One lock fell adorably across his forehead, and she imagined reaching out and pushing it back into place.

He was all business, scraping and stacking the dishes and filling the large farmhouse sink with soap and water. They worked in a companionable silence that was broken only occasionally by short phrases.

"Let me know if I missed anything."

"Here, take this."

"Oops. Quality control notes there's a little more pasta stuck on the inside of this pot."

After a while, the steam from the hot water created beads of sweat on David's brow, and Jessie felt her self-control slipping. What would David do if she reached up with her dishtowel and wiped his forehead? Somehow she managed to restrain herself from doing so, while thinking that this was what real life was all about—putting the babies to bed, washing the dishes after dinner, sharing small tasks and enjoying doing them because you are doing them with someone you love. Jessie felt a tightness in her heart and a sudden realization that she might be falling in love with David. What else could explain the strange thoughts she'd been having?

"All done," David announced as the water went down the drain with a whoosh. "Well, at least for the moment. Dishes aren't ever all done around here for very long." He turned to look directly at her, and Jessie felt as if he had reached out and touched her, the look was so direct and personal. "Feeling better after your nap?"

"Yes, and I'm sorry about shutting down earlier today."

"Perfectly natural," he replied, taking the dish towel she was holding to hang it above the sink. Then with a smile, he said jokingly, "The path to wellness isn't straight. It includes a lot of dips and curves. Just as long as you keep moving forward along your path, you'll be okay."

"Nice to hear." Jessie took a deep breath. "When will you be going back to Augusta?"

"I thought I'd stay through the weekend."

Happiness filtered through every fiber of her being, but a simple "Good," was all she said.

When Amelia and Mike came back downstairs, Jessie could tell that they were tired and ready for bed. "I think I'll head back over to my place," she said, "I'm still rather tired."

"I'll walk you over," David offered, making her heart skip a beat or two at the thought of being alone with him in the dark coolness of the workshop.

"No, I'll walk you over," Amelia stated firmly. "I want to make sure you've got everything you need to be comfortable over there."

Jessie felt a frisson of disappointment lasting only a second. "You are too kind, Amelia. By the way, thank you for hanging my painting in the bedroom. It was so nice to see it again when I walked in."

"See, Mike?" Amelia laughed. "I told you, it was important to get that picture hung this morning."

Over in Jessie's quarters, Amelia peered into the closet. "If there aren't enough hangers, let me know, and I'll give you more tomorrow. Want me to help you unpack your things?"

"No, I'd rather do it later."

"I hope you don't mind the window not having any covering. It seemed a shame to hide that view of the lake."

"I agree, and I doubt there are many peeping Toms out there on the lake."

"Jessie," Amelia said, sounding serious. "Mike and I want you to feel that you are at home here. I need help, but we're not expecting you to work a nine to five job. I understand you've taken up photography. Feel free to wander around taking pictures as much as you like. Sleep in as late as you want. Consider yourself more like family than a new hired hand."

"You don't know how much I appreciate your taking me in," Jessie said. "And, in particular, just a few days before Christmas. Please let me show my appreciation by helping as much as I can."

"You'll certainly have plenty of opportunities right off the bat with Mike being gone the next few days."

"I can't wait."

"Be careful what you wish for," Amelia laughed as she left, closing the door behind her.

CHAPTER 50

David was roused from sleep by a soft hand touching his face. For the briefest of seconds, his mind went to Jessie. But then the touch quickly became almost painful. He opened his eyes to see Davey pressing his palm into his uncle's cheek. Mike stood beside the bed, smiling broadly.

"You better be glad my nephew is here," David growled, "or I'd wipe that smile off your face."

"Yeah, you and who else? Come on, lazy bones, I need some help loading a chest of drawers into the trailer."

"Can I have five minutes to wake up first?"

"Five minutes? Sure. We'll be waiting for you downstairs."

Mike and David had put the chest of drawers on a trolley to roll out to the trailer

when the door at the top of the stairs
opened. Jessie started down the stairs,
wearing blue jeans and a yellow sweater.
Her hair was pulled back in a loose
ponytail that made her look about sixteen
years old.

"Days certainly start early in the
mountains," she commented dryly.

"This isn't early," Mike teased. "I've been
up since five o'clock. Now that's early."

"It's rather brisk outside," David said.
"You might want to get a jacket."

"Okay, I'll run up and get one. Then I'll
be happy to help you."

"Not unless you can bench press 200
pounds," Mike said.

"Hey, I don't think I can bench press 200
pounds," David said. "Does that mean you
don't need me?"

"Get over there on the other side of that
trolley," Mike ordered.

"I'll get out of your way, then," Jessie
said, turning toward the stairs to get her
jacket.

CHAPTER 51

Outside, Jessie was greeted by bright sunshine, along with a heavy chill. She walked hurriedly across the brown grass to the house, recalling how green everything had been on her last visit. Again, she wasn't sure whether to knock or enter. She knocked softly in case either of the twins was still sleeping and then went in, whispering "Hello" as she went.

Amelia was in the kitchen at the stove, and both boys were once again in their high chairs. "Good morning. I hope you don't mind me just walking in," Jessie said from the doorway.

"Good morning to you, too," Amelia answer gaily. "You live here now, so why would you knock? You want to supervise the boys' breakfast while I run upstairs?"

"Sure. How do I do that?"

"When food fights start, take the food away. And if they're not eating, try to coax them into eating."

"Sounds simple enough. I can do that," Jessie said.

Ten minutes or so later, Jessie realized that supervising the eating of two toddlers wasn't easy. One twin was always trying to throw food at the other or somewhere else, and neither seemed to want to eat the oatmeal their mother expected them to eat. Amelia flitted around the house and into the kitchen to check on their progress.

When Mike was ready to leave, he and David returned to the kitchen. Mike moved toward the boys and Amelia to kiss them good-bye. Jessie watched with envy at the genuine sadness both Mike and Amelia seemed to feel about being away from each other for even a day or so. She couldn't help remembering how Nick always gave her a quick peck on the lips before heading out the door and never looked back regardless of whether he was going to be gone for the day or for several days.

"Have you eaten anything?" David asked her, and before she could answer, he said, "I'm starving."

"I could eat something," she replied.

"How about eggs and toast?" David asked, and Jessie gave a thumbs up sign before starting to sweet talk little Michael into taking a bite of his oatmeal.

About the time David had breakfast ready, the boys had reached their limit in the high chairs. Jessie watched in amazement as David grabbed a clean cloth, wiped both boys down, and sniffed the air around Davey. "Whew! This one is rank!" he said. "I'll take him upstairs and change him."

David pulled the high chair tray out, then he grabbed Davey under the arms to avoid having to handle his bottom. "Can you get Michael out?" he asked.

"Sure," she replied, not really sure, but hoping for the best.

When Amelia surfaced a few minutes later, Jessie was holding Michael with one leg out of the high chair and the other seemingly stuck between the slats in the back of the chair. Michael seemed to think this experience was a new and delightful game. He was giggling wildly as Jessie wiggled him this way and that, trying to extricate his leg.

"These chairs are tricky," Amelia said, coming over to help get him out. "They probably wouldn't pass safety standards these days, but I found them at a yard sale and fell in love with them. Oh, no, your breakfast is getting cold."

"I'll wait for David, since he did the cooking."

"I'm here," David said, carrying Davey as if he were a football under one arm while Davey giggled uncontrollably.

Jessie was amazed at how fast the day flew by between helping Amelia with her chores and taking care of the boys. It was laundry day, and Amelia didn't have a dryer. Despite the chilly wind, the clothes had to be hung on lines stretched between trees behind the house. Luckily, the sun was out, making the outdoor clothes-drying activity better than it would have been otherwise. Jessie could hang only one wet garment for every three that Amelia could hang. Compared to Amelia's small, deft fingers, Jessie's fingers seemed large and clumsy.

The boys were bundled up in jackets and climbed happily in and out of the laundry baskets. When that activity lost its allure, they began to wander toward the chickens at the edge of the yard, clearly with mischief on their minds.

Amelia yelled to Uncle David to come from the workshop and rescue the chickens. As he came around the corner, Jessie said, "I don't know how you can do this on your own. There are three of us, and

I feel like we are barely keeping ahead of the two of them."

Amelia smiled. "Believe me, life has gotten more challenging since the boys started walking and became so adventurous. That's why I need help!"

Jessie watched as David scooped up one boy, then the other, and spun around in a circle. "Okay, you two, no escapees on Uncle David's watch," he said, and the boys shrieked with laughter. Jessie gazed at David's smiling and charmingly handsome mouth and hurriedly reached for more clothes to hang up. She realized she was standing there staring at David like a lovesick teenager.

CHAPTER 52

Even with a twin under each arm, David's senses still sharpened as he noticed Jessie's continued gaze. He felt that she was almost reaching out and touching him with her eyes. He looked down at the two squirming boys. He couldn't hold them for long. "I'll take the boys into the workshop to play for a while," he said.

He was surprised when he heard Jessie say to Amelia, "Let me finish hanging up these last few shirts. I think I've got the hang of it, and I'm sure you have other things you could be doing."

"Okay!" Amelia said enthusiastically. "You don't have to twist my arm." She began walking briskly to the house.

David didn't want to leave Jessie there alone. He put the boys back in the now-empty laundry basket and threw some toys from the ground in with them. Fortunately, they seemed happy once again. David walked up behind Jessie. Her fresh, earthy smell wafted towards him.

"What's this?" Jessie asked. "You don't trust me to hang the shirts correctly?" A smile hovered at the corners of her eyes.

"Maybe," David smiled in return. He grabbed a couple of clothespins from a bag hanging between them and began clipping the corners of the shirt Jessie was holding up in front of the clothes line. In response, Jessie held up another shirt, and David clipped it to the line. Standing close, working in tandem, they soon had all of the shirts hanging on the line. A couple of times their hands almost touched, and David was amazingly disappointed that they hadn't in fact made contact.

He felt enthralled by the way the tiny streaks of gold in Jessie's hair sparkled in the winter sunshine and by the earnest look on her face as she worked. Suddenly he wanted nothing more than to take her in his arms and kiss her senseless, but those feelings scared him shitless. He'd always believed that psychiatrists who developed personal relationships with patients were scum, taking advantage of them when they were most vulnerable.

"I can't believe Amelia does this wash every week," Jessie said, interrupting David's train of thought.

Still struggling with his newfound awareness of his attraction to her, David said flippantly, "My sister is a hippie."

Jessie immediately came to Amelia's defense. "I don't think she's a hippie. I admire her and Mike for being so dedicated to their philosophy of sustainability."

"Yeah, me too," he agreed. Noticing that one of the twins had climbed out of the basket and was heading toward the chickens again, he decided to put some space between himself and Jessie to think things over.

"The boys seem to be tired of playing out here," he said. "I'm going to take them into the workshop."

Jessie nodded. Was that a look of disappointment David saw cross her face as he was leaving?

The rest of the day and night, David stayed busy overseeing the boys while Jessie helped Amelia in the kitchen. First, they baked an Italian cream cake and then prepared the dressing and the rolls for their Christmas dinner. They brought David in occasionally for a male opinion. He was happy each time to see how well the two women seemed to be working together.

Sitting by a roaring fire that night, listening to the forecast of a white

Christmas on the radio, David kept going over his complicated relationship with Jessie. His first feelings for her had been steeped in guilt. They had progressed into genuine caring as he gotten to know her better. Was he now on the verge of falling in love with her? He knew that intimacy sometimes developed between therapists and patients undergoing long-term, intensive therapy. Perhaps that's all that this feeling was, and he just needed to remain vigilant until his feelings returned to normal. Still, he needed now more than ever to officially hand her therapy over to Andy. Once that transition was taken care of, perhaps then he might feel comfortable considering where a potential relationship with Jessie might go.

When Jessie rose to go back to her room over the workshop, David didn't offer to walk her across the way. Amelia seemed surprised but said nothing. She looked back and forth between the two of them, and David knew his sister well enough to understand that she suspected something strange was going on between himself and Jessie.

CHAPTER 53

Christmas Eve dawned with grey skies, and by noon, snow was blowing hard. Jessie was thrilled by the sight of the flakes falling heavy and fast even though she knew Amelia was worried because Mike wasn't home yet. By the time Mike's truck came lumbering up the driveway, the brown grass around the house had been painted a frosty, clean white.

"Merry Christmas, everyone!" Mike roared as he came through the front door.

"Well, it is now that you're here," Amelia said, giving him a big hug. "I've been so worried."

"Roads were fine. It hasn't been cold enough lately for the snow to stick. And that couple was so happy with their furniture. They said it was the best Christmas present they'd ever given to each other, and they insisted on presenting me with a big tip for getting it made and delivered in time."

At the mention of presents, Jessie felt troubled. She had been so wrapped up in the drama of going to Atlanta and of getting away from her mother that she hadn't remembered that it was Christmas until she'd arrived at Mike and Amelia's house. Now here she was, accepting their hospitality, and she didn't even have a Christmas present to offer them.

"Let's go get our Christmas tree," Mike announced to no one in particular.

"Oh, Mike, the boys just went down for their nap," Amelia said, disappointed. "We'll have to wait for a couple of hours."

""Well," Mike rolled his eyes suggestively, "how about you and I go take a little nap, too? I didn't sleep very well last night without you beside me."

Amelia blushed and said nothing.

"Jessie and I could go look for a Christmas tree," David suggested, indicating that it might be nice to give the two of them some privacy.

"Great idea," Mike said. "Take some of the red ribbon lying there in the floor and mark two or three trees. It will save us time later when we go out with the boys. Come on, woman, get up those stairs."

The crunch of their boots was the only sound as Jessie and David stomped through the silent woods. "Brrr. It's gotten a lot colder, hasn't it?" Jessie asked, just to break the silence.

"Are you too cold to do this? You can go back if you want."

"No, no, I didn't mean that." She reached for her camera hanging around her neck and snapped a couple of pictures of a small evergreen dotted with white crescents of snow. "You know, I didn't think about it being Christmas when I imposed myself on your sister and Mike."

"You aren't imposing on them," David said, sounding somewhat exasperated. "They invited you. However, don't worry. We'll decorate the tree tonight and have a great Christmas lunch tomorrow afternoon. Mike and Amelia aren't big into gift exchanges or anything. I did get them a microwave oven just because I thought they needed one. It's wrapped in the trunk of my car. I'll put your name on it, too."

"No, I don't want you to do that. I'll come up with an idea for something later."

David stopped beside a cedar tree that was probably eight or nine feet tall. "What about this one?"

Jessie thought David looked very manly standing next to the tree, so she focused the camera on him and took a picture. Then she considered the tree from all sides, before pulling the bright red ribbon out of her pocket and tying it around one of the boughs.

They continued walking. A few feet further, Jessie saw a tree of about the same size, but with fuller branches. "This one looks even better to me," she said.

David nodded in agreement, and she pulled out the ribbon and tied it on this tree as she had the last one.

They walked on in silence for a while. Jessie wondered if she'd done something to irritate David, as he seemed unusually terse. Finally she had to ask, "Is everything okay?"

"Yes, why?"

"You've not seemed like yourself since we were hanging the clothes yesterday. Is it something I've done?"

"Of course not. What could you possibly have done?"

"I don't know. I was thinking maybe you were having second thoughts about bringing me here."

"Damn it, Jessie. I'm a person, too. You've just not been around me long enough to see that sometimes I get tired and grumpy."

"Okay," she said quietly. They walked on for five more minutes before Jessie's foot sank deep into a hole hidden in the snow. "Ouch!" She pulled on her foot, which remained stubbornly immobile. "I think it's stuck."

David bent over her leg to help extricate her foot. As he began to pull on her foot, she started to fall forward and caught herself by putting her hand on his shoulder. Was it her imagination, or did her hand tingle slightly when she touched him?

"You've really gotten your foot tangled in some roots or something down there," he said.

"Would it help to take off my boot?"

"Probably. Hold on to me while I unlace it."

David was all business now, Jessie thought, as she added her other hand to his back to steady herself. She wished she could somehow capture that stern expression with her camera, but it took all her attention to keep her balance and remain standing.

"Pull your foot straight up now," David commanded, and Jessie felt her foot slide free. She looked down to see David bent over, still pulling on her shoe, with her foot balancing in the air above his head, as though they were in the advanced stages of a game of Twister. She couldn't help herself. She felt a giggle beginning.

"Something funny?" he asked, looking up at her.

Jessie shook her head, but the giggles wouldn't stop.

David looked at their entangled limbs, and then a smile started at the corners of his mouth. "I guess we'd look pretty silly if anyone saw us, huh?"

Jessie nodded, still giggling.

"But not as silly as this!" and David gave her a gentle push onto her backside.

"How dare you!" Jessie sputtered, feeling the cold snow beginning to seep through her non-waterproof pants. "That's freezing!" She picked up a handful of snow and threw it right in his face.

"So that's how it's going to be, eh?" David asked, already bending to scoop up a double handful of snow.

"David! Wait! I've got my camera, and I don't want snow on...." and then she was interrupted by a dusting of snow that rained down over her head. She glared up at him, speechless.

CHAPTER 54

When David looked down at Jessie sprawling on the ground, with snow sprinkled over her hair like a fine layer of dust and one sock foot held up in the air, he immediately felt remorseful. What had he been thinking? She was likely freezing and might have a bruised or twisted ankle. He went back to the hole and was able to get her shoe out quickly once he didn't have to worry about which way he was turning and pulling on the attached foot.

He sat down on a log beside her and lifted her foot to examine it. Startled blue eyes watched as he pushed and prodded her foot and ankle. Everything seemed all right since she wasn't experiencing any pain from his explorations. Her sock was damp, but there was nothing to do but unlace the boot and slide it onto her foot. When he was done lacing the boot, he ran his hand up her leg, feeling the calf and watching her face for any signs of pain. Her sudden intake of breath made him realize that she was definitely not feeling any pain. A desire that was stronger than the warning bells going off inside him made him decide to explore the leg further and see what else might happen.

As David moved from massaging her calf up to her thigh, he watched as her eyes grew stormy. He knew he was playing with fire, but at that particular moment, he didn't care. Watching her eyes darken in reaction to what his hands were doing was one of the most sensuous experiences he'd ever had.

He reached the top of her thigh. Oh hell, he thought, and shifted positions so that he could lean in and place his lips on hers. It was what he'd been wanting to do for days—no, if he were honest with himself, for weeks. He saw her surprised eyes right before he delved into her silken mouth. His hand went behind her head, pulling her more closely to him so that he could really explore.

Then, he pulled away. He waited, wanting to see what her reaction to his kiss might be. He had to wait only a few seconds before she reached up to place one soft, timid hand behind his head to bring his lips back to hers. Her lips were warm and more than willing, and soon he realized he was moments away from pressing her down in the snow and taking her right where they lay. He groaned and reluctantly pulled away from her. She looked confused by his sudden withdrawal.

"Jessie," David said softly. "That first kiss wasn't a good idea, but I couldn't help myself. You looked so perfect lying there in the snow, and you've been driving me crazy these past couple of days."

"I have?" she asked. David watched her face light up. "David, it's okay. I've been feeling the same way," she said shyly. "You don't have to stop."

David laughed, "Well, unless you want your butt to get a lot colder than it already is, I do have to stop while I still can." He watched as her face turned an adorable shade of pink. "I'm sorry. I didn't mean to sound so crude." He took several deep breaths of the pine-scented air, which seemed to clear his head a little and bring some control back to his body. "I am still your doctor so this is wrong. And I don't want to do anything that's going to impede your recovery."

He watched as various emotions played over her face. "I don't understand," she finally said, moving up next to him on the log. "This feels right. How could it impede my recovery?"

"Yes," he agreed. "It does feel right. But there's a lot of research showing that these intense feelings happen sometimes between psychotherapists and patients. Affairs are common. The research also states that indulging in such behavior is rarely, if ever, a good thing for the patient's long-term mental health."

Jessie said sharply, "What are you saying? This is just some doctor-patient thing that's come up between us?"

"I'm saying," David said, "that I need to get you settled into treatment with Andy or another doctor, and then if things still seem right between us, we'll pick up where we left off here in the woods. But until then, this is as far as it goes."

CHAPTER 55

"David! Jessie!" Amelia called from far off in the distance.

"We'd better get ourselves straightened up." David stood and shook the snow off. Then he held out a hand to Jessie.

She looked at David's hand for a moment before allowing him to pull her to her feet. All of her old insecurities came flooding back. His reasons for rejecting her love might sound good and noble, but all Jessie felt was that she had been rejected once again.

"Aren't you going to brush yourself off?" he asked just about the time Amelia, Mike, and the boys came within sight.

"What happened to Jessie?" Amelia asked in a concerned voice, seeing her wet coat and snow-covered hair.

"I had an accident," Jessie said tonelessly.

"Yeah, be careful," David said. "She stepped into that hole right there and got her foot stuck."

"Oh, you poor dear, you're drenched," Amelia said. "Come on, let's get you back to the house and warmed up. The guys can get the tree by themselves."

Later, sitting before the fire and drinking hot chocolate, Jessie reflected on what had happened in the woods. She had read stories about getting lost in lovemaking, but she had never experienced that feeling before today. If David had been feeling what she had been feeling, there would have been no way he could have pulled back from her as he had. Therefore, it must not have been the same for him as it had been for her.

She recalled how MJ had said that David was a womanizer. Maybe she was just a convenient woman, and maybe he'd forgotten for a few moments that she was also one of his patients, which was where he drew the line with his womanizing.

Amelia insisted that Jessie continue to rest for the remainder of the afternoon, a decision that suited Jessie's mood completely. From her chair in the corner, she focused her camera on the tree and the adults attempting to decorate the tree, as well as on the two little boys attempting to undecorate it. In spite of the funk she was in, she couldn't help feeling slightly amused at the twins' antics. At first they had been intimidated by the tree's size, but that response didn't last for long. Breakable ornaments had to be moved higher on the tree when little hands reached for them, and those same little hands had to be spanked several more times before the twins finally got the message that the tree was for looking at and not for touching.

Jessie studiously avoided eye contact with David, responding only when he directly asked her a question.

"Are there enough ornaments here?"

"I think so," Jessie said.

"Does the star look straight?"

"Looks straight to me," Jessie replied.

David was, in fact, acting as if nothing was different, and Jessie wondered if he were following his own "fake it until you make it" prescription, or if nothing had really changed for him.

Finally, she realized that she owed it to Amelia and Mike and their children to do her part in the Christmas Eve festivities. She rose from her chair when the decorating was finished and insisted on helping Amelia with dinner.

In the kitchen, Amelia turned the radio to Christmas music and pulled a large pitcher of eggnog out of the refrigerator. Without asking, she poured them each a large glass and sprinkled nutmeg liberally on the top. There was something magical about this kitchen, Jessie thought. Just being in it, surrounded by all of the color and smells and warmth brought a surge of happiness back into her soul. When Amelia picked up her glass and motioned for Jessie to do the same, Jessie said seriously, "Thank you for sharing your Christmas with me. It's very special."

Amelia replied, "I feel blessed to have you here with us this year."

Jessie took a sip of the eggnog and felt the emptiness she'd been experiencing fade. She was moved both by Amelia's genuine affection and by the rich, warm glow of the alcohol in the drink. If Amelia considered her to be a blessing, she was going to make sure she was one!

Dinner was to be a simple affair of cheese quiche, candied apples, and green beans that Amelia had preserved herself in the fall. Dessert was snow cream. Helping to prepare the quiche, Jessie rolled out her very first pie crust under Amelia's tutelage and felt a sense of pride that it didn't look too uneven. While the quiche was baking, Jessie went back to her room to freshen up while Amelia did the same. Mike, David, and the twins seemed content, playing with blocks in the den floor.

Standing at her big picture window, staring out at the moonlight's reflected luminescence on the lake, Jessie felt a semblance of peace return. Perhaps, as David said, what she was feeling was the result of their intimacy over the past six months. If so, then David's putting the brakes on today was the best thing for her. She had to trust that David considered her mental well-being to be his number one priority and that he hadn't been rejecting her because he felt nothing for her. Still, when she turned toward the big, soft, downy bed, she remembered the feel of his hands on her leg through her pants. She knew that, if given the chance, she'd gladly trade her future mental health to see what those hands felt like when there was nothing between them and her skin.

CHAPTER 56

For the Christmas Eve dinner, Jessie wore a deep red dress that showed off every perfect curve of her body and made her hair glow like burnished gold in the firelight. She seemed to have recovered emotionally from the afternoon and was back to acting as what David perceived as normal for her. He felt charmed by how proud she was of the quiche she had made and by her eagerness to see if others approved of her work. He had to remind himself every other moment that she was strictly off limits to him, and he was even more eager to talk to Andy about shifting her treatment to him or to someone else.

After dinner, they left the dishes on the table and ate their snow cream in front of the Christmas tree in the den. The white lights on the tree and the flickering light from the fireplace created a spell over the room that even the twins seemed hesitant to break as they messily enjoyed their special dessert treat. When Amelia began to hum along to the faint sound of "Silent Night" coming from the kitchen, Mike joined in, singing in a surprisingly beautiful bass voice, and David felt compelled to add his voice to the mix.

"You're not singing," Mike said to Jessie when the song was nearly done.

"And you should be grateful that I'm not," she joked as the last strains of the carol faded away.

"Seems like a good time to put the boys down." Amelia rose. "Come on, Mike."

"I guess we're on dish duty again tonight, Jessie," David said.

Amelia stopped on her way out the door. "Did you forget that Jessie helped cook? I think she deserves a reprieve from kitchen duty."

"I don't minding helping," Jessie replied and then said to David, "I'll clear the table."

"Put on my apron," Amelia said. "You wouldn't want to get anything on that fabulous dress."

An uncomfortable silence filled the kitchen as David and Jessie worked like two polite strangers. David was acutely aware of her movements at his side. It was almost as if an electric current ran between them, sparking occasionally when an accidental movement brought them too close together.

"Whoops, sorry," she said when he turned unexpectedly to hand her a pot and her elbow collided with his arm.

When Amelia returned to the kitchen, they were just finishing up. "Okay, you two, you're dismissed. Skedaddle. I've got some wrapping to do in here."

"Amelia," Jessie began hesitantly, "I don't have any presents for you and Mike."

"Who said I had any for you?" Amelia asked. "Go on. I've sent Mike to the workshop to put the finishing touches on the swing set. Why don't you two go hang out over there with him for a while?"

David, not knowing what else to do other than agree with his sister, went to get their coats at the back door. After bundling up, they went out, as silent as the stillness of the night around them.

David turned to her about halfway across the yard, finally unable to continue the awkward silence anymore. "Jessie, what are you thinking?"

She made no reply for a heartbeat or two, and then in a cracked voice she said, "I find it hard to think at all when you're around me."

Joy, unexpected, sluiced through every fiber of David's being. "I know. Me, too," he said.

She stopped, and in the bright moonlight David could clearly see her face. It wasn't a happy face, "Then, why are we fighting this attraction we have for each other?" she asked in a loud, angry voice. "We're adults, and you've warned me that this might not be a forever kind of thing. But I feel better and more clear-headed than I've felt in my life, and I want to be with you. Regardless of what else happens, I'll always be grateful to you for making my life good again."

David swallowed hard, surprised by the intensity in her voice. Here she was fighting for something she wanted, far different from the passivity shown by the withdrawn woman who had walked into his office only a few months ago, barely able to speak for herself. How he longed to take her in his arms and reward her newfound strength! But her last words sent a shiver of fear through him.

"Jessie, you may say that now," he said quietly. "But you might feel very different if things don't end well between us. Your life can't be good because of me. Do you understand that?" His voice went up a notch louder. "You need to believe that your life is good because you've worked hard to change and because you are a wonderful person who deserves happiness—who is worthy of happiness."

"Hey, you two," Mike said, coming out of the workshop on his way to the house. "I don't know what you're arguing about out here, but why don't you come inside the workshop and out of the cold? Remember, it's Christmas Eve. Peace on earth, right?"

CHAPTER 57

Jessie was embarrassed by Mike's sudden appearance and prayed that he hadn't been able to hear what they were fighting about while he was inside the workshop.

"Yeah, yeah, we were just going inside," David said. "Come on, Jessie."

She followed him inside the brightly lit workshop. The darkness had lent her a bravado that disappeared with the light. She waited expectantly for David to do something, say something, but seconds ticked by with exquisite slowness as he stood looking at her. She watched as a multitude of emotions played upon his face. He opened his mouth to speak but closed it again. She felt her bravery return as she saw how conflicted he was, somewhat like a lost little boy.

She reached up and put her arms around his neck. "I don't care," she said in a soft voice. "I've never felt like this before, and I'm not going to resist it anymore." She pulled his head down until their lips touched, and then she leaned into him and their bodies merged together. She felt powerful when he shuddered and then sighed deeply into her mouth.

"Ah, excuse me," Mike said. David immediately jumped back from Jessie. "I guess you two have kissed and made up, huh? Anyway, David, the twins are asleep, so I was wondering if you could help me move the swing set out into the back yard now."

"Oh, yeah, I forgot we were going to do that," David said, not looking at Jessie. When he did, his eyes looked determined. "I'll see you in the morning, Jessie. And, uh, Merry Christmas."

Jessie felt as though she'd been punched in the stomach. How was he able to switch gears so easily? "Yeah, Merry Christmas," Jessie said sarcastically as she turned and headed up the stairs to her very lonely room.

She stomped around angrily as she got ready for bed. Then, she looked out at the Christmas Eve moon shining brightly on the lake and waited futilely for the peace she had found there earlier in the night. She wondered how Rita's open house had gone. Perhaps there had been so many guests that no one had even noticed her absence. Perhaps her mother had enjoyed her not being there to distract from the party atmosphere. Then Jessie felt a sliver of sadness that she and her mother had never shared a Christmas Eve together as special as the one she'd just spent with David's family.

When Jessie opened her eyes the next morning, she was struck by the way the sunlight coming through the glass window danced on the wooden walls. She realized that this room, so starkly furnished, was one of the most beautiful places she'd ever stayed. Suddenly, a sense of hope filled her. It was Christmas Day, after all. And last night her Christmas prayer had been that she and David would be able to work things out, whatever that meant. Today she felt convinced that they would be able to do so.

She looked at the time and realized she'd slept in. She jumped up, dressed quickly in jeans and a red sweater, and combed her hair. No time to do any other primping. She'd decided late last night that she had to give Mike and Amelia something. She'd brought a book from her house in Atlanta— a mystery novel. She was going to give that to Mike. And she had an almost full bottle of perfume to give to Amelia. She had found some shelf liner paper in the bathroom cabinet and wrapped the presents as best she could, holding the paper in place with her hairbands, since she had no tape.

She hadn't come up with anything suitable for David. She had no other books to give away, and none of her other possessions were right for a man. She thought about how she used to make coupon books for her father as presents. If things were different between herself and David, Jessie imagined what fun she might have had resurrecting that practice. Instead, she pulled on her jacket, gathered up the presents for Mike and Amelia, and walked quickly across the yard.

She opened the door to a crackling fire and the smell of cinnamon. Gifts, beribboned and with bits of greenery tucked in, circled the twinkling Christmas tree. Jessie added her meager offerings to the pile and headed back to join the raucous group in the kitchen. The boys were in their high chairs, all smiles, stuffing cinnamon roll pieces into their mouths. The three adults had huge, steaming mugs of coffee in front of them. Amelia came immediately to give Jessie a hug. "Merry Christmas, Jess! Have some coffee and a cinnamon roll."

No one but her father had ever called her affectionately "Jess." Amelia's saying it so casually was like a sudden, warm embrace from her father on this Christmas morning. A shot of pure happiness went through Jessie, and she felt her eyes fill with tears.

"I think you're magic," Jessie said to Amelia. "How do you do it?"

"Do what?"

"Everything. Everything is just better because you are around."

Mike groaned. "Please don't say stuff like that. She's already impossible to live with as it is."

Amelia smiled slightly. "Remember what I told you the first time we met? I do these things because I enjoy doing them." Then her expression turned more serious. "When David and I were growing up, we were always moving from one military housing project to another. Our mother died when I was just two, and our stepmother never tried to improve anything in those places. They always seemed barren and lifeless to me. I swore that when I had a home of my own, it would be filled with life—good smells, colors, and love. All of the things I wanted desperately as a child."

Jessie's admiration of Amelia went up another notch. "I'm sorry about your mother. What did she die from?"

"Our mother was very fragile, right, David? In fact, I'm sure David went into psychiatry because of our mother."

"Amelia, let's don't go dragging all the family skeletons out of the closet," David said.

Jessie looked at him curiously. "I'd really like to hear more about your mother."

"She was beautiful." Amelia went to a drawer and pulled out a picture of a lovely, dark-headed woman standing next to a 1950's Chevrolet sedan.

"She was," Jessie agreed.

"If she'd lived somewhere else, she might have been a model or a movie star. But in Northwest Florida, women got married and had babies, and so she did. Only she had more miscarriages than babies. I think with each one, she became more unhinged, right, David?" Amelia looked at David again for confirmation, and he nodded.

"Did she ever get any treatment?" Jessie asked.

"No, our dad didn't believe in psychiatry," David said harshly. "So our mother lived an anxiety-ridden and fearful life until she died from a self-inflicted gunshot to the head."

It took a moment for the meaning behind David's words to sink in. Their mother had committed suicide. "I'm sorry," Jessie said. "I shouldn't have pried."

Mike, who had been standing silently during all of this, said, "Hey, Christmas morning isn't the time for sad tales. It's time for us to make some happy memories for ourselves and the twins. So let's get this show on the road."

Amelia touched David's hand briefly as a shared understanding seemed to pass between brother and sister. Then she turned to the group and said gaily, "Hey, Michael, Davey, do you want to open some presents?" Then chaos erupted.

CHAPTER 58

Amelia turned the radio to Christmas carols, and they moved to the den where Mike threw another log on the fire. "Let's wait," Amelia said, "until the end to show the boys what's outside. Otherwise, we might as well forget about the tree presents."

The boys were enjoying the box and the ribbon in which two fire trucks had been wrapped when they heard what sounded like a car coming up the driveway. Mike stood up to look out the window. "Anyone know someone with a white Range Rover?"

Jessie's heart dropped. "Yeah, my mother." Her next thought was, *How did she find me*?

David joined Mike at the front window. "I'll get my jacket," he said.

"Wait!" Jessie stood up. "I think I should go talk to her alone first."

After walking outside, Jessie held up her hand to keep Rita from getting out of the car. She hurried to the passenger side and got in. She was shocked by Rita's haggard appearance. Pieces of hair dangled out of Rita's normally perfectly-coiffed twist, and her lipstick was pink even though she was wearing apricot colored pants.

"Quite a Christmas surprise," Jessie began.

Rita's eyes narrowed, and her eyebrows indicated fury. "Yes, I'm sure, it is. You can't imagine what I went through to arrive here bright and early on Christmas morning. Not many places in the mountains of North Georgia take in guests on Christmas Eve. Those that do, well... let's not talk about the accommodations."

"Why are you here? What about your party last night?"

"I know you will find this hard to believe, but I was actually concerned about you. When you didn't answer your phone or return my messages, and you'd made no more withdrawals from your checking account or charges to your credit card, I thought something might have happened to you. I was hoping you were hiding at your house in Atlanta. I canceled my open house and drove to Atlanta to get you."

Jessie was incredulous. She couldn't imagine anything that would make her mother cancel her traditional open house.

"I got to your house in early afternoon, but, of course, you weren't there. Thank goodness, your neighbors were kind enough to explain that you were fine after your little fainting spell, and that you had left with a Dr. David Miller."

"How did you find David's sister?"

"Oh, I called a private detective that I've used on a few occasions and asked him to find out everything he could about our wonderful Dr. Miller," Rita said tartly. "You don't know how much I had to pay this man to work on Christmas Eve."

"You didn't need to do that."

"Really? What if this doctor, about whom we really know nothing, had absconded with you? What if he were some sadistic maniac? People are crazy, Jessie, and you are such an innocent."

"David's not like that, and he's not crazy, Mother. He brought me here to his sister's house because he didn't think I should be alone at the house in Atlanta. I've been entirely safe and have been treated wonderfully by him and his family."

"It is David now, is it? I have serious problems with a doctor who creates such personal relationships with his patients and also one who doesn't realize how hard it is on a mother when her daughter disappears."

"I didn't disappear. I told you on the phone that I needed some time away from you to figure things out. I wanted some time to think. Couldn't you have given me that?"

"If only you'd answered your phone, maybe. And couldn't you have waited until after Christmas, I mean, really? And when I couldn't track your phone, I got seriously worried. I've always been able to track you by looking at your credit cards or your phone records. Without those sources of information, it was like you'd suddenly disappeared."

Jessie felt a sliver of anger, thinking about her mother tracking her every move, unknown to her over the years. "I'm sorry, Mother," she said sarcastically. "I didn't realize what close tabs you keep on me when you hardly seem to notice me when I'm right there in front of you. But as you can see, I'm fine."

Then, because it was Christmas and she was still feeling the warm glow from the morning, she said in a nicer voice, "Today is Christmas. Why don't we put what's happened this week behind us? I'd like to take you inside and introduce you to David's family—his sister and her husband and their twins. We were just getting ready to open presents. I don't want to spoil their morning by making them wait for me to return."

"I'd like nothing better than to put this all behind us," Rita said. "But yesterday, while I was checking into David Miller's background, I came across some information about him that you need to know."

Jessie felt fear uncurl within her, but she said casually, "I'm sure that anything I need to know about David, he's already told me."

Rita eyebrows went up. "Do you know about his role in your accident?"

Jessie felt relieved. "Yes, he told me. He didn't recognize me at first, and it wasn't until I started talking about the accident that he made the connection."

"And you chose not to tell me this very important fact?" Rita's voice was brittle. "Seems like this doctor has been encouraging you to lie to me since the day you started seeing him."

"Mother, please stop!"

"Well, what about his role in his mother's death?"

Jessie was startled. "I know his mother committed suicide when he was a young boy. I don't want to listen to any more, Mother. Come inside, and you'll see how nice he and his family are." Jessie reached for the door handle.

"Wait!" Rita reached for her arm. "It wasn't suicide. David shot his mother. It was ruled accidental, but the coroner's report speculated that David might have pulled the trigger."

Jessie was having trouble comprehending the words coming out of her mother's mouth. "Are you suggesting that a seven-year-old child intentionally shot his mother?"

"Yes, as a matter of fact, I am."

Jessie stuttered uncomprehendingly. "I...I am not going to sit here and listen to more of this nonsense."

"And wasn't it quite a coincidence that he moved to Augusta where you were after the accident?" Rita hurried on. "Isn't this all beginning to sound a little creepy? Like one of those Lifetime movies? If he would shoot his mother, what else is he capable of doing?"

Jessie felt confused. Her mother had never been a liar as far as she knew. Rita prided herself on being brutally honest. What in the world was she saying?"

With her head spinning, Jessie said, "But he's never done anything except try to help me."

"Maybe, maybe not," Rita sneered. "Perhaps he has a long-term plan. He probably discovered that you come from wealth and saw an opportunity to worm his way into your affections. Then, perhaps one day not too long after your wedding, there will be another fatal accident."

All of Jessie's doubts and insecurities came rushing back. Could it be that David had been playing an elaborate game with her? Perhaps, like Nick, he was hiding the real David from her until after they were married so that he could get his hands on her mother's money.

Tears welled up in Jessie's eyes. "Mother, what's wrong with me?"

Rita looked at her, steely-eyed, "It's time to grow up, Jessie, and see the world the way it really is."

Jessie saw the front door open. "Oh, no, here comes David. I can't talk to him now. Will you please take me home?"

As Rita started the car, she said, "That's what I had planned to do all along."

CHAPTER 59

David had been watching from the window long enough. Rita always went for the jugular, and he was afraid to think about what Jessie might be undergoing at the hands of her mother.

"I'm sorry, guys, that we've had to pause Christmas," he said, putting on his jacket. "Let me see what's going on. I hope it won't take more than a few minutes."

"Should we all go out and invite Jessie's mother to come in?" Amelia asked. "Maybe she doesn't want to impose on us by visiting on Christmas morning."

David turned to Amelia. "I can promise you one thing. If Rita Forrester wanted to come in, she'd already be in here, with or without an invitation."

Much to David's surprise, just as he started down the steps of the house, he saw the Range Rover jerk backward, and then the wheels started spinning in the soft snow. *She's taking Jessie away,* he realized suddenly. He started waving his hands and running toward the car, but to no avail. Once the wheels gained traction, the car went speeding down the driveway, taking Jessie away from David.

After the car disappeared in the distance, David stood for a few minutes, stunned. Had Rita just kidnapped her daughter? Or had Jessie gone willingly?

CHAPTER 60

Out on the highway, Rita grimaced, "As soon as we get back to Augusta, I'm calling James Douglas and filing charges against Dr. David Miller. I don't know if he's done anything criminal, but his lack of ethics certainly should result in nothing less than a loss of his license to practice psychiatry in the State of Georgia. If not for the publicity that you and I would have to endure, I'd also file a civil lawsuit against him."

Rita's words permeated Jessie's jumbled thoughts. Regardless of how she felt right now about David's actions toward her, she didn't want her mother to ruin him. "No, Mother," she said in a determined voice. "Please don't. The bottom line is that I am better than I've been in a long time, and it's all due to him. So I want you to promise me that you won't hurt him in any way."

"I don't think running away from your mother and lying indicate that you're better."

Jessie sighed. "I wasn't running away, I was just trying to prove to myself that I could stand on my own two feet. That's what going to Atlanta was all about." She paused, trying to decide if she should continue, but then thought, *Why not*? For too long, she'd let her mother dictate everything she did and said.

"Mother," she said, "you were the one trying to punish me for my independence by cutting off my money, remember? How was I to know that you really hadn't cut off my credit cards and phone?"

Rita looked hard at Jessie. "I just wanted you to come home. I wanted to protect you."

"Why? Ten minutes ago, weren't you telling me that I need to grow up? Wouldn't that involve doing things on my own?"

Rita sputtered, "Well...well.... I'm your mother. Of course I want to protect you."

For once, Jessie felt totally in control of a conversation with her mother. Where was the anger that typically simmered right below the surface and made her lose control? Calmly, she asked, "Why couldn't you ever just love me?"

"Why, you ungrateful.... How can you ask such a question?"

"Because I never felt that you loved me. You never did things with me like other mothers did. I used to pretend when I was little that MJ's mother was my mother."

For just a second, Jessie thought she saw pain flicker across Rita's face, but then her face hardened. "Your father did more than enough with you for both of us."

"You sound jealous," Jessie said incredulously.

Anger mixed with sadness flickered across Rita's face. "Perhaps I was jealous of you. But I was more jealous of your father's first wife. It's difficult being the second wife when your husband was married to a saint the first time around." She gave a half-hearted laugh. "By the time you were born, I think your father was already regretting his rashness in marrying Rita Lou Tiller from Harrisburg."

"You grew up in *Harrisburg?*" Jessie asked, shocked. She was amazed that her perfectly dressed and coiffed mother had ever lived in the mill town located on the edge of downtown, an area that now had a shrinking population, many deteriorating houses, and a serious problem with crime and drugs. Her mother had never talked about her family. Jessie had always assumed that discussing it was too painful because Rita's whole family had died in a house fire, leaving Rita alone.

Rita looked from the road to Jessie and back again. "I guess you're old enough to know that my parents, your grandparents, were mill workers. The house I grew up in was very much like those ramshackle cottages that still exist down there on Broad Street. Just imagine, six of us lived in one of those places, not nearly as big as my master suite is now."

"What happened?" Jessie noticed that Rita's voice had taken on a rough edge as she talked, very uncharacteristic of her mother's usual polished tones.

"My dad fell asleep while smoking a cigarette in bed, and those little clapboard mill houses were all fire traps." Rita's voice became distant. "I was spending the night with a friend who lived around the corner. We woke up because of all the commotion, fire trucks, sirens, the works. When we went outside, flames were billowing up as high as the top of Enterprise Mill.

"When we rounded the corner, I realized it was my house on fire. I thought surely my family had gotten out. It was hard to get through the crowd. There were hundreds of people gathered in the street. I kept screaming for my momma as I made my way toward the house. Then someone grabbed me when I got to it and held me tight while I watched the house collapse into itself."

Jessie was having a hard time imagining her mother in the scene she was describing. "I'm sorry."

Jessie's voice seemed to bring Rita back to the present. "It was a long time ago. I was just seventeen years old. Almost seems like it happened to someone else when I think about it now."

"What did you do then?"

"The parents of my friend, Ada, took me in. It was just a few weeks before we graduated from high school. One of my teachers helped me get the job at your dad's bank." Rita smiled somewhat sardonically. "The rest is, as they say, history. His first wife died, and since I'd already found a million different ways to make his life easier at the bank, it wasn't that much more of a stretch for us to start dating."

Jessie couldn't stop herself from asking, "Having lost your parents like you did, couldn't you understand how I was feeling when Daddy died? Why did you send me away to boarding school?"

Seconds turned into minutes. Then Rita continued. "Your dad was twenty-five years older than me when we got married. I think, at first, he liked the excitement of a young wife. He enjoyed showing me the kind of life I'd never known existed. We traveled to places I'd only dreamed of— New York, Paris, and London. But when you were born, he was quite content to stay home and play with you."

"And you weren't?" Jessie asked harshly.

"No," Rita said in the driest of tones. "I suppose I was selfish then and even more so after your dad died." She gripped the steering wheel so tightly that Jessie saw her knuckles whiten. "I wanted some time to enjoy myself. Besides, it wasn't exactly as if I sent you off to an orphanage. I would have loved going to someplace like Huntington Hall when I was your age."

Jessie looked down. "I was so miserable that I felt like I was an orphan locked up in a prison."

Rita stiffened. "Poor little Jessica, poor little princess. Imagine how you would have felt if you'd been forced to move in with your best friend's family in an overcrowded shack because you literally had nowhere to go. Imagine living in fear of your best friend's father, who resented having one more mouth to feed and required that you pay for your rent in a very personal way. Imagine getting a professional job in a bank and having to go to work every day in the same dress. Imagine eating one boiled egg for lunch at your desk because there was never enough money for anything more."

Anger for what her mother had done to her and pity for what her mother had gone through warred within Jessie. Finally, pity won. "Okay, Mother you win. Your childhood trauma trumps my childhood trauma. I don't know what I would have done at seventeen in your place." Then anger surfaced again, "However, I can tell you one thing I do know for sure. I could never be happy not seeing a child of mine for months at a time."

Rita flushed and for once had no reply. As the silence stretched, Jessie noticed the fine lines around Rita's eyes in the classically-chiseled but very pale face, and the dark circles under her eyes. Compassion returned. "Do you think we can put the past behind us, and start fresh?"

Jessie thought she saw gratitude on Rita's face as she nodded. They rode in silence then, neither one wanting to break the uneasy truce they had achieved.

As the miles clicked off in silence, Jessie's thoughts returned to David. A man like David, who was so loving and supportive of his sister and her children, couldn't be the scoundrel that her mother had painted him to be. Yes, there had been some red flags, but nothing like with Nick. Why had she allowed her mother to take her away from David? She should have stayed and talked things through with him instead of running away.

"Mother, I've changed my mind. I'd like for you to turn around and go back. The only way we are going to get to the truth is by talking with David."

Rita continued to look straight ahead, almost as if she hadn't heard.

"Mother?" Jessie pushed. "I'm asking you to turn around."

"I need to get back to Augusta," Rita said.

"Please, I'm asking you to do this one thing for me."

When Rita finally looked at Jessie, her face was completely white and tightly constricted. "I've been having stomach pains on and off for several days. I thought it was just indigestion, but the pain has been getting progressively worse this morning."

Jessie realized that her mother wasn't joking. She appeared to be in serious pain. "Then you don't need to be driving. Pull over and let me take you to a hospital."

"All right." Rita put on the blinker and pulled over on the highway's edge.

Jessie looked at the car's navigation system and saw that they were still a couple of hours away from Augusta. "Perhaps we should look for a nearby hospital."

"I'd rather not chance the local hospitals. The place I stayed in last night was horrid enough. Just drive fast."

Jessie acquiesced. "Okay. Put your seat back and try to relax. I'll get us there as soon as I can."

CHAPTER 61

"Why don't you call her and see if she's coming back?" Amelia asked David as she calmly pulled wrapping paper out of one of the twin's mouth.

"She's not coming back," David replied, stone-faced. "Rita's got her now. Maybe that's for the best. I'm not sure Jessie was cut out for mountain living, anyway."

"I don't understand you," Amelia said. After studying David's face briefly, she turned to Mike. "Will you take the twins upstairs for a few minutes so David and I can talk?"

Mike looked from sister to brother, nodded, and without a word grabbed a squealing twin under each arm.

"What's going on between you and Jessie?" Amelia asked after the room was empty. "Don't say 'nothing romantic' because Mike told me he caught you two kissing in the workshop last night."

David flushed. "Yes. Look, I know, I know. She's my patient, and I crossed a line. And I'm talking to Andy on Monday about taking over her treatment."

"I don't think you'd risk your career for a casual fling. Jessie must be important to you."

"I don't know," he said nonchalantly. "There's definitely a physical thing between us."

Amelia's voice went up a notch. "And you think that's all? You know I'm a big believer in fate, right? It seems to me there's been an incredible amount of fate that has brought you and Jessie together. You almost had a head-on collision with that woman. Then out of all of the places in the world you could have moved after leaving the military, you picked Augusta, Georgia, where Jessie happened to be living. And of all the therapists in Augusta, she picked you, or at least her mother did. Don't you think that's an awful lot of coincidence?"

David shrugged.

"I think you're in love with her. I've never seen you so protective of someone other than the boys and me."

David was taken aback. "I'm not in love with her. I want to help her get better, because, because...."

"Because why?" Amelia asked, puzzled.

"Because I think I might have been responsible for her accident. I was talking to Mike on my cell phone just before it happened. I really don't remember what I was doing. I could have crossed the line and caused her husband to swerve off the road."

"You also don't know then that you did do anything wrong." Amelia waited for a few seconds and then continued. "Guilt can be powerful, I know. But my woman's intuition tells me that guilt isn't what's driving you right now. I think you are in love with her. And I think she's head over heels in love with you. I find it hard to believe that you're going to let her drive away without at least trying to find out what the truth is between the two of you."

David felt as if, in the massive puzzle that was his relationship with Jessie, an essential piece of the puzzle had suddenly clicked into place. Obviously, he'd never been in love before and hadn't known what it felt like. Now his inability to maintain his usual professionalism with her and his willingness to risk so much for her made sense.

He gave Amelia a swift, hard hug. "I love you, Mel. Now if you don't mind, I think I'll gather my things and go find Jessie. Merry Christmas!"

"Hallelujah," Amelia said with a smile, "And Merry Christmas to you, too!"

As David drove the four hours back to Augusta, he had plenty of time to think. Assuming that Amelia was correct, and Jessie was in love with him, Rita still presented a monumental challenge to his and Jessie's future. He would have to work hard to win her approval. Or he and Jessie would have to make a clean break from her mother, which would likely require a move from Augusta.

David thought a clean break would be easier than trying to build a relationship with Rita. However, Rita was Jessie's mother, so some sort of relationship would be best.

By the time David was back in Augusta, the sun was fading. He'd tried Jessie's new cell number as well as her old one before remembering that she'd left Amelia's house with nothing but her jacket. The only thing he could do was go to her house.

He felt apprehensive as he turned onto the cobblestone street where she lived. The uneasy feelings increased as he pulled into the empty circular driveway and parked his beat-up Toyota in front of the white-columned porch. When the doorbell chimed loudly like a grandfather clock, David fully expected the door to be opened by a tuxedo-clad butler. Instead, seconds turned into minutes until he finally realized that no one was going to open the door.

Were they not home? Were they hiding inside waiting for him to leave? Had Rita locked Jessie in her room? As the minutes slowly ticked by, David felt himself deflate. He'd been so eager to see Jessie, to talk to her. Now what should he do? He couldn't stand on their porch all night ringing the doorbell. He walked slowly back to his car. Merry Christmas, indeed.

CHAPTER 62

"Appendicitis is a heck of a Christmas present," the doctor said to Jessie in the waiting room of University Hospital. "We've got your mother sedated, and we're going to do surgery as soon as there's an operating room available."

Jessie was relieved. After all the horrific things she had contemplated while speeding as quickly as was safely possible back to Augusta, appendicitis seem fairly innocuous. Once her mother had stretched out in the passenger seat, she'd begun moaning and writhing in pain as Jessie had never seen anyone do. Had Jessie seen any other hospital signs, she would have stopped no matter how her mother begged her to drive on to Augusta.

They'd arrived at the emergency room just as her mother had thrown up.

"Oh, my God," Rita had moaned, continuing to shudder with dry heaves.

Jessie felt bile rise in her own throat as she slammed the car into park and ran to find help. She returned with two men and a gurney to see her mother attempting to get herself out of the car, having wiped off most of the vomit. Head held high, she insisted on walking into the emergency room until she was hit by another wave of pain and crumbled like a rag doll into the arms of one of the waiting men.

After her mother was taken away on the gurney, Jessie's first thought was of David. She wished she could call him, but all she had was her mother's cell phone, and she didn't know his number. She thought of Amelia's website that listed their home telephone number. She immediately did a Google search and, in a few minutes, heard the phone ringing at Amelia's house.

"Hello." Just the sound of Amelia's voice made Jessie feel better.

"It's Jessie."

"Jessie! I'm so glad you called. We've been worried."

"I'm sorry I left so abruptly," Jessie said. "It was very rude of me."

"Don't worry about it as long as you're okay."

"May I speak to David?"

"David?" Amelia's voice was suddenly hesitant. "I figured he'd be there with you by now."

Jessie's heart skipped a beat. "David's in Augusta?"

"Yes, he left probably fifteen minutes after you did."

"I'm at the hospital."

At the sudden intake of breath from Amelia, Jessie hurriedly said, "I'm fine. My mother is having her appendix taken out. Evidently, she's been in and out of pain for a while. I left everything including my cell phone at your house, so there's no way for me to let David know what's been going on."

"Oh, that's right. Do you want me to text you his number to this phone?"

"That would be great."

"Will do, as soon as we hang up. Let me know when you are coming back, or if you want me to send your things anywhere, okay?"

"Okay."

The telephone rang for the fifth time, and Jessie was starting to mentally prepare a message, when David answered.

Jessie felt her heart skip another beat at the sound of his voice, and for a moment she thought about hanging up. What could she say to him after running off like she had? At last she answered, "David, it's me, Jessie."

"Jessie! Where are you? I'm just leaving your house."

"I'm at the hospital with Mother, and she's having her appendix removed right now."

"Which hospital?"

"University."

"I'll be right there."

She saw him before he saw her standing at the door leading to the waiting room. He was still dressed in his brown corduroy pants and Christmas green shirt, his hair adorably messy. Then he saw her, and she rose from her seat as he approached.

"I'm sorry," she began, feeling her heart race at the mere sight of him. "I never should have gone with my mother."

"Why did you?" he asked, his brown eyes searching hers for answers.

"Old habits die hard," she offered in a faltering voice. *How could she explain that, for a few minutes, she had believed more in her mother's words than in David's integrity?* "I hope I didn't ruin Christmas for Amelia, Mike, and the boys."

"The boys were having a grand time playing with the boxes and tissue paper when I left," he said. "Let's sit down." He pointed toward two hard plastic chairs set away from the others in the room. From the television mounted in the corner above the chairs, a children's chorale sang "O Little Town of Bethlehem."

"You still haven't answered the question, Jessie. Why'd you go with her?"

The quietness of the waiting room was shattered when a sobbing woman walked in, accompanied by a man who was trying to comfort her.

Jessie opened her mouth, but words were hard to find. Finally, she said, "Mother was worried about me. She'd found out about your role in the accident, and she was angry that I hadn't told her. She started questioning the coincidence of you being in Augusta, and then she suggested all kinds of terrible things. She said you were trying to gain my trust to take advantage of me and get at her money."

"You believed her?" His brown eyes looked suddenly sad.

Jessie tried to find the right words. "I was confused for a little while. You have to admit that you weren't totally honest with me in the beginning. And my track record with Nick hasn't done much for my self-confidence." Seeing no softening in his face, she continued, "Still, all the time my mother was saying those horrible things about you, I knew, on some level, that what she was saying couldn't be true."

"And now?" his voice sounded resigned.

"Why do you think I called you? Would I have done that if I didn't trust you?"

Jessie waited for him to respond as the woman on the other side of the room continued to weep.

At last he said in a very quiet voice, "I'm going to ask Andy to recommend another doctor to take over your treatment. I'm sure that would be in your best interest."

Jessie wanted badly for him to stop looking at her so blankly. She reached for his hand lying on side of the chair, but he snatched it back as though she had burned him.

"Jessie, you've still got a lot of issues to work through, and it will be better for you if I'm not around complicating the situation," David said. "I want you to feel self-confident and to completely resolve your trust issues before we take our relationship any further."

Jessie could feel her eyes starting to burn with unshed tears. *Damn him, why was he doing this in a public place where she couldn't scream at him, or kiss him, or do something that would make him see how silly he was being?*

"I love you," Jessie whispered, suddenly unafraid to speak the feelings out loud to him that she hadn't even become accustomed to thinking to herself. "I need you. I don't need time alone to work on myself. I know that when I'm with you, everything is all right."

"There, you see," David said bitterly. "You've just proven my point." He stood up and walked through the waiting room's double doors without looking back at the tears streaking down Jessie's face.

CHAPTER 63

The doctor came in later to tell Jessie that Rita's surgery had been a success. If he noticed the tears in her eyes, he was too professional to mention them. When Jessie was admitted to the recovery room, she was shocked to see that the woman on the hospital bed only faintly resembled the larger than life Rita Forrester. Her silver-blonde hair was loose and tangled around her head. Her face was pale and almost skeletally thin around her large grey eyes.

Jessie waved awkwardly at her mother from the other side of a fairly large nurse who was checking a tube going into Rita's arm. The small recovery room space made Jessie feel claustrophobic, and she wasn't sure which way to move to get out of the nurse's way. At last the nurse said rather gruffly, "When we get her settled into her room, you can come and stay as long as you like. It'll probably be in a couple of hours."

"Okay, thank you," Jessie said and then, just in case her mother was more aware than she thought, she said, "Mother, I'll see you as soon as you are moved to your own room."

Instead of going back to the waiting room, she decided to go downstairs and get something to eat in the cafeteria. She hadn't eaten anything since the cinnamon roll at breakfast, and her head was aching slightly. Perhaps eating protein would make the ache go away. Stepping off the elevator, she was shocked to see David standing in the middle of the cafeteria, talking with an attractive brunette nurse. The woman was smiling and speaking animatedly, clearly flirting with him.

To Jessie, the situation seemed all too reminiscent of Nick. Perhaps David was a womanizer after all. Angrily, she did an about face and went back into the elevator.

She'd barely sat down in the waiting room before David was standing in front of her. "Why did you leave the cafeteria so abruptly?"

"I saw you flirting with a woman, and I've watched that scene before," she challenged.

"What you saw was me talking to a friend. It was no big deal. I'm not Nick."

"Why did you not turn me over to Andy when you realized who I was?" she demanded angrily. "Then I wouldn't be feeling as mixed up as I do now. I just don't understand."

David's voice rose a notch. "Damn it, Jessie! I've felt guilty about your accident since the night it happened. I was talking on my cell phone just before the crash. I don't know if I drifted over the line into your lane and caused Nick to go off the side of the road."

Jessie's breath caught at his words as she realized how obviously conflicted he was.

"I suppose because of the guilt I feel, I wanted to be the one to help you get better," David went on. "Besides, I really thought I knew what was best for you."

Anger flared up again as David spoke his last few words. Jessie suddenly realized that David was just like Nick, whether he was a womanizer or not. And David was just like her mother. He apparently wanted control over her life, too. How had she not seen this similarity before?

"I am so tired of people thinking that they know what's best for me!" she said in a low, intense voice. "Most of my life I've felt that I've not been in control, and I think that's why I've been depressed. But now, thanks to you, Dr. Miller, I realize that I must take control over my own life. To do that, I need to get away from my mother and away from you."

David's face paled with shock. Then, in a very flat tone, he said, "If that's what you want, Jessie."

Since she had won the argument, Jessie wondered why she didn't feel happier as she watched him turn, chalk-faced, and walk out of the waiting room.

CHAPTER 64

Andy was gone until after New Year's, visiting his in-laws, or David would have called him to warn him about the potentially explosive situation with Rita Forrester and to get some professional advice on how to go forward. David felt adrift, both professionally and personally. How had things with Jessie gone so terribly wrong?

On Monday, he returned to work. The holidays were always stressful, and not unexpectedly he had received emergency calls from several of his patients and a few of Andy's that he had to work into his planned schedule. Being busy kept him focused on other people's problems rather than his own.

Still, every so often, his thoughts wandered back to Jessie. The ball was in her court. She had wanted to be in control of her life, and now she was. On a professional level, David felt encouraged that Jessie had been strong in the face of the crisis with her mother and just as strong in arguing with him. The "old" Jessie would have withdrawn within herself.

The logical part of David knew that, if Jessie did love him as she had blurted out in the waiting room, and if she wasn't just experiencing co-dependency that she'd developed during therapy, she'd choose to give him the benefit of the doubt and reach out to him. If not? Well, he wasn't ready to consider that yet.

CHAPTER 65

After David's departure, Jessie found herself in an emotionally bittersweet place. Immediately following the surgery, her mother seemed to appreciate Jessie as she never had before, and having Rita dependent on her was gratifying. Jessie knew theirs was never going to be a traditional, loving, and supportive mother/daughter relationship, but perhaps now they might be able to forge a better relationship going forward.

However, painful reminders of David were everywhere, such as in the golden glint of a stranger's brown hair in the hospital lobby. *Is that him?* And then disappointment when she realized it wasn't him. She felt a visceral yearning for David's touch when she watched adoring lovers in the advertisements for New Year's Eve events. The ads seemed to run continuously on the television in Rita's hospital room. Jessie almost longed for the return of the depression that had kept her emotions muted for so long. Now she felt as though she were a raw, exposed nerve, too sensitive for everyday feelings.

The Sunday morning after she brought Rita home from the hospital, Jessie made coffee and fixed her mother toast, as it was Maggie's day off. When the food was ready, she carried the tray into her mother's bedroom.

"Good morning, Mother," Jessie said cheerfully, putting the tray down on the bed and going to the windows to open the drapes.

Rita was sitting up against several pillows, still looking pale but much more like her old self with her hair arranged in its traditional twist, and her cell phone, iPad, and several newspapers strewn carelessly around the bed. "You're getting to be almost as good as Maggie at fixing my breakfast. How about culinary school?"

Jessie shook her head and said, "No, I don't see cooking school in my future." One of their ongoing discussions was about what Jessie should do with the rest of her life. Her mother seemed adamant that photography wouldn't work. But all other choices were still available for consideration.

Talking about cooking made Jessie remember Amelia's homemade bread and pies, and then she thought about her car and her personal things still at Amelia and Mike's house. She supposed it was past time for her to contact Amelia and see about retrieving them. It was crazy how much she missed all of them after knowing them for such a short period of time. Yet she was hesitant about reconnecting with Amelia and Mike, considering the uproar she caused the last time she'd been with them.

"You're thinking of David, aren't you?" Rita asked caustically. "You have that *I just lost my dog* look on your face that you had for so long after you lost Jello."

Jessie didn't take offense at her mother's question or her reference to Jello, the dog that had run away from home when Jessie was seven. "As a matter of fact, I wasn't thinking about David but about his family," she answered. "I wish you could have met Amelia and Mike and their twins. They are really good and honest people. You would have realized that, with family like them, David couldn't be the sleazy opportunist that you painted him to be."

"I've known many good and honest people who had sleazy relatives," Rita remarked.

"I wish you'd give him a chance."

"I wish you would forget about him."

Jessie sighed, for she supposed neither of those wishes would come true.

CHAPTER 66

A couple of weeks into January, Andy charged into David's office with a look of fury on his face, the like of which David had never seen before. As soon as Andy returned from his vacation, David had confessed all about his relationship with Jessie and asked Andy to reach out to her about changing doctors and continuing her therapy. Andy had tried to do so, but Jessie had said she was too busy caring for her mother to consider going back to therapy. She did say that she would consider calling him back when she felt able.

"You're never going to believe what just happened at the bank!"

David had a sinking feeling that whatever had happened at the bank—the one that was partially owned by Rita Forrester—wasn't going to be good. "What?"

"I have a $100,000 line of credit with the bank that gets extended automatically at the end of its term as long as I make the interest payments. I got a call yesterday from them, telling me that they were no longer going to extend me this courtesy and that they are calling the loan in its entirety."

"I'm sorry," David began. "You and I both know this is Rita Forrester's doing. Look, I've got some money in a retirement account, so let me pay off your loan."

"*No!*" Andy said. "I've already been to another bank this morning, and they seemed more than happy to grant me a loan. I just wanted you to be aware of what Rita's capable of. Be careful, my friend."

That afternoon, despite its being a particularly chilly day, David decided to go for a run. Without making a conscious decision about the direction, he found himself heading toward the Forrester house. A part of him wanted to march right up to the door and demand to see Rita. *How dare she attack Andy the way she had?* But the thought of running into Jessie when she had yet to reach out to him kept him from taking that action. Instead, he kept running further and harder until his feelings of anger were overtaken by exhaustion.

Several days later, Andy returned to David's office, holding a free local newspaper. One of its columnists was famous for publishing sly innuendo and skating carefully over the truth. "Have you seen this?" he asked.

"No," David replied, the feeling of dread returning.

"There is an article in here that doesn't name names, but seems clearly to be referring to you and questioning your character and professional ethics. Seems you were right about Lillie. The quotes in the article obviously come from her, and they are such a bunch of bullshit. The article even implies that you left the military under suspicion after being involved in a car accident in Atlanta."

"What the hell? Andy, I can't let Rita Forrester go on with this vendetta. I've got to talk to her."

Andy snorted. "Like that would do any good."

"Well, I can't just sit here and wait for the next bad thing to happen. I'm going over to their house tonight and demand that she quit this stuff."

"What about Jessie?" Andy asked.

"Maybe if Jessie knows the full extent of what her mother is capable of, she'll realize Rita doesn't need her as a caretaker anymore, and she'll finally get away from her mother for good."

Andy shook his head. "One can hope, I guess."

The rest of the day was a struggle for David. He found it hard to listen to his patients when his mind returned again and again to the coming confrontation with Rita Forrester. After his last appointment, he walked over to Andy's office, but the door was still closed. *Oh, well, probably best.* Andy might have tried to talk David out of doing what he knew he had to do.

Once again David parked on the circular drive and stood before the enormous door, waiting for someone to open it. After what seemed like forever, it was finally opened by a middle-aged black woman in a white uniform. "May I help you?" she asked.

David decided instantly that professionalism might be his best bet for gaining entrance to the house. "I'm Dr. David Miller, and I want to talk to Mrs. Forrester about her daughter's treatment."

The woman said nothing for a moment as she looked him up and down. Finally she said, "Come in. You wait here." And she disappeared around a corner.

David found himself in a marble-tiled foyer where what appeared to be museum-quality artwork hung on every wall. He stood next to a round wooden table with a massive centerpiece of white and red flowers. He realized that the entrance to this house was about as big as the entire cottage he lived in. Then he heard footsteps, and Jessie came around the corner.

CHAPTER 67

"That Dr. Miller is in the foyer wanting to speak to your mother," Maggie had said. Jessie was bent over a bowl of pears on the granite counter top, arranging them for a photograph she was about to take.

Jessie was shocked. "David's here?" Her heart started pounding in her chest.

Maggie nodded her head. "Don't you think you should go talk to him?"

"Well, yes, of course." Jessie put her camera down and wished she could check her hair and makeup without the watchful eyes of Maggie on her.

When she rounded the corner, Jessie felt as though the breath had been knocked out of her. David looked so handsome standing there in the foyer, almost as if he had been placed there as part of the design.

"David?"

He looked surprised to see her. "I asked to speak to your mother."

"She's not here," Jessie said, disappointed that he didn't seem happy to see her. "But she should be back shortly." She wondered what kind of business David had with her mother.

"May I wait?"

"Of course." They stood awkwardly, and then Jessie asked. "How have you been?"

"Oh, just fine," he answered sarcastically.

"How are Amelia and everyone?"

"Fine," he said stiffly.

"You seem angry," Jessie asked, genuinely concerned.

"I am."

"What's wrong?"

"You need to ask your mother."

Jessie felt the beginnings of apprehension. "She promised me that she'd not do anything to harm you. What did she do?" Jessie heard the garage door opening and knew her mother was home. "Wait a minute. I'll be right back." Jessie turned and walked into the back of the house.

Rita was walking in with an armful of packages that she set down on the kitchen table. "Whose piece of junk is that out in the driveway?" she demanded.

"Mother, David is here, and he is upset. What have you been up to?"

"How dare he! I'm going to call the police." Rita walked to the phone.

"No!" Jessie ordered just as David walked into the kitchen.

"I got tired of waiting out there in the hall by myself. Hello, Rita," David said ominously.

"I'm calling the police unless you leave right now," Rita said. Jessie noticed that both eyebrows were up as high as they would go, but she wasn't exactly sure of their meaning.

"Put the phone down, Mother. I invited him here," Jessie said, hoping that Maggie wouldn't contradict her.

David wasn't waiting any longer to get to the point of the visit. "Rita," he said firmly, "you have to stop what you've been doing to Andy and to me."

"What have you been doing, Mother?" Jessie asked.

"I don't know what he's talking about," Rita snapped.

David folded his arms across his chest. "I suppose it's just a coincidence that Andy's loan at your bank got called in last week and that a slanderous column about me appeared in the local metro paper yesterday."

"Why would you think those things have anything to do with me?" Rita asked. "I don't run either the bank or that newspaper."

"Like hell you don't," David said and took a step toward her. "You just happen to own a controlling interest in both."

Jessie saw that he was really angry and stepped between them quickly. "Mother, what's the truth here?"

Rita gave a harsh laugh. "The truth? The truth is that you are never going to be able to get over this, this scoundrel as long as he is still hanging around Augusta. He needs to move on."

"But you promised me, Mother, that you wouldn't harm him." Jessie said incredulously.

"I was only doing what's best for you," Rita replied scathingly. "One day you'll thank me for this."

Jessie inhaled quickly, feeling as though she'd been sucker punched in the stomach. Then she said bitterly, "I've just realized that I've spent most of my life doing not what I wanted to do, nor what I should have been doing, but whatever you wanted me to do, Mother. And I've no one to blame but myself. But I'm done with letting you control my choices and my life."

She turned to David. "If Amelia still wants my help, I want to go back to the mountains and live there until my house in Atlanta sells." She saw David's eyes widen with surprise.

"You'll be sorry," Rita warned.

"No, Mother. You'll be sorry. Because one day you'll be a lonely old woman without any family around you. And I just hope to God your money holds out until you're gone. Because, if it doesn't, you might find your friends aren't there, either. And if you attempt anything else that harms David, his practice, or his family, your childhood history might just make the front page of the *Augusta Chronicle*."

Rita's face blanched white. "You wouldn't."

"Try me," Jessie said, looking her mother directly in the eye. She turned to David. "Would you mind giving me a ride to the mountains or to a rental car agency or really anywhere away from here?"

David shook his head, apparently dumbstruck.

"Great," Jessie said. "Give me a minute to collect a few things."

"Perhaps I'd best wait outside at the car," David suggested.

Jessie nodded in agreement and started toward the stairs. She began to shake after taking the first few steps, but she continued toward her room, hoping no one would notice her trembling. At the top of the stairs, she saw Maggie coming up behind her.

"Don't try to stop me," she warned Maggie as she pulled a suitcase out of her closet.

"Stop you? I've come to help you pack," Maggie replied before wrapping her arms around her. "I've never been prouder of you." Together they piled all of Jessie's jewelry and a few of her favorite clothes into the suitcase.

"Now all I need is my camera from the kitchen, and that's it."

When they came back down, Rita was nowhere to be seen. "Do you think she'll be all right?" Jessie asked Maggie.

"Never seen her not land on her feet. You just go on and start living your own life."

"I love you, Maggie."

"I love you, too, baby girl."

As Jessie walked by the portrait of her father in the den, she stopped. "You know what, Maggie? I'm not leaving Dad here, either. I'm taking him with me." She set her suitcase down and quickly slid the portrait up and off its hook on the wall.

Maggie was grinning from ear to ear as she picked up Jessie's suitcase. "I guess I better help you carry your stuff out to the car."

Outside, Jessie's heart swelled when she saw David waiting for her next to his beat-up old car. His warm expression gave her hope.

"Your father?" he asked, indicating the portrait she was holding.

"Yep. I decided I am taking him with me."

"Fine." David took the suitcase from Maggie and the portrait from Jessie, and put both into the trunk. Before he opened the car's squeaking passenger door for Jessie to get in, Jessie turned to give Maggie one last hard hug.

"Where are you taking me?" she asked after they were both settled inside the car.

"Anywhere you want. After that passionate declaration of independence in the kitchen, I'm sure you are a woman who knows her mind and exactly what she wants."

"You are so right!" Jessie exclaimed, feeling finally in control of her life and happier than she could ever remember feeling. "Why don't we go to your place?"

The surprised look on David's face made her laugh. "I want to finish what we started in the woods that day" Jessie said. Then she had to laugh again because there was definitely a red tint suddenly coloring David's smiling face.

EPILOGUE

His daughter slept soundly on the padded blanket while David watched over her to ensure protection from bugs, ants, and the splashes of the twins as they jumped one right after the other off the end of the dock into their father's waiting arms. David had finally attained that celebrated status of a married man with a child. And he couldn't have been happier about it all.

He looked up to see Jessie and Amelia coming back from the house with drinks and snacks, and his heart swelled in response. He was so blessed that Jessie had walked out of her mother's house and never once looked back. He was still amazed when he thought about how she'd faced her mother that day. Later, she'd told him she'd realized that her mother would never change and that she had to move on with her life without her mother as a part of it. Not much later though, she'd actually forgiven Rita for all that she'd done to make her life and David's life miserable, and offered to get together to talk. Rita's answer had been to leave town.

The year and a half that had passed since Jessie left her mother's house had been a time of growth and fulfillment for both David and Jessie. At first, they'd considered moving away from Augusta. But when no other place seemed as appealing, they decided to stay. Buying a house outside The Hill area had helped remove them from her mother's circle of influence, and Rita's long absences from Augusta also helped their transition into a new life.

Jessie had continued with photography, and her recent exhibition at the Morris Museum of Art had done quite well. She had received a commission to photograph scenes at the Augusta National for a Masters Golf Tournament coffee table book. David's practice had also continued to grow. Now he truly felt like Andy's partner.

In addition, David had finally achieved a peace that had eluded him for most of his life. Watching Jessie forgive her mother and move on had made him realize that he needed to do the same with his past. The little boy who had struggled to take a gun away from his mother had done all he could do to save her. It wasn't his fault that she had succeeded in pulling the gun away from him. By forgiving his mother for taking her own life, and his father's treatment of her, he'd finally been able to forgive himself as well.

He and Jessie had sent Rita an invitation to their wedding, but she did not appear. Later, they heard she'd gone to Europe for an extended stay—or, maybe not. There was a rumor that several people had seen a veiled woman about Rita's size slip into the back of the church after their wedding ceremony began. The same woman had left just as the bride and groom started walking back down the aisle.

Perhaps one day Rita would decide that seeing her granddaughter was worth swallowing some of her stiff-necked pride. Then again, maybe not. All David knew was that like everyone else, Rita had to make her own choices about what was important in her life. As for David, he knew that everything of any importance in his life was right there within arm's reach.

ALSO BY J.A. STONE

Life Unexpected

AUTHOR BIO

J.A. Stone is a pseudonym for Jo Ann Appleton. She has written one other novel—*Life Unexpected.* She lives in Georgia, works as a technical writer, and is already sketching out the plot for her next novel in this *Life* series.

Proof

Made in the USA
Charleston, SC
27 December 2015